Praise for *Face of Betrayal*

"This novel is a blast to read!"

—Bill O'Reilly, FOX TV and radio anchor

"Only a brilliant lawyer, prosecutor, and journalist like Lis Wiehl could put together a mystery this thrilling! The incredible characters and non-stop twists will leave you mesmerized. Open this book and find a comfortable seat because you won't want to put it down!"

—E. D. Hill, FOX News anchor

"Great characters, compelling storyline . . . a winning combination."

—Earl Merkel, co-host of *Money & More*

"Lis Wiehl's been there, done that and reported on it all. A riveting and revealing fast-paced look at our criminal justice system and the press who cover it."

—Dr. Michael Baden, current chief forensic pathologist for the New York State Police; former Chief Medical Examiner, NYC; host, HBO's *Autopsy*

"Wiehl exposes the malevolent side of power in this murderous thriller. A harrowing tale ripped from the headlines!"

—Catherine Crier, former judge, journalist, and best-selling author

"A real thrill ride! Filled with twists and turns you won't see coming."

—Rita Crosby, Emmy award-winning TV personality (formerly with MSNBC)

"An incredible read. The story grips you from the get-go and reveals a stunning look at what happens when crime and the media meet head-on!"

—Nancy Grace, CNN anchor and former prosecutor

"Feels fresher than today's headline story. One of the best suspense novels of 2009."

—Sean Hannity, FOX anchor

"Three smart women crack the big cases! Makes perfect sense to me. This book blew me away!

—Jeanine Pirro, former DA; hosts The CW's
daytime court television reality show
Judge Jeanine Pirro

"Lis Wiehl has done it again! I'm a big fan of her nonfiction books and now the multitalented Wiehl lets loose with this juicy political mystery! A fine mixture of all this savvy commentator has to offer . . . including politics, law, friendship, and even motherhood! Lis is a quadruple threat in my book!"

—Hannah Storm, ESPN; former CBS anchor

"A smart, fast-paced debut. If you like the Women's Murder Club books, you will really enjoy this."

—Deborah Sinclaire, Editor-in-Chief
(Book of the Month Club).

One of Top Ten Best Books of 2009
—Suspense Magazine

"[A] sizzling political thriller. The seamless plot offers a plethora of twists and turns."

—Publishers Weekly

"[A] tense, brisk plot that crime novel fans will love."
—CBA Retailers & Resources

"Page-turning thriller . . . Her novel displays the new face of Christian publishing, where characters wrestle with faith but don't have to undergo an overt conversion within the pages of the book."
—World Magazine

FACE OF
BETRAYAL

FACE OF
BETRAYAL

A Triple Threat Novel

LIS WIEHL
with APRIL HENRY

THOMAS NELSON
Since 1798

NASHVILLE DALLAS MEXICO CITY RIO DE JANEIRO

Published in Nashville, Tennessee. Thomas Nelson is a registered trademark of Thomas Nelson, Inc.

Thomas Nelson, Inc., titles may be purchased in bulk for educational, business, fund-raising, or sales promotional use. For information, please e-mail SpecialMarkets@ThomasNelson.com.

HOLY BIBLE: NEW INTERNATIONAL VERSION®. © 1973, 1978, 1984 by International Bible Society. Used by permission of Zondervan Publishing House. All rights reserved.

NEW AMERICAN STANDARD BIBLE®. © The Lockman Foundation 1960, 1962, 1963, 1968, 1971, 1972, 1975, 1977. Used by permission.

"The Sick Rose" by William Blake, published in *Songs of Experience* in 1794.

ISBN 978-1-5955-4817-7 (TP)

Library of Congress Cataloging-in-Publication Data

Wiehl, Lis W.
  Face of betrayal : a triple threat novel / Lis Wiehl and April Henry.
    p. cm.
  ISBN 978-1-59554-705-7 (hardcover)
  1. Women lawyers—Fiction. 2. Women television journalists—Fiction. 3. Female friendship—Fiction. 4. Stalking—Fiction. 5. Spousal abuse—Fiction. 6. Abused women—Fiction. 7. Murder—Investigation—Fiction. I. Henry, April. II. Title.
  PS3623.I382F33 2009
  813'.6—dc22

                                        2009000122

Printed in the United States of America

11 12 13 QG 6 5 4 3 2

With love for Dani, Jacob, and Mickey,
LIS

With love for Sadie and Randy,
APRIL

Come on, Jalapeño!"

Katie Converse jerked the dog's leash. Reluctantly, the black Lab mix lifted his nose and followed her. Katie wanted to hurry, but everything seemed to invite Jalapeño to stop, sniff, and lift his leg. And there was no time for that now. Not today.

She had grown up less than two miles from here, but this afternoon everything looked different. It was winter, for one thing, nearly Christmas. And she wasn't the same person she had been the last time she was here, not a month earlier. Then she had been a little girl playing at being a grown-up. Now she was a woman.

Finally, she reached the agreed-upon spot. She was still shaking from what she had said less than two hours earlier. What she had demanded.

Now there was nothing to do but wait. Not an easy task for an impatient seventeen-year-old.

She heard the scuff of footsteps behind her. Unable to suppress a grin, Katie called his name as she turned around.

At the sight of the face, contorted with rage, Jalapeño growled.

As she walked to the courtroom podium, federal prosecutor Allison Pierce touched the tiny silver cross she wore on a fine chain. The cross was hidden under her cream-colored silk blouse, but it was always there, close to Allison's heart. Her father had given it to her for her sixteenth birthday.

Allison was dressed in what she thought of as her "court uniform," a navy blue suit with a skirt that, even on her long legs, hit below the knee. This morning she had tamed her curly brown hair into a low bun and put on small silver hoops. She was thirty-three, but in court she wanted to make sure no one thought of her as young or unseasoned.

She took a deep breath and looked up at Judge Fitzpatrick. "Your Honor, I ask for the maximum sentence for Frank Archer. He coldly, calculatedly, and callously plotted his wife's murder. If Mr. Archer had been dealing with a real hired killer instead of an FBI agent, Toni Archer would be dead today. Instead, she is in hiding and in fear for her life."

A year earlier Frank Archer had had what he told friends was a five-foot-four problem. Toni. She wanted a divorce. Archer was an engineer, and he was good at math. A divorce meant splitting all their worldly goods and paying for child support. But if Toni were to die? Then not only would Archer avoid a divorce settlement, but he would benefit from Toni's $300,000 life insurance policy.

Archer asked an old friend from high school—who also happened to be an ex-con—if he knew anyone who could help. The old friend found Rod Emerick, but Rod wasn't a hired killer—he was an FBI agent. Archer agreed to meet Rod in a hotel room, which the FBI bugged. In a windowless van parked outside, Allison monitored the grainy black-and-white feed, all shadows and snow, waiting until they had enough to make an arrest before she gave the order. With gritted teeth, she had watched Archer hand over a snapshot of Toni, her license number, her work schedule, and $5,000 in fifties and hundreds. She sometimes understood those who killed from passion—but killers motivated by greed left her cold.

Given the strength of the evidence, Archer had had no choice but to plead guilty. Now, as Allison advocated for the maximum possible sentence, she didn't look over at him once. He was a small man, with thinning blonde hair and glasses. He looked nothing like a killer. But after five years as a federal prosecutor, Allison had learned that few killers did.

After she finished, she rejoined Rod at the prosecutor's table and listened to the defense attorney's sad litany of excuses. Archer hadn't known what he was doing, he was distraught, he was under a lot of stress, he wasn't sleeping well, and he never intended to go through with it—lies that everyone in the crowded courtroom could see through.

"Do you have anything you would like to say to the court before sentencing?" Judge Fitzpatrick asked Archer.

Archer got to his feet, eyes brimming with crocodile tears. "I'm very, very sorry. Words cannot describe how I feel. It was all a huge mistake. I love Toni very much."

Allison didn't realize she was shaking her head until she felt Rod's size 12 loafer squishing the toe of her sensible navy blue pump.

They all rose for the sentence.

"Frank Archer, you have pled guilty to the cowardly and despicable act of plotting to have your spouse murdered." Judge Fitzpatrick's face was like a stone. "Today's sentence should send a strong message to cowards who think they can hide by hiring a stranger to commit an act of violence. I hereby sentence you to ten years for attempted capital murder-for-hire, to be followed by two years of supervised release."

Allison felt a sense of relief. She had an excellent track record, but the previous case she had prosecuted had shaken her confidence. The date rapist had been pronounced innocent, which had left his victim stunned, fearful, and angry—and left Allison feeling guilty that she hadn't been able to put him away for years. Today, at least, she had made the world a safer place.

A second later, her mood was shattered.

"It's all your fault!" Archer shouted. He wasn't yelling at Toni—his ex-wife was too afraid to be in the courtroom. Instead, he was pointing at Allison and Rod. "You set me up!"

Archer was dragged from the courtroom, and Rod patted Allison's arm. "Don't worry," he said. "We'll keep an eye on him."

She nodded and managed a smile. Still, she felt a pulse of fear. Ten years from now, would the man come back to take his revenge?

Shaking off the feeling of foreboding, Allison walked out of the courthouse—known to Portlanders as the "Schick Razor Building" because of its curved, overhanging roof—while she called Toni with the good news. In the parking lot, she pressed the fob on her key chain, unlocked her car door, and slid behind the wheel, still talking.

Only after she had accepted Toni's thanks and said good-bye did she see the folded paper underneath her windshield wiper. Muttering under her breath about junk advertising, she got back out of the car and tugged the paper free.

Then she unfolded it.

The professional part of Allison immediately began to take notes. For one thing, except in a movie, she had never actually seen a threat written in letters cut from a magazine. For another, were her own fingerprints obscuring those of the person who had done this?

But the human side of Allison couldn't help trembling. For all her detachment, she couldn't tamp down her horror as she read the message.

I'M GOING TO RAPE YOU. AND YOU'RE GOING TO LIKE IT. AND THEN I'M GOING TO CUT YOU INTO LITTLE PIECES. AND I'M GOING TO LIKE IT.

Hi! I'm a Senate page on Capitol Hill. This blog will tell about my experiences here in Pageland.

Washington DC is all tall buildings, honking cabs & humidity that feels like someone wrapped you up in a blanket of steam. Plus it smells funky. Like hot garbage.

It turns out that the Vietnam Memorial & the Washington Monument & the statue of Lincoln are all a couple of blocks apart. My stepmom V has been trying to get me to all the famous sites, even though there will be trips every other weekend just for the pages. (Now she's asleep & I'm writing this in the bathroom of the hotel, which has free wireless.)

I can't believe that the whole time we've been here it's been raining. For some reason, I never thought it would rain in DC. Luckily some guy on the street was selling umbrellas.

After all the sightseeing, we went out to dinner with Senator X. He got me this internship, but I probably won't see him very much. I'll be working for all the senators, especially the 50 Republicans, not just him. (Working in the Senate is better than working in the House. I hear they have to stare at hundreds of photos so they can memorize all the faces & names in their party. Compared to that, 50 is a piece of cake.)

We ate at an elegant Japanese restaurant, where I had many things that

I can't pronounce. Not only are the Japanese people good at anime, but they know how to cook.

Before our food came, V told these people at the next table to keep their toddler under control. He had a cup of Cheerios & was throwing some on the floor. So of course she had to boss them around. Then V started telling the senator that he had better keep an eye on me & not let me talk to boys. I just wanted to crawl under the table, even though they both pretended she was joking.

Doesn't she realize that I'm not a little kid anymore? In eight days, I'm going to be seventeen!

Allison set the pregnancy test on the edge of the tub. Marshall was in the living room, stretching in front of the TV news, getting ready to go for a run.

All afternoon, this moment had been in the back of her mind, providing a welcome distraction from her anxiety whenever she thought about the threatening note. Rod had come as soon as she called and had taken the document away as evidence. He asked her if she had any enemies, but they both knew the question was a joke.

Of course Allison had made enemies, most recently Archer. She was a third-generation prosecutor, so she knew it came with the territory.

The so-called blue-collar criminals—bank robbers and drug dealers—weren't so bad to deal with. For them, getting caught and doing time was an accepted risk, a cost of doing business. They were professionals, like she was. In a weird way, they understood that Allison was just doing her job.

It was the other ones, the ones who had been fairly upstanding citizens until they snapped at dinner and stabbed their spouse or decided that bank robbery was a perfect way to balance the family budget. Those were the ones you needed to watch out for. Their feelings for Allison were personal. Personal—and dangerous. For now, she would be extra careful, and Rod had alerted the Portland police to make additional patrols past her house.

Her watch said 6:21. She told herself that she wouldn't pick up the white stick again until 6:30. The test only took three minutes, but she wanted to be sure. How many times had she watched one of these stupid tests, willing two crossed lines to show up in the results window but seeing only one?

"I'll be back in about forty minutes, honey," Marshall called from the living room. She heard the sound of the front door closing.

Allison hadn't told him she was going to take the test today. She was four days late, but she had been four days late before. After so many failed tests, so many months in which being even a day late had filled her with feverish speculation, Marshall no longer inquired too closely into the details.

When they started this journey two years ago, she had been sure that she and Marshall would conceive easily. Any teenager could have a baby. How hard could it be? She and Marshall had always been scrupulous about birth control. Now it seemed like a bitter joke. She had wasted hundreds of dollars preventing something that would never have happened anyway.

They had started trying a month after her thirty-first birthday, giddy to be "playing without a net." At the end of the first month, Allison was sure she was pregnant: her breasts felt different, the taste of food changed, and she often felt dizzy when she stood up. But then her period arrived on schedule.

As the months passed she got more serious, tracked her temperature, made charts. Even though she had read all the statistics about how fertility declined with every passing year, it hadn't seemed like they applied to her.

How many crime victims had she met who had never believed that anything bad could happen to *them*? Because they were special?

"It's in your hands, Lord," she murmured. The idea was one she struggled with every day, at home and at work. How much was she responsible for? How much was out of her control? She had never been good at letting go.

To distract herself, Allison turned on the small TV they kept in the bedroom on top of an oak highboy. After a Subaru commercial, the Channel Four news anchor said, "And now we have a special bulletin from our crime reporter, Cassidy Shaw. Cassidy?"

Allison's old friend stood in front of a beautiful white Victorian house. She wore a coral suit that set off her blonde shoulder-length hair. Her blue eyes looked startlingly topaz—either she was wearing colored contacts or the TV set needed to be adjusted.

"A family is asking for your help in finding a teenager who has been missing from Northwest Portland since yesterday afternoon," Cassidy said, wearing the expression reporters reserved for serious events. "Seventeen-year-old Katie Converse left her parents a note saying she was taking the family dog for a walk—and she has not been seen since. Here's a recent photo of Katie, who is on winter break from the United States Senate's page program."

The camera cut to a photograph of a pretty blonde girl with a snub nose and a dusting of freckles. Allison caught her breath. Even though Katie was blonde and Lindsay had dark hair, it was almost like looking at her sister when she was Katie's age. The nose was the same, the shape of her eyes, even the same shy half smile. Lindsay, back when she was young and innocent and full of life.

Cassidy continued, "Katie is five feet, two inches tall and weighs 105 pounds. She has blue eyes, blonde hair, and freckles. She was last seen wearing a black sweater, blue jeans, a navy blue Columbia parka, and Nike tennis shoes. The dog, named Jalapeño, is a black Lab mix.

"Authorities are investigating. The family asks that if you have seen Katie, to please call the number on your screen. This is Cassidy Shaw, reporting from Northwest Portland."

Allison said a quick prayer that the girl would be safe. But a young woman like that would have no reason to run away, not if she was already living away from home. Nor was she likely to be out partying. Allison knew a little bit about the page program. It was fiercely competitive, attracting smart, serious, college-bound students whose idea of fun was the mock state legislature. The kind of kid Allison had been, back when she and Cassidy were in high school.

She looked at her watch and was surprised to see it was already 6:29. She made herself wait until the clock clicked over to 6:30, then reached for the pregnancy test. The first time she had bought only one, sure that was all she would need. Now, two years later, she bought them in multi-packs at Costco.

In the control window was a pink horizontal line. And in the other window, the results window, were pink crosshairs.

Not single pink lines in both windows.

She was pregnant.

The words popped up on FBI special agent Nicole Hedges's screen.

PDXer: WHATS UR FAVORITE SUBJECT?

Nic—using the screen name BubbleBeth—and some guy going by the name PDXer were in a private area of a chat room called Younger Girls/Older Men.

BubbleBeth: LUNCH

It was what Nic always answered. She could disconnect from her fingers, from the reality behind her keyboard and the words that appeared on her screen. Which was good. Because if she thought about it too much, she would go crazy.

At first, working for Innocent Images, the FBI's cyber-crime squad's effort to take down online predators, had seemed like a perfect fit. Regular hours, which were kind of a must when you were a single parent. The downside was that she spent all day exposed to vile men eager to have sex with a girl who barely qualified as a teen.

Most people were surprised that it wasn't the creepy guy in the raincoat who went online trolling for young girls. If only. In real life it was the teacher, the doctor, the grandpa, the restaurant manager. The average offender was a professional white male aged twenty-five to forty-five.

PDXer: How OLD R U?

BubbleBeth: 13

In Oregon, eighteen was the age of consent. But prosecutors preferred to keep it clear-cut to make it easier for the jury to convict. So Nic told the guys she met online that she was thirteen or fourteen, never older. Some typed L8R—later—as soon as Nic told them her imaginary age. For the rest, it was like throwing a piece of raw meat into a dog kennel.

PDXer: KEWL

Surveys had shown that one in seven kids had received an online sexual solicitation in the past year. It was Nic's job to find the places where the chances weren't one in seven, but 100 percent, which meant going to chat rooms.

Sure, that kind of thing happened on MySpace, but the FBI didn't have the time to put together pages that would fool anyone. They never looked as good as the real thing. Real kids spent hours on their MySpaces, tweaking them with photos and music and blogs. Real predators went there, too, but it was hard to catch them without some kind of tip.

But there were plenty of chat rooms. Nic's being there was predicated on the chat room name (Not Too Young to Have Fun, for example) or a kid's report of having been solicited.

Sometimes she took over from a true victim, but usually she just started out fresh—went into a chat room and announced her presence. The first thing you noticed upon entering a chat room was the absence of any actual chat. The point of being there was to start up a private conversation. It never took longer than five or ten minutes before someone approached her.

PDXer: R UR PARENTS TOGETHER?

BubbleBeth: No. I LIVE W/MY MOM. ONLY C DAD SOMETIMES.

It was what she always said. Guys like PDXer loved kids with one parent and unfettered access to the Internet. It was like that line in *Casablanca*. "*This could be the beginning of a beautiful friendship.*"

PDXer: DO YOU HAVE ANY BROTHERS OR SISTERS?

BubbleBeth: 1. SHES 3.

Young enough that Nicole's imaginary mom would have her hands full.

Nic let Makayla play Neopets online. But only when she was in the room with her. And her daughter knew that at any time her mom could come to her and ask to see what she was typing, and Makayla would have to show her right away.

PDXer: R U A COP?

Nic smiled. *Got ya.*

BubbleBeth: No!

Nic went on answering PDXer's questions, not even paying that much attention. It was better if she didn't. Didn't think about this sick jerk sinking his hooks into a girl. Grooming her. Better if she didn't wonder how many there had been before her. Girls who really *were* thirteen or fourteen.

PDXer: CAN U SEND ME A PIC?

Since they never used pictures of real kids, Nic would send him a picture of herself, morphed back to look like she was thirteen. The morphing wasn't accurate because it didn't take into account three years of braces and four pulled teeth. When she had really been BubbleBeth's age, everyone had made fun of her buckteeth.

PDXer: WANT 2 GO 2 A MOVIE SOMETIME?

BubbleBeth: SURE, THAT WOULD BE COOL.

Nic had to backspace and retype the last words, changing them to B KEWL.

PDXer: ANYTHING U REALLY WANT TO C?

BubbleBeth: MEAT MARKET.

It was rated R, which meant technically she couldn't get in. Well, BubbleBeth couldn't. Sometimes Nic forgot to distance herself. She wasn't thirteen, she wasn't going to school, she didn't fight with her mom.

PDXer: GR8. R U WEARING ANY UNDIES RIGHT NOW?

Bingo.

CHANNEL FOUR
December 15

With varying degrees of dread, TV crime reporter Cassidy Shaw and five other people seated in swivel chairs in Channel Four's dressing room watched Jessica Lear. Jessica was a high-definition makeup consultant the station had flown up from LA to teach them how to prepare for the high definition-era.

HD was five times sharper than regular TV. That meant every line, spot, and lopsided lip would be in sharp focus. You could even see nose hairs, which made Cassidy shudder just thinking about it.

HD also allowed TV sets to show more colors. For years, government standards had limited the range of colors available to broadcasters. But HD allowed the use of some formerly forbidden shades of red. That meant that every blotch, pimple, and tiny broken vein showed up on-screen with the brutal clarity of a surgery textbook.

When she first started out on TV, Cassidy had been taught that she needed to define her face with eyeliner, eyebrow pencil, lip liner, blush, etc. It was almost like paint-by-number. Because studio lights made everyone look pale and washed out, the end result still looked natural on-screen. But that era had come to an end. It had started with the national programs, but as more and more viewers made the switch to HD, it had begun filtering down to all the regional markets—including Portland.

Now all of the on-camera talent had gathered in the dressing room for a makeup application lesson. After the consultant left, they would be on their own. The guys were used to a quick swipe of pancake to hide five o'clock shadow. The men who worked in the field weren't even asked to do that. But now everyone—anchors, reporters, even the weather and sports guys—needed to learn how to look good on the new HD sets.

Jessica, who could have been any age from thirty to fifty, said, "Traditional makeup looks too theatrical in HD. It looks cakey and fake. But wearing no makeup at all would look"—she paused while she found a diplomatic term—"*distracting.*"

Old, Cassidy translated. *Old and ugly.* And Cassidy was determined never to be old and ugly.

Her parents had raised her to believe that being beautiful was a woman's top priority. Good grades had meant little to them, but let Cassidy gain five pounds or go without makeup, and she heard about it. Her bone-deep determination to stay beautiful was what kept her a size 2—well, maybe a 4, if she was being honest, but she was a size 2 on her good days.

The drive not to be old and ugly got her butt into a spinning class six days a week. It made her go to the dermatologist for another round of Botox and laser treatments. It led to regular trips to the nail salon, hair salon, and spray-on tan place. It maxed out her credit card. But it was better than the alternative.

"This is an arms race," Jessica said. "We'd all like to go back to the old days. But we need new weapons. We can't slap on powder when every grain looks like a boulder."

"What about plastic surgery?" asked anchor Brad Buffet (Boo-fay, as he insisted on pronouncing it). He turned sideways to regard his sagging jowls.

Jessica shook her head. "That's iffy too. In HD, when you've had work done, you can actually see the seams. You could end up looking like Frankenstein."

"So basically, this is like being naked," Anne Forster, another reporter, complained.

"It's only like being naked if you don't learn how to cover everything up," Jessica said, and then named a big star in movie comedies. "On regular TV, she still looks great, as sexy as ever. But in HD, she's nothing but a mass of wrinkles and unfortunate pockmarks."

Cassidy leaned closer to the mirror. In HD, the faint wrinkles at the corners of her eyes would probably look like folds of origami and her pores like giant shell-blasted craters.

"So," Jessica said, holding up a metal gizmo about six inches long with an open bowl on the top to hold liquid, "we airbrush." The applicator looked like something a house painter might use to paint the home of an elf. "Can I have a volunteer?"

Cassidy was the first to wave a hand in the air. After pinning back her hair, Jessica told her to close her eyes and hold her breath. The air compressor fired up, making a weird bubbling sound as it aerated the liquid.

Two minutes later Cassidy was so close to the mirror she could kiss it, the way she used to do when she was twelve and desperately wanted a boyfriend. Her skin looked perfect, a flawless sunny beige. No wrinkles, no bumps, no broken veins, no blemishes. It was all still there, of course, but it was now covered with a very thin layer of paint.

If Richard Nixon had had this, Cassidy thought, *Kennedy would never have been elected.*

This morning, V took me to the place where I'll be living for the next five months: the Daniel Webster Senate Page Residence.

There's one floor for girls & one for guys. On each floor there's a community day room, which sounds like something in a mental hospital. Down in the basement is where we'll go to school, plus do laundry & eat.

I'm sharing one tiny room with three other girls: one from North Carolina, one from Texas & one from Idaho. They are all nice. And pretty. And talented. (Just in case they ever read this.) We get to share two sets of bunk beds, two totally crammed closets, one bathroom with two sinks & one phone. Thank goodness V & Daddy let me bring my cell phone & bought me this laptop. They think I'm just going to use it for homework. They're kind of clueless, so they'll never figure out about this blog. (Once V even called the Internet the "world wide interweb.")

I couldn't wait for V to leave. None of the other girls still had their parents with them. When she finally left, she asked the Capitol policeman how close an eye they keep on the pages or, as she put it, "these kids."

The cop told her that she didn't need to worry about her "sister" being safe. There's a security alarm system & pass cards & a twenty-four hour post here. And everyone has to go through metal detectors to get into Webster Hall or the Capitol.

(V didn't correct him about the sister thing, which was typical, but annoying. She's only fifteen years older than me. She likes it when people think we're sisters, but really, we don't look anything alike. I look like my real mom. I'm blonde & five foot two, she's brunette & five foot eight.)

As soon as I got back into our room, the girl from Texas started talking about how this place used to be a funeral home & how down in the basement is where they embalmed the bodies & about how they still keep some of the old equipment in a locked closet. It gave me the creeps.

And I tried not to, but it made me think of my mother. I mean, they must have done that stuff to her after she was dead. Flushed out her blood, pumped her full of chemicals.

The thing is, our room does have a weird smell.

Normally she would have walked the five blocks to Jake's Grill, but tonight Allison decided to drive. As she pulled into a parking lot behind a Subaru with a "Keep Portland Weird" bumper sticker, she told herself it was because she was too tired. But part of it was that she also felt vulnerable, even if the streets were crowded with Christmas shoppers. As she hurried inside the restaurant, she urged herself not to be so paranoid. She had received death threats before.

But never one hand-delivered to her car.

Under a high, white plaster ceiling, the large room was all dark wood and white tablecloths; unchanged for decades, the kind of place where you could still smoke at the bar. Jake's was just loud enough that you wouldn't be overheard, but not so loud you had to shout. Allison had chosen it because she thought it was the perfect place to talk shop.

Trying not to breathe in the odor of beer and stale cigarettes, she made her way past the bar and to the back of the dining room. Since she had found out she was pregnant, her sense of smell had gone into overdrive. In court this morning she had been aware of the witnesses' shampoo and cologne, even the court reporter's mouthwash. She'd had to throw away her lemon poppyseed muffin uneaten because it smelled too *lemony*.

Cassidy and Nicole were already at a booth in the back, but they hadn't yet noticed her. Cassidy was clearly telling a story, all gestures and animation. No doubt describing some amusing scrape she had recently gotten herself into. She had shrugged off the cardigan of her violet cashmere sweater set, revealing—perhaps not inadvertently—her toned and tanned upper arms. Her short blonde bob was perfect in the front and tousled in the back, which meant she had been ruminating. Whenever Cassidy was stymied, she twisted strands of hair at the back of her head— a spot the camera never saw.

As she listened to Cassidy, Nicole rested her glass of wine against her cheek, half hiding her mouth. Fifteen years earlier, when the three of them had attended Catlin Gabel, Nicole had stood out by virtue of being one of a handful of African-Americans at the private school. Given her prominent overbite, some of the crueler kids had dubbed her Mrs. Ed. When she spoke, she had cupped one hand in front of her mouth, muffling her speech.

Somewhere in the years since high school, Nicole had had her teeth straightened. With her dark, smooth skin and slightly slanted eyes, she had always been pretty. Now she was beautiful. Still, old habits died hard.

Nicole caught sight of Allison and waved. "Hey, girl!"

Still thirty feet away, Allison lip-read the words as much as heard them. As she unbuttoned her coat, she announced, "The Triple Threat Club is now in session."

The three women hadn't been close in high school. After graduation, they didn't see each other again until their tenth reunion, where their common interest in crime—Cassidy's in covering it, Nicole's in fighting it, and Allison's in prosecuting it—had drawn them together. A month later, Allison had suggested they meet for dinner. A friendship had begun over a shared dessert called Triple Threat Chocolate Cake, which featured devil's food cake filled with rich chocolate mousse and topped with shaved chocolate.

As Allison pulled out a chair, Cassidy said, "I was beginning to think you weren't coming. And you were the one who picked this place."

"Sorry. I was in a meeting that ran long."

"We saved you some onion rings." Cassidy pushed a plate toward Allison. Her lips were shiny with grease.

Suddenly feeling a little queasy, Allison shook her head. "That's okay."

"We've already ordered," Nicole said, "but I kept a menu if you need one."

"I already know what I want."

The menu never changed. Jake's served comfort food, all of it tasting of her childhood, back when her dad was still alive and her mom still cooked and Lindsay could still be counted on to come home at night. Pot roast, sirloin steak, prime rib, meat loaf with potatoes and gravy.

When the waiter came, Allison ordered the pork chop.

"You've got to try some of this Cab. It's just"—Nicole let out a long sigh—"relaxing." She filled Allison's glass. "Let me tell you about this case someone else in cyber crimes is handling. He's working with Jack in your office on it, Allison. What happens is: Husband and wife get a divorce. He moves out of state. Then he goes online and puts an ad on an adult sex site. And in the ad, he claims to be the ex-wife. He says, 'This is my name, this is my phone number, this is my address, this is where I work, this is the kind of car I drive and the license number, and here's my picture.' But all the info he gives is hers. And then he says, 'Oh, and my fantasy is to be stalked and raped.'"

Allison shook her head. How could someone who had promised to love and honor another human replace that with a rage so intense it caught things on fire?

Nicole continued, "So another guy answers the post. Of course, he thinks he's talking to the ex-wife. And the ex-husband pretends to be her and says, 'Yeah, this is my biggest fantasy, ha-ha. If you do it, I'll pretend to resist because it just enhances the excitement.'"

Cassidy squirmed in her seat like a little kid. "Then what happened?"

"So this guy breaks in while the ex-wife is asleep one night. And he's got a dozen roses and a box of See's candy and a gag and a pair of handcuffs. And the whole time she's fighting him off, he's getting more excited, because it's just like she said it would be. He gets one handcuff on her, but before he can cuff her to the bed, she beans him with the bedside lamp. When he wakes up, he's under arrest and he's the one wearing the cuffs." Nicole looked at Allison. "The dilemma for your office is, what do we charge him with? Attempted rape? Or what?"

"I want in on this one," Cassidy said.

Nicole wagged a finger at her. "I don't want you to give anyone ideas. All I need is a bunch of bitter ex-husbands setting it up so that some stranger kills their ex."

Cassidy looked self-righteous. "The public has a right to know."

Nicole snorted. "Don't give me that. It's just pure titillation. There's nothing a potential victim could do to stop this. All you're doing is giving bad guys ideas."

Taking on the familiar role of peacemaker, Allison changed the subject. "I saw you on TV last night, Cassidy." She picked up her wine glass, remembered the baby, put it down. "On that segment about the missing girl."

"Blink, and you would have missed it." Cassidy set down her own glass, already empty.

"I must have missed it." Nicole tipped some more wine into her own glass and then Cassidy's. "So—a little kid? I didn't hear anything about that."

Cassidy shook her head. "No, a high school junior—seventeen years old. She went out to walk the dog and never came home. When we filmed the story, she'd only been gone a little over twenty-four hours. Now it's been more than forty-eight, and there's still no sign of her. When the parents contacted me, the locals weren't taking them too seriously. But something about it didn't feel right to me. This girl, Katie Converse, is home on break from being a Senate page in DC. Her parents told me there's only about a hundred kids who get to do it from around the whole country. Someone like that would be responsible."

"Maybe she's just holed up with some boy, and now she'll never live it down," Nicole said.

Cassidy reached for a piece of bread. "Oh, like kids now care about that. Nobody even bothers to get married before they have a baby anymore, or haven't you noticed?"

Allison watched as Cassidy winced, belatedly remembering Makayla, Nicole's nine-year-old. No father was ever mentioned.

Cassidy said rapidly, "Although in Katie's case, maybe they would. Her family seems pretty rigid. Going on and on about how she was such a good girl and would never get in trouble."

Allison said, "If she's been missing for more than forty-eight hours, then maybe the reason she hasn't come home is because she can't."

Nicole nodded. "With stranger abductions, they are usually dead within three or four hours. It's very rare to find them alive and okay."

Cassidy fingered a red string she wore around her wrist. "Don't say that. Don't put that kind of energy out there into the universe."

Nicole pointed at Cassidy's wrist. "What's with the string?"

"Kabbalah."

"Isn't that for Jews?"

"You don't have to be Jewish," Cassidy said. "You can be anything. It's not about being a member of a formal religion. It's about getting in touch with spiritual forces that are active in our lives whether we acknowledge them or not."

"What do you do exactly?" Allison asked, trying to be open to Cassidy's latest transitory spiritual enthusiasm.

"You meditate on the cosmic energy of the Hebrew alphabet."

Nicole's expression was dubious. "And where does the red string come in?"

"It helps protect you."

Nicole shook her head. "Might as well drape chicken guts around your neck."

Cassidy slipped her cardigan back on, hiding her slender wrist. "Allison goes to church, and you don't tease *her*."

"At least she's consistent." Nicole gestured with her wine glass. "You have a new thing you're into every month. It's feng shui or a palm reader or some new ritual you read about in a magazine."

Nicole was smiling, but there was an edge to it that made Allison anxious. She liked them both so much, but sometimes it felt like they needed her as a buffer. The three of them had much in common—women trying to make their way in a man's world of crime and punishment—but there were times their differences were all too apparent.

"Well, I think it's good to be open to new ideas," Cassidy said. "I don't think there's only one answer, like Allison. And I don't think there are no answers, like you do, Nic. You won't admit that there are things we can't see or touch, but that still exist. You don't leave any room for magic or serendipity."

Sometimes Allison thought they were still locked in the same roles they had held in high school. Cassidy was still the cheerleader. Her enthusiasm was intense—and short-lived. Nicole was still a realist. As a black woman living in an overwhelmingly white city, she strove to be better than the best. And Allison herself? She guessed she was still the good girl, smoothing things over, cleaning up other people's messes. The one who put herself last. She reached out and put her hand on Cassidy's wrist, asking her without words to pull back a little.

"I do believe in something," Nicole declared. "I believe if you think the universe is looking out for you or that God is watching over you or whatever, then life's going to come around and bite you in the butt. That red string doesn't protect you any more than Allison's going to church on Sunday protects her."

Nicole took another sip of wine, but as she tipped her head back, Allison thought her eyes looked lost and sad.

"I think you're wrong, Nic." Cassidy shook her head. "Maybe it's not the church, and maybe it's not the string. But sometimes if you believe there's a force at work for good, it can change your perspective."

Their food arrived, and for a minute they were all quiet as they ate.

Eventually Nicole picked up the wine bottle and gestured toward Cassidy. "More wine?" It was a peace offering.

"I'll have a splash. What about you, Allison? You haven't even touched your glass."

Allison opened her mouth, but nothing came out. She hadn't prepared any statements yet. She wasn't ready.

Cassidy narrowed her eyes. "You're not!"

Her friend leaped to the truth so fast it made Allison feel even more off balance.

"Sh! I don't want to jinx it. It doesn't feel real yet." She was surprised to feel the prick of tears.

"So you're sure?"

"I know how to pee on a stick. I've had lots of practice."

"Marshall must be over the moon," Nicole said with a grin. But when Allison didn't say anything, she tilted her head. "Don't tell me you haven't told him."

"I was going to, but when I went out to talk to him, he was on the phone with a client who wanted to change an ad at the last minute, and I could tell he was going to be in a bad mood when he got off. And then I was going to tell him this morning, but he had an early meeting and was rushing around." Allison realized she was spinning her plain gold wedding ring around her finger. "I'll tell him tonight."

"This calls for a celebration." Cassidy waved the waiter over. "Do you have any sparkling cider?"

He shook his head. "The closest I've got is Italian soda."

Cassidy looked at Nicole. "Maybe *we* should order another bottle."

Nicole shook her head. "I'm already past my limit. You know how rigid the Bureau is."

FBI agents were required to be "fit for duty" at all times—which meant that having more than one or two drinks, even on weekends, was out.

"All right then," Cassidy said. "Italian sodas all the way around. Oh, and one Chocolate Bag—and three spoons."

It was Jake's signature dessert: dark chocolate molded to look like a small paper bag and filled with white chocolate mousse and fresh berries.

When their Italian sodas came, the three women clinked their glasses together.

As her friends smiled at her and dipped their spoons into the dessert, Allison's mind raced. Was she really ready? What if something went wrong? And should she be bringing a child into a world where bright, beautiful girls went missing?

Do you have any news?" shouted a woman standing in the Converses' driveway. She wore a bright blue Columbia parka embroidered with the logo for Channel Two. Pushing the microphone into Nic's face, she said, "It's been three days since Katie disappeared." Just as she ignored the few snowflakes lazily drifting from the sky, Nic paid no attention to the reporter or the cameraman filming them.

In her work with Innocent Images, Nic had gotten a reputation for working well with parents of missing or exploited children.

"These Converse people are high maintenance," her supervisor had told her. "You're good at that."

An hour earlier, Nic had called Katie's parents and asked to meet. Now she walked up the front stairs of the Converses' white Victorian home. The oversized front door was nearly covered by a giant poster reading: HAVE YOU SEEN THIS GIRL? It showed Katie dressed in her navy blue page uniform, with a smaller inset of a grinning black dog. Except for its size, the poster was a twin to the posters now stapled to hundreds of telephone poles all over town.

A tall woman in her early thirties answered Nic's knock. Her dark hair was cut in a chin-length bob, and her eyes looked like bruises. Pinned to her sweater was an oversized button with a color photograph of Katie, with the word *Missing* stamped in white on the bottom.

"Nicole Hedges, FBI." Nic held out her badge.

"Come in." The woman closed the door behind them. "I'm Valerie Converse." A tall, thin man with short gray-blonde hair hurried into the entryway. "This is my husband, Wayne."

Wayne looked about fifty, his face weather-beaten. Behind gold wire-framed glasses, his blue eyes swam, wet and reddened. He too was wearing a button. "Have you heard anything?" he asked urgently. "Anything at all?"

Nic had to shake her head. "We don't have any news, but this morning we formed a task force with city, county, and state police, as well as the FBI."

A task force when there was no evidence of foul play was unusual, but Wayne and Valerie had the power to pull some strings, and the fact that Katie was sponsored by Senator Fairview had been underlined. And the more the locals had looked, the less they thought Katie was a runaway.

"We're examining footage from all the ATM, traffic signal, and parking lot cameras within a three-mile radius. We've got teams showing Katie's picture at every restaurant, store, and bar in Northwest Portland. We've set up a hotline and are asking the media to publicize it. And we're talking to every sexual predator within a five-mile radius."

"Dear God," Wayne said, "do you think Katie's dead?" He grabbed Nic's arm, squeezing until his fingers pinched her bones. "Is that what you think? That some monster took our little girl and now she's dead?"

"We have no evidence of that," Nic said, and Wayne released her.

The truth was, they had no evidence of anything. It was as if Katie had walked out of her parents' house three days ago and vanished.

"Where were you people when Katie first went missing?" Valerie demanded. "I can't sleep. I can't eat. Last night, Wayne never even went to bed. He was searching all the Dumpsters in the neighborhood, wondering if he'd find her body. Her body!" She pressed closer, her breath sour.

Nic took a half step back until her shoulders brushed the door.

"A beautiful young girl goes missing, and you wouldn't help us! Didn't you people learn anything from Candy Lane?"

Candy Lane was an unfortunately named fifteen-year-old who had been branded a chronic runaway. When she didn't come home from school, Portland police hadn't taken it seriously. Then Candy was found in a child molester's basement, half dead, on a live Web cam. Several cops—including the chief of police—had turned in their badges over the case.

Now the locals might have screwed up again. But if Katie's disappearance turned into another debacle, in this case there would be plenty of people to share the blame. And Nic could be first in line if she didn't handle these people with kid gloves.

With her back pressed against the door, she was beginning to feel claustrophobic. "Perhaps we could sit down?"

Wayne blinked rapidly. "I'm forgetting my manners."

The living room had cream-colored walls, a twelve-foot ceiling, and bay windows that bracketed a fireplace built of river rock. The furniture was either very good reproduction mission or the real thing. Nic took a seat on a chocolate brown leather armchair. As the Converses sat down on the opposite ends of a leather couch, she made a mental note of the distance between them. Some couples pulled together during a crisis, while others drew apart.

Nic pulled out her notebook and said, "You two have done a great job getting those signs up all over Portland."

"It's the kids from Lincoln," Wayne said. "When they heard that Katie was missing, kids and their parents volunteered to put up signs as far south as Eugene and all the way up I-5 to Seattle. Tomorrow they're holding a vigil at the high school."

"What time will that be?" Nic would go, of course. It wasn't unknown for the killer to join in the search. And later, to show up at the funeral.

"At 7:00 p.m." Wayne's voice broke. "People have been so generous. They're donating food for the volunteers, putting up posters, passing out buttons, and contributing to the reward fund."

From her briefcase, Nic took out a notebook and pen. Then she handed a sheaf of papers to Wayne. "This is a warrant for you to sign so we can get a trap and trace on Katie's phone. Then the phone company can research which numbers have called her phone and any numbers she's been calling."

Without reading it, Wayne scribbled his name and handed the papers back. His eyes never left her face.

"Do you have caller ID at home?"

"I already looked," Wayne said, following Nic's train of thought. "No number on there that I didn't recognize before she disappeared."

"Then why don't we start," she said, "with you telling me a little bit more about your daughter."

"We've been over this before." Valerie sighed heavily. "More than once."

"I know, I know, Mrs. Converse, and I appreciate that, but sometimes a fresh pair of eyes and ears can pick up something that has previously been missed."

They painted a sweet, uncomplicated picture. Nic took notes, listening for what they didn't say as well as what they did. At home, Katie was known as Katie-bird. She played the piano. She collected designer shoes and liked to draw. Her favorite movie was *Legally Blonde*, and her favorite color was purple. In February she would rejoin the rest of her junior class at Lincoln High.

"She's a sprinter on the track team," Wayne said. "She's small but fast. She wouldn't have been taken easily. If she wasn't immobilized, she would have fought or run."

"So what do you think happened?"

Nic watched him carefully. It wasn't impossible that Wayne actually *knew* what had happened because he had done it. Even killers could break down in tears, not believing what they had done, not believing they couldn't undo it. And people were much more likely to be harmed by a family member than by a stranger.

Wayne took a shuddering breath. "There must have been more than one of them. Maybe they had a van. And probably a gun."

"What about her dog?" Nic asked. "Wouldn't he have bitten anyone who tried to attack her?"

"Jalapeño?" Valerie snapped. "That dog is stupid. He'd be as likely to lick a kidnapper's face as bite him."

The local cops had put out a bulletin to the pound and all the shelters within a twenty-mile radius, but so far, nothing. The dog was chipped, which made the search easier. It would be hell if the family had to keep driving from shelter to shelter, looking at dogs that weren't theirs. Of course, it would be far worse to hear that a body had been found—only to learn that it wasn't your sister, your daughter, your wife.

"He's really Whitney's dog." Wayne pushed himself off the couch and started pacing. "Now he's gone, and Whitney has to endure not knowing where her sister *or* her dog is. I just hope they're together. Then Katie wouldn't be too lonely."

Nic turned a page in her notebook. "Can you walk me through what she did that day up until the time she left with the dog?"

"You're wasting time asking all this again," Valerie snapped.

Wayne shot her an anxious glance.

"Precious minutes, precious hours. Why aren't you out there finding the person who did it?" She covered her face with her hands.

"Please," Nic said. "It could be useful."

"She was still sleeping when I left," Wayne said. For a second, he stopped pacing. A shudder ran through his body. "I didn't even get to say good-bye to her. I never got to tell her I loved her one last time."

"Don't say that," Valerie ordered, uncovering her face. "We don't know that." She turned to Nic and took over the story. "Katie didn't get up until after her sister went to school. I would have thought she would have been wide awake, given the three-hour time difference between Portland and New York, but she had the pillow over her head and she didn't want to get up."

Nic remembered those days, when she was fifteen or sixteen and could have slept half the day and then not gone to bed until two in the morning. She had a feeling Valerie wouldn't stand for either of those things.

"She had Life cereal for breakfast and read the newspaper," Valerie continued. "She's not like most kids, who don't read the paper at all, or only read the comics and the celebrity gossip. Katie is interested in national news, international news." She pressed her lips together until they turned white. "Then she took a shower and got dressed. Around eleven, I left for my volunteer work—I run the clothes closet at a local outreach center. We help women getting off the street who don't have a working wardrobe. We give them the clothes they need to look present-able again. When I got back around four, I found a note from Katie saying she had taken Jalapeño for a walk. I started calling her cell phone about a half hour later. It was already getting dark. But she never answered."

"What route does she normally take?" Nic was careful to use the pres-ent tense. She would never promise that Katie was alive, but she wouldn't rest until the girl was found. What would it be like to lose Makayla? It was a thought she kept coming back to, like a tongue probing a sore tooth.

Valerie tipped her head to one side, thinking. "She likes to window-shop. I'm guessing she went up Twenty-third and came back on Twenty-first."

It was the same good news–bad news answer Katie's parents had ear-lier told the locals. The two streets were probably the busiest in Portland, with plenty of foot traffic. Cops had already walked the same route, done a neighborhood canvass, talked to every person along the way. Nada. But it wasn't surprising. Would one girl, bundled up against the cold, walking a nondescript dog, have attracted any attention among hundreds of shoppers intent on finding the perfect Christmas gift?

Wayne clenched his fists. "It's like she went out that door and stepped into a black hole."

"Has Katie seemed any different since she came home?"

"She's seemed lost in thought. I'll say something to her, and she won't answer me until I ask it a second time."

Valerie nodded. "I think she's depressed. She's been sleeping a lot and only picking at her food. I thought maybe she was just missing school and her friends in DC. But when I tried to ask her about it, she said nothing was wrong."

"Have you looked to see if anything is missing?" Nic asked. "Her purse? Her keys? Any kind of backpack or bag?"

Valerie massaged the space between her eyebrows. "Just the things you would think she would take. Her cell phone and her keys."

"This might seem insensitive, but we need honest answers to help us find her. Does Katie drink or use drugs that you know of?"

Valerie stiffened. "That we know of! She's not some latchkey child. We make it our business to know what Katie is doing and with whom. She doesn't smoke, she doesn't drink, and she most certainly does not use drugs. We've already discussed these things with the other policemen. Why are you wasting time asking the same questions over and over?"

The woman was like an injured dog, biting anyone who tried to help.

"Please, just bear with me. Does Katie have a boyfriend?"

"No," Wayne said. "Katie knows we don't want her to date until she's out of high school."

What the parents wanted and what the kids did could be two very different things.

Watching Valerie pinch her lips together, Nic asked, "And who would you say her friends are?"

Valerie said, "Her best friend is a girl named Lily, but I don't know if they've been in touch since Katie came home. They've known each other since preschool, but Katie has kind of outgrown Lily, if you know what I mean."

"Why don't you tell me?"

"Oh, Lily's turned into one of those Goth girls, all dressed in black. She wasn't brought up that way, but she's a bit of a rebel. Not like Katie. Katie has, has—*goals*."

"She's so focused," Wayne said, his voice cracking. "So focused and smart and funny. And now some sick creep has taken her."

"We don't know that, Mr. Converse." Nic had to say it, although her gut told her he was right.

His eyes were haunted. "You may not know it, but I do." His hands curled into fists. "If I could only get my hands on the guy who took my little girl!" With a roar, he pivoted and punched the wall. A dimple appeared, and then the paint fell away, revealing plaster held in place by chicken wire. White dust swirled in the air. Wayne shook his hand as both women sprang to their feet.

"That's not going to help!" Valerie shouted.

"Did you hurt yourself?" Nic asked.

When Wayne mutely shook his head, she took his hand between her own. His skin was cold. She ran her finger across his knuckles, which were red and already starting to swell. Bruised, but not broken, if she was any judge. When something hot plopped onto her arm, she flinched and looked up. Wayne was crying, his mouth so wide that she could see the silver flash of fillings on his back teeth. His face was red and his whole body shook with sobs, but he was eerily silent. She let go of his hand.

Finally, Valerie reached out for her husband and pulled him to her. As Wayne buried his face in her neck, Valerie stared at Nic over his shoulder. Her eyes were blank, unseeing.

Five minutes later, Nicole followed Katie's parents up the stairs. While Wayne held a bag of frozen peas across his bruised knuckles, Valerie pushed open the door at the end of the hall. Katie's bedroom had pink curtains, apple-green walls, and a window seat.

Nic said, "Sometimes I find it helps me to spend some time alone in a person's room. It helps me absorb their spirit."

She sounded all New Agey, like Cassidy. The truth was that she just wanted the parents out of the room in case she found something—like pot or a vibrator—that would upset them.

They both nodded, Valerie more slowly.

Nic closed the door. First, she surveyed the room. Everything was so neat. The furniture was dusted, and the clothes were hung on evenly spaced hangers in the walk-in closet, instead of strewn on the floor the way Makayla's always were. It was so clean that even the trash basket was empty.

Where another girl might have had a poster of a popular band, Katie had a poster of Condoleezza Rice. The top of a chest of drawers held a framed photograph of herself—complete with braces—shaking hands with President Bush. There was also a mounted wooden gavel. Nic read the brass plate. *To Katie Converse, for exemplary leadership in the State of Oregon Mock Legislature.*

She took a pair of latex gloves from her pocket and pulled them on.

The chances that this was a crime scene, that someone had been in here with Katie and forced her to go with them—or simply enticed her—were small. But if they didn't come up with something soon, she would bring in the fingerprint specialists to see if there was anything in the room that didn't match up.

Methodically, Nic began to search. She checked the pockets of Katie's clothes. No Abercrombie & Fitch or American Eagle for this girl, but Nordstrom and Saks. Each pocket was flat and empty. The only surprise in the back of the closet was the hundred shoe boxes in wooden cubbies. The front of each box bore a stapled Polaroid of the contents, ranging from ballet flats to totteringly high heels.

On the bookshelf were a half dozen teen novels—the kind that looked more serious than racy—and a book of poetry. From it, the green edge of a Post-it peeked out. Nic opened the book.

The Sick Rose
by William Blake

O Rose, thou art sick.
The invisible worm,
That flies in the night
In the howling storm:

Has found out thy bed
Of crimson joy:
And his dark secret love
Does thy life destroy.

After reading the poem through twice, Nic closed the book and put it back. Was Katie as virginal as her parents imagined? Or was it Katie herself who had done the imagining?

A search of the drawers yielded no rolling papers, phone numbers, diaries, loose pills, porn, or hidden cigarette packs. The only thing she noticed was that the panties on top of the underwear drawer were all silky thongs, while those underneath were cotton Jockey briefs. There was nothing taped underneath the drawers. Nic was pushing the last one back into place when she saw the slim white Macintosh laptop sitting underneath a pile of folders on the desk.

Her heart started to race. In today's world, a computer held everything. E-mail, IM log, journal, calendar, shopping lists, even last time on the computer. With the latter, they might be able to nail down the last time Katie was in the house.

Nic pulled out her cell phone and called the computer forensics lab.

"Hey, Katie Converse had a laptop. I'm bringing it in."

At the lab, the techs would be able to bring up all the laptop's past history, even if it had been erased. Everything that came across the machine was cached in little nooks and crannies that the average user knew nothing about. With the right tools, any secrets could come spilling out. There could be a clue in an e-mail—an invitation to meet or even a threat.

The computer was already on, so she opened it up. On the Internet browser she looked to see the last place Katie had visited. It was myspace .com/theDCpage. Nic clicked. And there she was. Katie. A photo of her striking a pose wearing a fedora, more sexy than disguise. But was that sadness Nic saw in Katie's eyes? From the angle, she guessed Katie had taken the photo herself with her cell phone.

On the left of the page were lists of the books and movies and music the girl liked. On the right, blog entries and a series of comments from friends. Music began to play, a song Nic vaguely recognized as having been very popular over the summer. Now, so close to the shortest day of the year, it seemed like it had never been summer and never would be again.

Alive on the screen. Nic just hoped Katie was alive in real life. She clicked on one of the blog entries at random. It was labeled simply "Rules."

I'm exhausted. And hot! My clothes stick to my skin. I never understood what humidity really meant. They might as well just say "sauna."

This morning I made myself drink three cups of coffee. It tasted burnt. But I figured I needed it, b/c it was five thirty in the morning! I haven't gotten up that early since I believed in Santa Claus. A couple of guys at my table were really cute (I'm not naming names, just in case).

After breakfast the Senate Page Director explained the program to the thirty of us. There are lots of little rules like not breaking curfew, getting good grades & keeping your room clean. Anytime we're someplace not patrolled by the Capitol police, we have to be with another page or an adult, even if it's just to go to the Starbucks across the street.

If we break any of the big rules, we can be kicked out without warning. Like last year I guess this guy was caught stealing. That same day, he was put in a car & driven directly to the airport. Can you imagine how humiliating that would be?! The director said that everything that happens in Washington gets in the paper, so if we screw up, we jeopardize the entire page program.

He also said they monitored our Internet when we're on the government's computers, although he didn't say exactly how much they could see. He did say if you go to a porn site & are there for more than a few seconds, they'll know. He didn't say anything about MySpace on my personal computer, though & I didn't ask, so this is legal—right? ;-)

As he was talking, I looked around the room. We look like the pod people. All of us in navy blue pantsuits, white long-sleeved shirts, dark socks & black lace-up shoes. (Do you know how hard it is to find women's black lace-up shoes? Which, by the way, are the ugliest shoes I have ever seen. I finally had to mail-order them & they didn't show up until two days before I left for DC.) The only difference between the girls & the guys is that the guys have to wear ties.

At lunch, a lot of the other pages grumbled about all the rules.

Me? No matter how many rules there are, it's better than being home. V is always yelling at me. Not at my sister, of course, b/c she's perfect.

The last thing we learned was how to put on a gas mask. Mine smelled funny inside. Even though they said you could breathe with it on just fine, I couldn't. I felt like I was smothering. There just wasn't any air.

I finally had to tear it off.

Allison sat in the kitchen nook, drinking the one real cup of coffee she had decided to allow herself per day. With real sugar, since she had sworn off the artificial stuff. Around her, the rest of the house was in darkness. Sleet lashed the black rectangles of the windows.

Floyd the cat sprawled on her lap, deliriously kneading her thigh with his sharp claws. His pupils were so wide there was only a fine rim of yellow around them. He had been in a whiny, obnoxious mood since she had gotten up. The only way to quiet him was to hold him. Not wanting to wake Marshall, she had pulled the cat onto her lap. Fine preparation for parenthood, Allison thought, stroking Floyd with more annoyance than affection.

Ever since she had learned that she was pregnant, she had been filled with uncertainty about becoming a mother, but it was too late to step off now. One minute she couldn't believe it was really happening, the next minute she was worried that it was all too much.

She had pushed aside Marshall's latest comps for a shoe ad to make room for her coffee cup and her Bible. Allison turned the pages until she found the verse she was looking for in Philippians. *"Do not be anxious about anything, but in everything, by prayer and petition, with thanksgiving, present your requests to God. And the peace of God, which transcends all understanding, will guard your hearts and your minds in Christ Jesus."*

Still keeping one hand on Floyd, Allison raised the other one and began to pray in a soft murmur. Her arm was stretched high overhead, her hand pressing up as if it carried a weight. It was the physical expression of the emotional and spiritual load she had felt since she saw the two crossed lines on the pregnancy test.

"Oh, God, I offer you up the burden I'm carrying, the burden of this pregnancy. I thought when it finally happened I would feel so happy, and I do, but I'm also scared. I know I need to be taking care of myself, and get more sleep, but I can't stop thinking about this girl Katie. She looks so much like Lindsay at that age."

Her arm began to ache. Allison let it relax a few inches. "And what if this baby *isn't* born healthy? And I keep putting off telling Marshall, even though I don't know why, and what am I going to do for child care, and how will I manage to breastfeed *and* work? And what if my work just gets too dangerous?"

In the midst of pouring out her fears and requests, Allison remembered the other half of the verse. *Thanksgiving.* It took real effort to get the words out. "But thank you, Lord, for this pregnancy, for this baby growing inside me." As she heard herself murmuring the words, she felt a thrill of wonder and awe. She *was* pregnant, after all this time.

As of today, she was five weeks along. Allison clung to that number now, even though only last week it had seemed silly when she had learned that they counted from the first day of your last menstrual cycle. She hadn't had any morning sickness, hadn't been especially tired, hadn't had to go to the bathroom more often. The only things that were different were her heightened sense of smell and her sore breasts. Whenever she was alone in her office or in a restroom stall, she would roughly run one hand across them, making sure they were still tender. She had read someplace that if you were going to miscarry, then your breasts would stop hurting first, before the blood began.

Allison realized she had fallen silent, and that both hands were back in her lap. She had given the burden back to God.

Behind the closed bedroom door, the bed creaked, and she heard Marshall roll over and put his feet on the floor. Taking a deep breath, Allison thought of her prayers.

As soon as the door opened, she said, "Marshall. I have something for you." Ignoring the cat's cry of protest, she pushed him off her lap and stood up.

"What?" He pushed his black hair out of his half-closed eyes. Marshall wasn't a morning person.

"I got you an early Christmas present."

Allison handed him the small package she had wrapped this morning. It felt too light to contain all their dreams.

Marshall shot her a puzzled look. They weren't the kind of people who stretched out Christmas celebrations. They didn't even have a tree up yet.

He hefted it experimentally and then tore open the wrapper. Inside was the white plastic pregnancy test. The crossed pink lines were still visible in the window.

Slowly, Marshall's mouth opened. No words came out. Her heart beating in her ears, Allison watched as comprehension spread up his features. His eyes widened. His eyebrows lifted. Finally, he turned toward her. He had to clear his throat before he could get the words out. "You're—you're pregnant?"

Allison nodded.

He caught her wrist and pulled her to him, wrapping his arms around her. His body was still warm from the bedclothes. With his mouth pressed against her hair, Marshall murmured, "We've been waiting for so long. I can't believe it."

She could feel his heartbeat underneath her ear. Finally, finally, Allison began to feel herself relax. No matter how hard things were, Marshall would always hold her up. He offered her a safe place where she could take off her armor and show the vulnerable woman underneath.

"I love you," she murmured.

Instead of answering, Marshall kissed the top of her head, a million tiny kisses. His fingers lightly grazed her belly.

"I can't wait," he said, and his voice wavered between laughter and tears.

Allison grinned up at him.

Even four blocks away from the school, Allison could hear the singing. She couldn't make out the words, but the tune was old and familiar: "Amazing Grace." She wrapped her coat more tightly around her.

When she had heard on the radio about the vigil for Katie Converse, Allison had decided to attend. Every time she saw Katie's photo on the news or in the paper, she was reminded of her sister. It wasn't just the superficial resemblance, the unfinished look of the snub nose and the big eyes. Before their father died, Lindsay had been filled with the same enthusiasm, the same hope that maybe she could be the one to change the world. After he was gone, she started to hang out with a different crowd. Allison felt she should have done something to save her, but she had ignored the danger signs. By attending the vigil, Allison felt like she was doing something, no matter how small, to help Katie.

Obviously, she wasn't the only one who felt some kind of connection to the missing girl. The school parking lot was completely full, forcing her to park four blocks away. As Allison hurried to the school, she tried to put some distance between herself and the shabbily dressed man who had parked directly behind her. He wore a navy blue ski jacket, the hood cinched tight against the cold so that she couldn't even see his face. There was something about him that made her uneasy, but she told herself that a vigil would attract all kinds.

After she had walked a block, she turned to look over her shoulder.

The man was matching her step for step, no closer, but not any farther away. She thought of the note she had found on her car. Walking faster, she snaked her hand inside her coat and touched her cell phone, clipped to her belt. She was relieved when she joined the crowd—she guessed there were more than three hundred—congregated in front of Lincoln High.

Allison had come straight from work, so she didn't have a candle. But as soon as she came up to the edge of the crowd, a girl with black-rimmed eyes handed her a candle and a large button with Katie's picture on it. After Allison pinned the button to her coat, an older man standing next to her lit her candle with his own while she shielded the flame.

The crowd had stopped singing, and it was eerily quiet, except for some muffled sobbing. It was like they were all waiting for something to happen. Waiting for Katie to come home. Or, failing that, waiting for news. For answers, for a sign, for their hopes to be fulfilled—or their nightmares to come true.

Allison spotted Cassidy at the edge of the crowd in a bright circle of TV lights. She was interviewing a man whom Allison recognized from the newspaper as Katie's father. She edged closer so that she could hear.

Wayne Converse was in the middle of an appeal. "Katie, honey, if you can hear this, we love you. Please call us." His glasses reflected the light. "And if you are someone who has Katie against her will, please let her go. Please." His voice broke. "If anyone has any information that can help us, that can lead Katie to us or us to Katie, please call the FBI or any police agency. Our family is absolutely devastated."

As he spoke, Cassidy nodded solemnly. Afterward the camera turned its eye to her while she wrapped up the segment, leaving Katie's stricken father literally in the dark. Then a dapper man whom Allison recognized as Senator Fairview put his arm around Katie's father and drew him away, murmuring softly. They were joined by a tall, slender woman whom Allison guessed must be Katie's mom.

On an easel near the school's front doors, a huge blown-up photo of

Katie watched the crowd. She was grinning, her eyes as blue as the bright sky behind her. The photo had been blown up so large that every one of her freckles was clear. Allison joined the others gathered before the make-shift shrine erected in front of the photo. More than a dozen votive candles flickered inside glass enclosures. Heaped around them were stuffed animals, snapshots of Katie, a drawing of a dove held in place by a pebble, a ceramic kneeling angel, and a dozen bouquets of flowers, still wrapped in plastic.

On each side of Allison, girls stood in clumps, their arms around each other, their faces shiny with tears as they contemplated the potential loss of their friend. Their tears, Allison thought, came as much from disbelief as they did from pain. And maybe there was a measure of fear, too, fear that whoever had snatched Katie could come for them next.

Allison closed her eyes and prayed wordlessly.

When she opened her eyes, she saw a woman slowly walking along the edge of the crowd, filming people's faces with a digital video camera small enough to fit into her palm. Scanning the rest of the gathering, Allison picked out two men dressed in plainclothes, filming the faces that glowed in the light of candles. A uniformed police officer approached one, indicating a part of the crowd with a jerk of his chin. The camera-man turned. Allison tried to figure out who they were looking at, but she couldn't tell. She suddenly remembered the man in the navy blue parka, but when she looked around the crowd, she couldn't see him anymore.

She did spot Nicole, who acknowledged her with a nod and then went back to watching the crowd, her expression fierce and alert. Nicole was here for professional reasons, while Allison's were more complicated, personal as well as professional. She thought about the fragility of life, about Katie and Lindsay and the new life inside her.

The crowd began to sing "How Great Thou Art." In the flickering, golden light of the candles, their faces looked serene and ghostly. Their voices raised gooseflesh on Allison's arms, despite her warm coat. Without a piano or even a pitch pipe, they were perfectly in tune. Without a director, they still found the same rhythm, still started and stopped each line at the same time.

In their unrehearsed and implausible perfection, Allison felt the presence of the Holy Spirit.

But when she looked out at the blackness that surrounded them, she felt something else. Evil. Waiting.

As she drove to the Converses' house, Nic felt exhausted. She had stayed at the vigil until every last person had gone, paying particularly close attention to those who lingered, those who wept until they could barely stand—and those who caught a glimpse of one of the cameras filming the crowd and quickly turned their backs.

And she knew this was only the beginning. Today was a Saturday, but for the time being, weekends were only a theory. You worked this kind of case until it was finished, and until then there weren't any days off. This could eat her life up—bones and all—before it was over. She had already made arrangements for Makayla to temporarily stay with her own parents. She hadn't seen her daughter since the day before yesterday. Nic was giving up time with her own precious child to help another family find theirs.

At least she had been in the FBI long enough that she was no longer considered a rookie. When you were the newest agent, you got handed a stack of cases no one else wanted to work, took the territory no one else wanted to drive, and drove it using the oldest car in the fleet. When everyone else went to lunch, you stayed behind to answer the phones. When they executed a search warrant, you were assigned the spot the bad guy was least likely to exit through.

Being asked to be a liaison to the Converses was a sign that someone in the Bureau wanted her to go further up the ladder. The thing was—Nic wasn't sure she wanted to go. Not when Makayla was so young and she saw her so little as it was. The next step would be being named a field supervisor, but the Bureau had recently gotten serious about its five and out policy. Supervisors at a field office could only be there for five years before they were required to take an assignment at headquarters. If they didn't, they had to step back down in rank or quit. There was no way Nic would take Makayla to DC. She couldn't afford private schools, not on what the FBI paid, and she would never put her daughter in public school there.

As a black woman in the Bureau, Nic was in a double minority. They liked to trot her out as an example, but everything she did was also scrutinized. Nic's achievements didn't seem to add up as fast as a guy's. At the same time, she sometimes thought that if she made a mistake, it would be broadcast on a loudspeaker all over the office.

Sometimes it felt like she had to be twice as good as a man to even compete—like Ginger Rogers, who had done everything Fred Astaire had, only backward and in high heels. Take the 2.5-minute shooting drills. Agents had to shoot while lying prone, from behind barricades, on their knees, reloading, switching hands, moving ever closer to the target. They were expected to get a score of 80, which meant they had to put 80 percent of their bullets in the kill zone.

Nicole's last score had been a 97.

She pulled up to the Converses' house. Now there were four camera crews out front. She parked in the narrow driveway behind Valerie's red Volvo station wagon—she didn't see Wayne's blue BMW sedan—and ignored the shouted questions as she went up the walk.

Nic was here to interview Whitney before Valerie drove her to her violin lesson. At first she had thought it was strange that the Converses insisted on keeping to Whitney's routine. In the last day, though, Nic had begun to see the wisdom of it. If she stayed home, Whitney would be reminded of her sister's absence every second. She would probably overhear speculation that would crush whatever innocent conceptions she still harbored about the world and the way it worked. These hours spent at her lessons might be her last chance to still be a child.

Valerie answered Nic's knock. Each day, her face looked more haggard. "Wayne's out with the searchers," she said. "He can't take sitting at home." She called upstairs. "Whitney! The lady from the FBI is here to talk to you."

Whitney bounced down the stairs. She was in that awkward stage of adolescence, springy and skinny, her limbs like rubber bands. Her hair was as dark as her sister's was blonde. Wasn't there a fairy tale about two sisters, one dark and one fair? Snow White and Rose Red, maybe that was it.

Valerie led them into the living room and then left.

Whitney kicked off her flats and curled her legs under her. She was dressed like all girls were these days—skinny jeans, a turquoise camisole long enough to show underneath a striped T-shirt, and a dark green hoodie. It was pretty much what Makayla wore, only because this girl was four years older, she had more of a figure. She looked at Nic with curious dark eyes.

"So tell me about Katie," Nic said gently.

"She's three years older than me. We haven't gone to the same school for a long time. But she's really smart. Every teacher that had her thinks I'm going to be as smart as her. But I'm not."

"It sounds like she casts a long shadow."

Whitney stared at Nic, a little puzzled, and then her brow smoothed out. "You mean is it hard being Katie Converse's little sister? It's not. She's nice to me. She gave me this manicure." Whitney spread out her pink-tipped fingers, but half of them had been nibbled on. She flushed and slipped her hands under her thighs. "She helps me with my homework, and sometimes she lets me borrow her shoes. We wear the same size."

Nic thought of the dozens of boxes in Katie's room.

"Do you think your sister could have run away?"

Whitney's face scrunched up. "Where would she go? Sometimes we see kids on the streets downtown, but Katie would never live like that.

You'd get really dirty. She likes to be clean. Besides, she really wanted to go back to the program. She said that she could go to bed whatever time she wanted, and eat whatever she wanted." She glanced at the doorway and lowered her voice. "See, our mom's kind of strict."

"Did you talk to her that morning?"

Whitney bit her lip. "She was still asleep when I went to school. I didn't see her at all." Tears sparkled in her eyes. She exhaled shakily. "That's what I don't understand. Why did she have to take Jalapeño for a walk?"

"What do you mean? Because you had already walked him that morning?"

"No. I mean, yeah, I did walk him that morning. But Jalapeño's my dog, not Katie's. I'm the one who takes him for walks. She doesn't even like him that much."

Nic felt a bolt of electricity race down her spine. The Converses had mentioned earlier that the dog was Whitney's, she was sure they had, but the meaning of it hadn't hit her until now.

The day Katie disappeared, she hadn't been walking the dog to give it some exercise.

She had been walking the dog to give herself an excuse.

But an excuse to do what?

Cassidy sat in the basement of the TV station, logging the tape she and Andy Oken the cameraman had shot this morning.

After the rally last night, they had rushed to the car to get the tape back for the eleven o'clock news. Except there had been a teensy problem. Cassidy's car was gone.

"I told you not to park here, Cassidy," said Andy, a weathered man who was really a little too old to be toting around such heavy equipment. He gave her a smug look. "But you said no one would notice. You said they would be too busy trying to find a bad guy to give a rat's—"

Cassidy cut off his rant with one of her own. "It wasn't really that close to the fire hydrant. And it's not like this is the time of year they have to worry about fires anyway."

"Well, we're in deep doo-doo. There's no way we'll get the tape back to the station in time."

Cassidy didn't waste her breath answering. Instead, she ran out into the middle of the street and forced a huge car, so old it had fins, to lurch to a stop. The driver leaned out to yell at her in a foreign language. But through a series of hand gestures in which she repeatedly pointed at the Channel Four logo on the camera and then at her watch, Cassidy managed to impress upon the guy, a fiftyish Russian immigrant—at least she thought he was Russian—that she and Andy needed to get back to the station and that it was an emergency.

"TV?" the driver asked with a grin, pointing at both Cassidy and Andy.
"TV," agreed Cassidy, pointing at just herself.

After several wrong turns, a hair-raising few minutes going the wrong
way on I-405, and an illegal U-turn, he had gotten them back to Channel
Four. With five minutes to spare.

This morning they had been out again, first to retrieve Cassidy's car
from the impound lot, then to interview a few of the Boy Scouts who
were now canvassing the area near Katie's house. They had also shot
B-roll—footage without a narration sound track that would run while
viewers listened to Cassidy or one of her interview subjects. The B-roll
added dimension. While Cassidy talked about the Boy Scouts, the B-roll
would show them knocking on doors and handing out fliers.

You always shot more footage than you could use. But to be able to
decide what part of the tape to use, you had to log it—record exactly what
was on the tape and the time it appeared. Logging narrowed things down,
weeded out the unusable. It allowed you to save time in the long run, searching for that elusive shot. But in the short run, it was tedious and time-
consuming. Just one of the thousand little tedious tasks that put the lie to
the "glamour" of being a reporter.

As she took another sip of coffee, Cassidy used the knob to shuttle
through some footage she was sure they wouldn't use. At the upper right
was a time code that showed how far into the footage that particular scene
started. She took notes about what was in each scene. When someone was
speaking, it was impossible to take down every word, so she only wrote
down the first and last few.

There was Nicole, clipping the microphone onto her collar. Cassidy
turned up the sound and listened to her friend say, "We've realized that
during our first canvass many renters did not disclose that they had other
people visiting or living with them. Sometimes there were two names on
the lease, and six people living in the apartment or friends of friends who
had been visiting. And some of these people have turned out to be fugi-
tives of one kind or another."

Nicole went on to explain law enforcement's version of Cassidy's grunt work. They now had to identify as many individuals as possible who had been in the area where Katie disappeared, and then either clear them by obtaining a valid alibi or gather enough information to justify a search warrant.

"We also are locating and interviewing every registered sex offender who lives in the area," Nicole continued. "But that's going to take time. There are approximately nine hundred registered sex offenders with Northwest Portland addresses."

That was her next angle, Cassidy realized. She could profile a few of the worst of those nine hundred. With luck, she could track down old victims who might be willing to talk if their faces and voices were altered. That kind of footage was actually more dramatic than filming the actual people, in Cassidy's opinion, so it was a win-win all the way around.

Next came some shots of Cassidy standing next to a poster of Katie that conveniently looked weather-beaten. It allowed her to pontificate about whether people were already forgetting about the girl. Cassidy watched her on-screen self critically. Had she talked too fast, swallowed consonants, sped past important points? Had she been clear, credible, and comfortable?

After all, this could be her big break. Did she really want to stay in Portland forever? Los Angeles sounded marvelous after months of gray skies. But then again, was she still young enough to make it in LA? Every time she saw her parents, they reminded her that she was, as her dad put it, no spring chicken.

Cassidy was so deep in thought that she didn't see Jerry, the station manager, until he was close enough to touch.

He cleared his throat.

She jumped and then tried to hide it. "Hey, Jer. What are you doing here on a Saturday?"

"Looking at these. Did you see the overnights?" He waved a printout under her nose.

Ratings haunted Channel Four. Theirs was a "metered market," which meant Nielsen had put meters in a sample of Portland's households to automatically measure viewership. But ratings were like getting a report card without any explanation from the teacher. You knew what you had, but you had to guess at the why.

But this time Jerry seemed to think he knew. "It's the Katie Converse thing. People are eating that up," he said. "Last night's program delivered a 9.7 household rating and a 15 percent share in the metered-market overnights. That's up 45 percent from a year ago. Forty-five!"

Cassidy was stunned. Such a huge jump for a news broadcast was nearly unheard of. More and more, people turned to the Internet for the news. A TV news broadcast was practically an anachronism, filled with "news" that people had already learned about hours earlier. The only way to fight back was with news that was more than just a recitation of dry facts. News that was more like the stories she had been doing about Katie Converse.

This was it, Cassidy realized. Really and truly it. The Katie Converse story could make or break her career.

And right now it was making it.

I got lost on my first official day of work. All those long corridors look alike. While I was trying to find Senator Y's office, I ran into Senator X—my senator. He walked me to the right office & asked me how it was going.

Just before lunch, this other page in the program, R, told me she had seen me talking to Senator X. She said she knew he was my sponsor, but that it seemed like I knew him personally.

Finally I gave in & told her that my parents were supporters of his & that V & I had dinner with him before the program started.

R sniffed. She has all these freckles. I've got some, but she looks like someone spattered her with olive-green paint. Then she said something about how a lot of the pages here seem to have some sort of "in" & don't really need to be qualified.

I couldn't believe her! I *am* qualified. Straight A's, debate, mock UN, mock state legislature, etc. How is it that on my first day of work I've already been branded a freeloader? I told her I still had to meet the same requirements as everybody else. It wasn't just a slam dunk.

Sometimes people think they know you, but they really have no idea.

Then the weird thing was that R asked if I wanted to go to lunch together. Like we were friends or something! We all have meal cards so we can eat in the Senate cafeteria. I told her I was meeting someone else. No way was I hanging out with her.

Of course, then I had to make sure we didn't show up at the cafeteria at the same time, so she wouldn't see that I was alone.

But guess who was there? Senator X! He asked if I wanted to sit with him. I didn't care if it looked like I was sucking up. I just said yes.

He wanted to know where I had heard about the program. I told him there was a guy at school a couple of years ago who had been a page. In fact, Senator X sponsored him, although he didn't seem to remember him that well.

While I was talking to Senator X, R walked by & stared at me. I knew what she was thinking.

But I am not a freeloader.

HEDGES RESIDENCE
December 19

You're taking Makayla to church?" Nic asked her mother.

"If your child is staying in my house, then of course she is going to church with me this morning." Berenice Hedges put her arm around Makayla's slender shoulders. She wasn't going to give up her granddaughter that easily.

"But, Mama, I'd rather she decide that kind of thing for herself when she gets older."

"'Train a child in the way he should go, and when he is old he will not turn from it,'" her mother retorted. Berenice was five inches shorter than Nic, but right now she seemed taller.

"Like that made any difference with me," Nic began, when her cell phone vibrated on her hip. She looked down. It was from the Converses. With a sigh she said, "I have to take this." Turning away as she pressed the talk button, she said, "This is Nicole Hedges."

"Can you come by the house?" Wayne Converse said in a rush. "There's someone we'd like you to talk to. Someone who might know something about what happened to Katie."

Nic's pulse began to race. "Who?"

"I'd rather wait until you get here to explain it to you."

Nic had to park four blocks away. Before she got out of the car, she slipped on her sunglasses and picked up a notebook and an empty Starbucks cup for protective camouflage.

The media filled the sidewalk for the length of the block and spilled out into the street. Three satellite trucks, guys with TV cameras on their shoulders or long-lensed cameras around their necks, others toting boom mikes, a couple of dozen people talking on cell phones or tapping away on their BlackBerries. All of them waiting for something to happen.

She twisted her way through them, her coffee and notebook a kind of disguise. There were so many reporters here now, many from out of town, that a new one wouldn't be remarked upon. Once she came back out of the house, it would be a different story. Nic was two steps from the Converses' walkway, two steps from private property, when someone grabbed her arm.

"Nicole," Cassidy hissed in her ear, no more eager to draw attention than Nic was herself. "What's happening?'"

Nic shook her off. "Later," she said out of the side of her mouth.

Cassidy fell back, a tiny smile tightening her lips, her turquoise eyes avid.

The minute Nic turned up the walk, the crowd turned and began to shout. She thought of a pack of wild dogs baying. Baying simply because the others were baying.

"Do you have news about Katie?"

"What about Katie?"

"Is there something new in the Katie Converse case?"

The front door opened, and she heard the cameras whirr. Wayne pulled her inside. Valerie was standing behind him. It was a relief to have the door click solidly into place behind her back, to have the shouts reduced to murmurs.

"Are you getting tired of having them camped out out there?" she asked.

Wayne pushed up his glasses and then pinched the bridge of his nose. "It's a balance. We have to figure out a way to keep them interested, keep the case alive, without having them lose focus—or go away completely."

Valerie rubbed her temples. "We learned our lesson when we let one in to use the bathroom. Next thing you know, she was boasting about having some kind of 'exclusive.'"

"The media can be on your side," Nic said, "but you have to be careful. Because finding Katie isn't their priority."

"Then what is their priority?" Wayne asked. "What could be more important than a missing girl?"

"Ratings," Valerie said flatly.

Nic nodded, thinking of Cassidy's eagerness. "Right. So if they can turn your life upside down and shake out some scandal, they'll do it. Anything for a new angle. Thanks to the Internet and CNN, we live in a twenty-four-hour news cycle. The only problem is that there aren't twenty-four hours' worth of news. So if there isn't anything new, they have to make something up." She remembered why she was here. "Anyway, who is it you want me to talk to?"

"We didn't want you to be skeptical," Wayne said in a rush. "But once you meet her and hear what she has to say, then . . ."

Nic's heart started to sink. With difficulty she kept her face neutral.

"It's Lorena Macy. I understand she's quite well-known to law enforcement personnel," Valerie said. "She says she's even helped your agency before."

Nic kept quiet. She had never heard of Lorena Macy. But she already knew what was coming.

Wayne's voice was low. "She came to us and said she's been having dreams since the day Kate disappeared. Even before it was on the news. Then when Lorena did see it on TV, she knew her dreams were really about Katie. She says she can get in touch with Katie by holding something of hers. But we wanted you to be here. In case she says something you can act on right away."

"Where is she?" Nic tried hard to keep the anger out of her voice.

"In the kitchen," Wayne said.

Nic took a deep breath. "Look, Mr. and Mrs. Converse. Let me be blunt. These kinds of people are already crawling out of the woodwork. We're getting dozens of tips every day based on people's dreams and visions. And 99 percent of them want attention or they want money. And then there are a few who just really, really want to help, even though they have no clue what happened."

Wayne raised his eyebrows. "Lorena's not asking for money. She said she would refuse it even if we pushed it into her hands."

Nic wanted to shake him. "Of course she did. Just by taking her seriously, you're putting money in her pocket. Do you think she won't leave here and go right out front and talk to all those people? Once they hear about how you asked her to help on the Katie Converse case, more people will want their palms read or their cards done or whatever it is she does. They'll think that if the FBI consulted with her, then she must be good. I bet she was the one who asked if I could be here, right?"

She could tell by their uneasy exchange of glances that she was. "She'll drum up business, with Katie as her calling card."

Nic hated to do this to the Converses when they were so desperate, but she tried to make it quick and clean, like pulling off a bandage. "Have you said anything to her that's not generally known? Because let me warn you—don't tell her one thing she doesn't already know."

"But what if she does know?" Wayne asked. "What if she knows *already*? That's why she's here. To tell us what she knows. Not the other way around."

So much for quick and clean. "All right. Let's go hear what she has to say."

Lorena was a plump woman, sixtyish, with dyed red hair. She looked like she had fallen in a paint box. There was a bright circle of red on each cheek, turquoise shadow on eyes rimmed with black liner, and so much mascara that she looked half asleep.

And then Nic figured it out. The makeup wasn't so much for the Converses. It was for the TV cameras outside.

After the four of them sat down around the kitchen table, Nic said, "Can you spell your name for me?" She hadn't flashed her badge, hadn't given her own name. Her goal was to give this phony as little as possible.

Lorena did. There was something high-pitched and artificial about her voice that set Nicole's teeth on edge.

"And you contacted the Converses because . . ."

Lorena patted her ample bosom. "I've been having visions and dreams since the very hour Katie went missing. When I saw Cassidy Shaw on the TV, and she said Katie was missing, I knew in my marrow that was who I was dreaming about. But to get to the truth, I need to be able to hold something of hers. Something she might have worn would be good."

Nic was glad that they had already taken away something for the dogs, should they ever need them. If they ever got to a point where they could narrow this down to an area smaller than Portland.

"Just a second," Valerie said. She left the kitchen and they heard her footsteps go upstairs.

"So how does this work?" Nic asked while they waited.

Lorena simpered, not at all deterred by Nic's glare. "When I'm in one of my trances, I don't see or hear in a traditional way. It's energy. I receive an impression of the energy the person is sending out. It doesn't matter if they're dead. They're not dead to me."

Valerie reappeared holding a red sweater. "Katie wore this two days before she left. It hasn't been washed."

With eager hands, Lorena pressed it to her chest. "I'm going to go inside myself now. Don't be worried if you hear me make strange sounds. I lose myself when I'm in one of my trances."

Wayne murmured, "Okay," and Valerie nodded. It was all Nic could do not to roll her eyes. *What would you do if it were Makayla?* she scolded herself. *How far would you go?*

Lorena closed her eyes. She rubbed the sweater over her face and then let her hands and the sweater drop into her lap. "Okay, Katie, tell me where you are. Tell me where you are, baby. I can help you. Katie, where are you?" As Lorena spoke, she rocked forward and back, her upper body following a small circle.

There was a long silence. Nic looked at her watch. One minute ticked by. Two. Three. When Lorena finally spoke, the three of them jumped. Her voice was slower, lower-pitched, like a sleepwalker's.

"I see an old car. There's something on top of it. Maybe it's an Oldsmobile?"

Despite herself, Nicole felt her skin prickle. She saw Katie, not sitting in a car, but sprawled unmoving in the trunk. A spill of honey-blonde hair across her open, staring eyes.

"Katie, tell me what I'm looking at, sweetie. Come on. Tell me where you are. Are you in the car?" Her plump hands, with rings on every finger, kneaded the sweater.

There was a long silence. Lorena cocked her head to one side, as if listening. "There are trees where she is. A lot of them."

Good guess, Lorena. Oregon is nothing but trees.

"But is she alive?" Wayne demanded.

"Water. She's near water."

Near water. Give me a break. Every place in Portland is near water. We've got the Columbia and Willamette rivers and countless creeks and streams. Not to mention the rain.

But Valerie and Wayne had grabbed each other's hands.

"I see something green. A duffle bag? And I'm hearing a name like Larry." She drew the name out, giving it an extra syllable. "Lar-er-y. Or something like that." Her face screwed up. "Katie, where are you? Are you with someone named Larry? No, that's not it, is it? But something close. Is it someone you know?"

Good choice, Lorena. How many names rhyme with Larry? Mary, Harry, Carrie, Barry, Jeri, Terry? Half the city probably qualifies.

"Mmm," Lorena moaned. The pitch of her voice had changed, arced higher. Her head was loose, her neck boneless. "Mmm."

The three of them stared at her.

"Mommy." Her voice was high-pitched and breathy. "Mommy. Where are you?"

The back of Nic's neck prickled. *Stop it!* she warned herself. *Don't fall for this crap.* Despite knowing it was a bunch of hooey, there was something about the woman's voice that was getting to her.

Valerie leaned forward and tentatively touched Lorena's arm. "I'm right here, honey. I'm right here."

"It's dark," Lorena whimpered. "I'm scared." She whimpered again. "Mommy? Mommy?"

Then it was like the older woman had touched a live wire. Her body jerked upright, and her arms and legs stiffened, breaking contact with Valerie. Her eyes snapped open.

"What did you see?" Wayne's voice broke. "Tell me. Is she alive?"

Lorena's voice was soft and slurred, as if she was only slowly coming back from where she had been. "I saw Katie laughing and smiling."

Nic stiffened. This was cruel. This was downright cruel. *Katie laughing and smiling?* Why give these poor people false hope?

Valerie's hand shot out and gripped Lorena's forearm, her fingers digging in. "She's alive, then?" Her voice was ragged.

"Sometimes I see the future and sometimes I see the past." Lorena sounded exhausted. "And sometimes I see the present."

"Was she with someone?" Wayne asked. His hand closed on Lorena's other wrist. "What was she wearing? Was it this time of year?"

"Did she look older or younger?" Valerie asked.

The three of them were in a tight knot. Only Nic leaned away from what was going on. At some point, although she didn't remember doing it, she had crossed her arms.

"I don't know," Lorena murmured. "I don't know. The spirits didn't reveal that to me."

"At the end, she sounded so scared," Valerie said. Her eyes shone with tears—the first time Nic had seen her close to crying. "Was she scared where she was?"

"I couldn't see anything at that point." Lorena covered her eyes with her fingers. "It was like I went blind."

"Katie calls you Mom," Wayne said to Valerie. "Not Mommy. Never Mommy."

Valerie blinked, and a single tear ran down her perfectly made-up face. "No. That's what she called Cindy."

"Who's Cindy?" Nic asked.

Wayne turned to her with a look of surprise, as if he had forgotten she was there. "My first wife. Katie's mom. She died when Katie was eighteen months old." His wet eyes implored Lorena. "Do you think"—his voice broke—"do you think she's with Cindy? Do you think Katie's dead?"

"What I think," Nic said, pushing herself away from the table and getting to her feet, "is that Lorena is using your personal nightmare to make money." She leaned over the table, getting within a foot of the psychic's face.

Lorena's eyes widened.

"Let me ask you something. If I start checking up on you, what am I going to find? Is everything squeaky clean and aboveboard? Or is something going to come crawling out from under a rock?"

Lorena opened her mouth, but no words came out. Wayne and Valerie looked nervously back and forth between the two of them.

"That's what I thought," Nic said, finally straightening up. "When you leave, I suggest you keep your head down and not say one word to anyone. And if I find out that you have defrauded the Converses in any way, or if you try to use this to make some kind of profit, then so help me, I will start digging. And I have a feeling you won't like what I will do when I find something."

After the vigil, Allison went to her boss and asked to be assigned to Katie's case. Assuming it was a case. But it was, she was sure of it. She could feel it in her bones. "This one really speaks to me, Dan," she had said. "And you know I've done homicides."

"We don't know that it's a homicide." Dan picked up a pen on his desk, fiddled with it, put it down. Then added, when Allison wouldn't look away, "Yet."

"I know I'm not out of line," she said, working Dan as hard as she had ever worked any jury. "I deserve this."

It was sure to be a high-profile case, with all the potential for success—as well as failure—that entailed. Big cases made big names for prosecutors—which could lead to big bucks if they ever decided to jump the fence and become defense attorneys. Even if they stayed put, big cases also led to promotions. And good publicity if they ever decided they wanted to run for district attorney.

But that wasn't why Allison wanted this case. She only wanted to do right by this girl. If someone had hurt Katie, Allison wanted to bring that person to justice.

Dan closed his eyes and rested his chin on his thumbs and his forehead on his steepled fingers.

Finally, he took a deep breath, opened his eyes, and said one word. "Okay."

Now Allison had teamed up with Nicole to question Lily Rangel, Katie's old best friend. Lily was a plump girl who Allison thought was trying a little too hard to look dangerous. She had skin as white as a vampire's, and there was a silver stud just underneath her black-lipsticked lips. Her hair had been dyed black, straightened, and then brushed forward so that it covered her forehead and cheeks in long spikes. A streak of electric blue hung over her left eye. Her clothes were all layers of black, except for black-and-red-striped socks that stretched above her knees.

"You just let me know if you girls need anything. It's no trouble to make coffee." With a little wave, Lily's mom left the room. She was a plain, sweet, and essentially colorless woman.

It wasn't too hard to guess what Lily was rebelling against.

Lily sighed. "My mom is clueless. She thinks Katie and me are still friends. She keeps asking me if I know where Katie really is."

Allison and Nicole exchanged a look. Allison said, "Katie's mom told us you were Katie's oldest friend."

Lily made a dismissive sound and shook her head. "We've known each other since we were like, in diapers." She looked down, fingering the black choker that cut into the soft flesh of her neck. "But that's not the same thing as being tight."

Allison decided to start with the big picture. "Tell me, what was Katie like?"

Lily's head jerked up, and her startled eyes, rimmed with black liner a quarter inch wide, met Allison's. "You mean, what *is* she like? You said *was.*"

This girl was more perceptive than she looked.

"*Is,*" Allison said, mentally kicking herself. "Sorry. What *is* Katie like?"

"She's nice."

Nicole made a skeptical sound in the back of her throat, half question mark and half laugh. "Nice? That sounds like what you say when you really don't like someone."

Lily shifted, and when she spoke again, it was to her knees. "Katie and me, we *were* friends when we were really little. Our moms met in some kind of 'mommy and me' class when we were like two. But we got older and we got different."

Nicole said, "Translate that for me."

Lily twisted the silver ring on her left thumb. "To be honest, Katie's kind of a suck-up. Adults like her more than kids do."

"A suck-up?"

"You know, an overachiever. She wants to get straight A's, she wants to go to Harvard, she wants to be a lawyer. She has this whole plan. She says she's going to be president someday."

A thought occurred to Allison. "So did she run for office at Lincoln High?"

A roll of the eyes. "Last year. Ran—and lost. I tried to warn her. It's like everything else at school. It's not how good your ideas are, it's a popularity contest. Katie kept saying she had a great, what'd she call it, a great platform. Only it's not about your *platform*. It's about how many friends you have."

"Are you saying Katie didn't—" Allison corrected herself. "Doesn't have any friends?"

"She has friends," Lily admitted reluctantly. "Friends like her. So of course there aren't a lot."

Allison couldn't imagine that Lily herself had that many friends.

"Have you been in touch since she left for the program?" Allison asked.

"Sometimes Katie texted me if she saw someone famous. You know, like an actor or something came to the Senate. It was like she was trying to impress me. Which is stupid. She's the one that gets to go off to DC and live on her own. And I'm stuck in Puddletown." She sighed. "I can't wait until I can move out on my own."

"So Katie just texts you, then," Nicole said patiently. "She doesn't call you."

"She called me once in October. It was like, right before Halloween. And she said she had a boyfriend."

Allison straightened up. "Who was he? Do you know?"

"She wouldn't tell me his name. But she did say he was somebody important. Somebody everyone's heard of." Lily shrugged. "At first I kind of thought she was lying."

Lying? Allison thought of Katie's blog. Katie had known that others might read it. Which meant she might have shaded the truth. Allison had known that. But until now, Allison had never considered that Katie's hints of a boyfriend could have been conjured up from her imagination. At that age, you might be tempted to mimic the drama you saw all your friends going through.

"Why did you think she might be lying?"

"I wasn't there, was I? In DC, I mean. She could say anything she wanted about what it was like there, and how would I know? I mean, if it were me, I would come back and tell the best stories about what I had done there. You know, like about how I had eaten dinner with the president and his family. And no one would know they weren't true."

"So what did Katie tell you about this guy? Her boyfriend?"

"She mostly just bragged about having one. She'd never really had a boyfriend before. Not a serious one. And when I asked her who he was, she said that all she could tell me was that he was famous. And I was like—famous? You know, 'cause we're juniors in high school, not like rock stars or anything. But she said he took her to expensive restaurants and he drove an expensive car and he bought her a bracelet."

Nicole and Allison exchanged glances. Someone rich and famous. Was it true? Or was the whole thing like Lily thought—an elaborate lie to make Katie feel better?

"So is that when you thought she might be lying?" Nicole asked.

Lily nodded. "I figured she was probably just staying in her room and doing her homework. You know how sometimes you say something and it's not true, but to make people believe it's true you have to tell more and more lies?"

Allison nodded. As a prosecutor, she had met a lot of people who did exactly that.

"You said 'at first,'" Nicole said. "At first you thought Katie was lying. So did something change to make you think she was telling the truth?"

Lily nodded. "I saw her the second day after she came back home for Christmas break. The day before she disappeared. Her mom came over to have coffee with my mom and brought Katie with her. We went up to my room, but we really didn't have that much to talk about. She didn't care what was happening at Lincoln, even though she's coming back in February. She just kept wanting to talk about this guy. But it wasn't like it was in October, when she was bragging about how wonderful he was. She kept saying it was complicated, but that it was true love, and that was all that mattered."

"Oh?" Allison asked.

True love. Kids were the only ones innocent enough to believe in that idea. That two people, no matter how mismatched, were fated to be together despite any obstacles.

"And how did Katie act when she was telling you this?" Nicole asked.

"She just seemed sad, you know. She was thin, but it wasn't pretty thin. It was like, bony. And then she showed me that gold bracelet he had given her. And how it had a 24K stamped on the inside, which means it's the best kind."

"Is there anything you're not telling us, Lily?" Allison asked gently.

Chances were faint, but if this girl knew if Katie was hiding out, or that Katie was in some kind of trouble, they had to make sure she told them.

"Whatever you say can't get you in trouble, and it can't get Katie in trouble. We just need to find her. And nothing you say could surprise us. So if there's something you're holding back, please don't."

Lily hesitated, then said in a rush, "Well, who would it be that had an expensive car and took her expensive places and gave her expensive gifts?

Who was famous? No one our age, that's for sure. So I figured it was some old guy. And since she wouldn't tell me who it was, I figured it was some old guy who's married."

"Did you ask Katie if that were true?" Allison asked.

Lily looked down at the toes of her high-top Converse. "Not exactly."

"What did you say?" Nicole asked.

"Nothing really. Just that she better be careful."

"And . . . ," Nicole pressed.

"And I told her one thing I knew that she didn't."

"What's that?"

Lily turned her head toward the doorway, listening for her mom. After hearing nothing, she spoke in a voice not much louder than a whisper. "A long time ago, I heard my mom talking to my dad about her mom. Katie's mom. Only she's not her real mom. Valerie's her stepmom. Her real mom died from cancer when she was a baby. Everybody knows that. But what Katie didn't know—what hardly anyone knows—is that her stepmom started out as *her* babysitter. *Katie's* babysitter. And she ended up having sex with Katie's dad after Katie's mom died. Which is just so messed up. And she got pregnant and had to get married, and then had the baby, and that's Whitney."

Allison looked at Nicole. Even Nic, whose face rarely betrayed emotion, looked shocked. Allison was pretty sure her own mouth was hanging open.

"So I told Katie she had to be careful. I told her she didn't want to screw up her life like Valerie had. I mean, my mom said something about her having to get married while she was still in high school. She didn't even graduate. I don't want to get married until I'm like thirty or something." Lily said the word *thirty* as if it were synonymous with *dead*.

Allison asked, "How did Katie react when you told her this?"

"She was really mad. She says Valerie is always lecturing her about waiting until she gets married. She couldn't believe Valerie was such a hypocrite."

"So," Nicole said, "what do you think happened to Katie?"

Lily took a deep breath, let it out. "Something bad. I think something bad happened."

"You said Katie was sad, that she had lost weight," Allison said. "Do you think she was depressed enough to kill herself?"

Lily pursed her lips and blew her bangs out of her eyes. "I keep thinking about that, but no. Not unless she thought she was going to lose everything."

It was hard to believe that it had been less than a week since she had first heard Katie's name, Nic thought. Now she was more than just a missing girl—she was a project that had taken on a weight and momentum of its own. The Katie Converse task force had set up a command post in a hotel ballroom downtown. The huge room was filled with people from every branch of law enforcement as well as database experts, stenographers, dog handlers, search-and-rescue teams, topography experts, reconnaissance pilots, and media reps.

Half of the room was set up theater-style, with rows of chairs facing a head table and a whiteboard. At the rear of the room a table was piled with reports, documents, and copies of Katie's photograph for investigators to take as needed. The walls were lined with photocopiers, computers, printers, and boxes of paper. Timelines, maps, photographs, and lists were tacked above. Nicole was at the back of the room, part of a group of FBI agents and cops at a table fielding telephoned tips.

"If you find her, send me something of hers, like her watch or a shoe. The murder weapon would be perfect," a hotline caller told Nic.

The woman was a psychic, or so she had said. The same claim had been made by the last three people Nic had spoken with.

"I'm sure I could tell you who did it then."

"We'll keep that in mind. Thank you very much for your call," Nic said.

She hung up and pulled the headset from her head. Her ear itched. Her head itched. Her whole body felt irritated. She wanted to be out doing something, not answering the phone.

Fielding anonymous tips on a hotline was considered too important to be done by civilians. Yet everyone knew 99 percent of it was a waste of time. The lonely, crazy, and vengeful came out of the woodwork for this kind of case. The hotline had had more than a thousand tips. Unfortunately, more than eight hundred had come from psychics or people who had had a dream about Katie. But just in case a real tip did sneak through, the agents all put in time answering calls.

Next to her, Leif Larson took off his own headset and looked at her sympathetically. "Another crazy?"

"She says she's a psychic." Nic sighed and tried to stretch the kinks out of her neck. She couldn't turn her head without wincing. "You should have seen the charlatan the Converses made me talk to. After I left, I did a little online search of her 'revelations.' One boy she said was dead turned out to be alive and part of a cult. So of course she now says she saw his 'spiritual death.' The closest she's come to being right is when she told the parents of a three-year-old that their daughter was submerged in water, trapped beneath a metal grate. There had been a lot of rain, and everyone thought the girl had wandered away and fallen into a drainage ditch. It was probably just her best guess."

"So what really happened?"

"She had been raped and strangled by her neighbor, and then he stuffed her under his waterbed. So now this lady says on her Web site that she was right—it was just the spirits who were a little vague about the whole water and grate business."

"Well, my last caller had a dream about a man in a house next to trees and a road," Leif said. "And she's sure it's something to do with Katie."

"Now we've finally got something we can act on!" Nic pumped her fist in mock excitement. "Trees and a road! That certainly narrows it down." She was so frustrated she was getting giddy.

Neither of them saw John Drood, the special agent in charge of Portland's FBI, standing behind them until it was too late. He was a pale man with graying hair and less than six months to go until he bumped up against the FBI's rule that forced agents to retire at fifty-seven. It was clear that he was having trouble even contemplating letting go, which had the unfortunate effect of making him more officious.

"I don't care if the tip comes in on a flaming arrow," he said, his hands on his narrow hips. "You investigate the tip first and the arrow second. We can't afford to discard anything. Not when we have nothing else to go on. And it's always possible that someone who is personally connected to the case may call and claim to be a psychic."

"That's true, sir," Nic said, nodding. "Someone who claims to have seen Katie in a dream may actually be the person who took her."

"Exactly." Looking mollified, Drood walked off.

"But not your lady," Leif added when Drood was out of earshot.

"No," Nic said. "Probably not."

So far, professionals and volunteers had canvassed Portland and the outlying suburbs. They tracked down rumors of a body seen in the river, a bundle of clothes in a ditch, a neighbor acting suspiciously. They had checked warehouses, docks, outbuildings, and vacant houses. The search had spread well past Portland. People were looking in woods and farms all over Oregon and Washington.

But they were finding nothing.

Nicole stood up to stretch, her holster catching briefly on the back of the cheap folding chair. After eight years in the FBI, her Glock was part of her. She was required to be armed, available, and fit for duty at all times, whether she was at work or not. She carried her gun on planes. She carried it when she met her friends for dinner. She took it to Makayla's fourth-grade play. Makayla was now the class celebrity, thanks to some kid sitting on the floor catching a glimpse of Nic's gun when her jacket fell open. It was underneath her left arm, snug against her side, just below her breast.

The FBI had trained her to shoot in all kinds of weather, during daylight and at night, in any position. She had drawn her weapon and fired her weapon hundreds of time. But she had never fired it at a human being.

At home, the gun went into the gun safe. Makayla knew she could ask to see the gun as often as she liked, but only when they were alone at home. She was never to touch it.

Luckily, Makayla didn't seem at all curious about it, or about Nicole's job in general. Which was good. Nicole didn't exactly want to explain to her daughter that there were men who liked girls Makayla's age.

As she turned her head from side to side and massaged her tense shoulders, she thought about how they had busted PDXer the day before. With a subpoena, Nicole had been able to trace the computer's address to the home of a fifty-two-year-old shoe salesman. BubbleBeth had agreed to meet him at a bus stop downtown. The FBI weren't allowed to use decoys to fool the perp, so there was no real girl to meet him. Instead, there were fifteen agents, including Nicole, all of them stationed around the stop.

PDXer turned out to be tubby, with a bad, graying perm. He paced up and down, holding a dozen roses, looking for the thirteen-year-old BubbleBeth but seeing only joggers, shoppers, construction workers, and people waiting for the bus.

Nicole walked up, pulled out her badge, and said, "I know why you're here."

He didn't even bother to hang his head. Some perps were relieved when their problems finally caught up with them. "Yeah, I'm here to meet a thirteen-year-old girl and take her to my house and have sex."

She had cuffed him a little tighter than was strictly necessary. The only thing that had helped curb her anger was knowing that Innocent Images had a 98 percent conviction rate.

Wincing in pain, Nicole pressed her fingers as far back along her neck and down her spine as she could. She hadn't noticed that Leif had stood up, too, until he said, "Hey, try this to get the kinks out. First, put your hands up." He turned to face her, and she was conscious of his height. A lot of guys in the Bureau were shorter than Nic, but Leif was well over six feet.

He held out his hands, palms facing forward, on either side of his head, looking like someone about to be arrested. "It's called a dorsal glide." He waited until Nic put her hands up, then tucked his chin as he slowly moved his back in a straight line. She did the same.

Something clicked into place between her shoulder blades. The pain wasn't gone, but it lessened remarkably.

"Hey," she said. "Thanks."

She saw a few of the other agents looking at them, and she grabbed her headset and quickly sat down. She liked Leif, and respected him, which weren't always the same thing, but she didn't want to send the wrong message. Being a single woman meant she was grist for the office rumor mill. Nicole knew what some of them said about her behind her back. That she was a lesbian. And/or a man-hater.

Nicole ignored Leif's sideways glance when he sat back down next to her. She had a reason for the way she acted. A better reason than she would ever tell any of them.

SAFE HARBOR SHELTER
December 21

Hello, you must be Sonika. I'm Allison Pierce. I'm a lawyer." When Allison stuck out her hand, the slender woman with huge, dark eyes flinched.

"Sorry," Sonika said. She hid her mouth with her hand, reminding Allison of Nicole. Only Sonika's teeth were already perfect, even and white. Glossy black hair framed her heart-shaped face.

The caseworker had told Allison that Sonika was a Cambodian immigrant without much English. And that her husband beat her. Sonika had come to the shelter several times, but always said she couldn't stay. She wouldn't even take a brochure, out of fear that her husband might find it. The hope was that Allison could get her to change her mind about accepting help.

Because of Lindsay, Allison had done a little research on domestic violence. It accounted for more injuries to women in America than anything else—more than heart attacks, cancer, strokes, car wrecks, muggings, and rapes combined. To try to help, Allison did a little pro bono work for the shelter. Not as much as she thought she should, but far more than she had time for. Especially now. But so many volunteers were unavailable so close to Christmas that the shelter had begged Allison to come today. To come right away, before this Sonika got too frightened. Allison had reluctantly agreed.

Once the baby came—the idea was now a refrain that played through

her mind every few seconds—Allison would probably have to stop volunteering altogether. She put her hand on her abdomen for a second,
then dropped it when she saw the other woman take it in. Sonika had the
hyperawareness typical of abused women.

They were in the children's room, but at the moment there were no
children in it. The smell of Play-Doh made Allison's mouth water,
which was better than her reaction to most smells these days. She sat on
a green plastic Playskool chair and gestured for Sonika to pull up the
red one.

Instead, Sonika sank down until she crouched on her heels. She held
the position easily, looking far more comfortable than Allison felt perched
on her tiny seat.

In two years of volunteering, Allison had learned the unspoken rules
for dealing with victims of domestic violence. You took your time. You
nodded when they said that he wasn't so bad, that it was complicated. You
told them to write down the hotline number next to a fake name, so that
no one would suspect. You didn't call a marriage an "abusive relationship" until they were ready. You didn't scare women by trying to force
them to go into the shelter. And you never berated them for not leaving—or for going back.

"What brings you here?" Allison asked.

Sonika's fingers hovered over the top button on her high-necked
blouse, then cupped her knees. "Very private."

Allison nodded. For five minutes, they sat in silence. Finally, Sonika
brought her fingers up to her blouse again. She unbuttoned the top button
and the next. Holding the edges of her blouse, she pulled them open and
turned her head away.

Small black bruises were lined up on each side of her neck. Someone
had tried to strangle her.

"I'm sorry," Allison said. "You can button your blouse back up."

Sonika did, her eyes still not meeting Allison's.

"Your husband?"

Sonika didn't answer, just pushed up her sleeve. More bruises brace-leted her wrist. These were older, a greenish-yellow.

"These my husband."

"Then who tried to . . ." Allison veered away from the word *strangle*—this woman was like a frightened deer. "Who hurt your neck?"

"My father."

"Your father?" Her voice betrayed her surprise. *Give me guidance, Lord.*

"I ask if I could live at home again. He say I bring shame on our fam-ily. He say better for me to be dead than disgrace."

"Where does your husband think you are right now?"

"Grocery store."

"I can help you. We can make it so that your father and your husband have to stay away from you. I am a lawyer. I can make the police and the courts protect you."

Sonika snorted and shook her head as if Allison had just said some-thing wryly funny. "The police! They want money. My father, my husband, they have money. Not me."

Allison had run into this problem before with immigrants from countries where justice was available to the highest bidder.

"Not here, Sonika. I can make it so that your husband and father won't be able to come near you without being put in jail. We can help you get housing, food stamps, eventually a job. We can help you get a new life, Sonika. One where nobody hurts you."

"You don't understand. My father was in army. He knows how to kill people. He knows how to make them disappear." Sonika flicked her slen-der hand to show how fast it could happen.

"But you're his daughter."

"He has five daughters. I am disobeying."

"But—," Allison started, when her phone buzzed on her waist.

She looked down at the display. Nicole. Nicole knew where Allison was, knew not to call unless it was an emergency.

"Excuse me," she said, knowing she was losing Sonika. Knowing she would have lost her anyway. "I have to take this."

She went out into the hall. "Yes?"

"Sorry to interrupt you, Allison. But it's about Katie Converse."

Her stomach felt like she was in an elevator that had lurched down half a foot. "You found her?"

"No. We found her dog."

Yesterday was my birthday. My roommates made a big fuss over me & took me to Starbucks for lemon squares & chai tea. I got a lot of stuff from my family in the mail & a CD from L, my best friend at home. Daddy sent me something separate. Even before I opened it I could tell it was from him. It was lumpy & had way too much tape.

Inside was a necklace from my mom. My real mom. She died from breast cancer when I was just a baby. I don't have many pictures of her. I'm pretty sure V threw them all away as soon as she married Daddy. The necklace is an amethyst on a silver chain. I'm wearing it right now. I'm never going to take it off.

The whole family talked to me, but finally Daddy took the phone & went out in the backyard to talk to me alone. On my birthday we always go for a hike in Forest Park together, just the two of us. When I get back home we'll still have to go on our hike, just a few months late. Just him & me. And I'll tell him I've been thinking I could be a senator myself one day, the way Senator X says. Maybe even president.

At dinner, one of the other pages asked where I was from & told me I had a cute accent. That made me smile. Do I really have an accent? In the state I'm from, we pretty much talk like TV newscasters. On the other hand, you should hear him. And just in case he's reading this, let me say that *he's* the one with an accent.

Later we were in the dayroom together with a bunch of other people watching TV. Eventually everyone left, until we were the only ones there.

And that's all I'm going to say about my birthday.

BLUE MOON TAVERN
December 21

Allison found herself scanning the faces of the people on the sidewalks as she hunted for one of Northwest Portland's scarce parking spaces. Knowing she wouldn't see Katie, but all too aware that another day had gone by without a break in the case.

As she walked down the poorly lit sidewalk toward McMenamin's Blue Moon Tavern, the restaurant Cassidy had chosen, Allison's thoughts took another, even darker, turn. Whoever had put the threatening note on her car could be anyplace. She interlaced her keys between the fingers of her left hand and held her cell phone ready in her right. Her heels ticktocked on the sidewalk of the deserted side street. But once she was on the busy main street she relaxed, at least a little.

She found Nicole inside the restaurant, and the two women ordered. About twenty minutes later Cassidy turned heads as she rushed in. Her customary bright colors—including an orange raincoat—stood out among the jeans and dark parkas.

"Sorry I'm late," she said, leaning over to hug Nicole. "The bridge was up." She gave Allison an air kiss, then stepped back to appraise her. "So how are you feeling?"

"Fine. The only difference I've noticed is that I can smell things a lot better. I was in PetSmart, and I could smell the shavings in the hamsters' cages and the chemicals in the fish tanks."

And Cassidy's perfume bordered on overwhelming, but Allison decided not to mention that.

Cassidy went up to the counter. From the guy behind the beer taps she ordered a Wilbur's Jumbo Deluxe Burger, a pint of Hammerhead, and an order of McMenamin's famous fries.

Nicole called out, "Cass, we already have fries!"

"I need my own," Cassidy answered, taking the glass of beer and walking back to the table. "Why do you think I picked this place anyway?"

The Blue Moon had been in Northwest Portland long before the neighborhood's housing values shot out of sight. Now its funky artwork and battered wooden chairs were a throwback to the time when the area had been a cheap refuge for artists and college students.

When Cassidy looped her heavy Coach purse over the back of her chair, the seat went up on two legs. With an ease born of long experience, she caught the purse with one hand while slipping out of her coat and draping it over the back of the chair with the other. Just before the whole thing tipped over, she sat down.

Nicole snorted. "Ever thought of getting a purse with luggage wheels?"

"Oh, shut up! If you ever need a Band-Aid or a complete change of clothes, don't come crying to me." Cassidy turned back to Allison. "Have you been to the doctor yet?"

"I have an appointment in three weeks. They want to be able to hear the baby's heart rate, and they can't do that until it's bigger."

Allison had been surprised by how casually the receptionist at her doctor's office had treated her. Did they really think that she could do the right thing all by herself? She had spent the last couple of evenings reading *What to Expect When You're Expecting* instead of the files she had lugged home from work.

"So how big is it now?" Cassidy reached over to help herself to some of their fries. "Do you know?"

"According to what I'm reading, I've already gone through the grain of rice and green pea stages. I think it's somewhere between pinto bean and olive size."

"Why is it always food?" Nicole pointed a french fry at Allison. "At this rate, you're going to give birth to a fryer chicken."

"Stop talking about food," Cassidy said, snatching up more of their fries. "I'm hungry!"

Nicole lightly slapped Cassidy's hand. "You've got a bad habit of eating off other people's plates, you know that?"

Cassidy's grin was unrepentant. "In grade school kids used to make a big production out of licking their food in front of me so I wouldn't eat it."

"Did that stop you?" Allison asked.

Cassidy raised one eyebrow. "What do you think?"

The three women laughed.

Turning serious, Cassidy added, "I didn't just pick this restaurant for the quality of its grease. It's also close to where Katie disappeared. I saw both of you at the vigil." She lifted her beer glass in Nicole's direction. "And I heard that you've been handpicked to be the liaison with Katie's parents. Congrats! The Triple Threat Club is on the case!" She raised her glass and leaned forward.

Allison tapped each of their glasses with her own. She was trying to drink more milk for calcium and eat more leafy greens for vitamin K—the existence of which she had only learned about this week. As a result, her dinner tonight was a Cajun Cobb salad and a glass of milk. McMenamin's, which wasn't exactly known for restraint, had dressed the salad in about a half cup of blue cheese dressing.

Her newfound hunger sometimes shocked her, especially since it alternated with bouts of nausea. Three hours after breakfast this morning, she had felt an overwhelming urge to eat. She ended up in the third-floor cafeteria, tucked away in a corner, her back to the empty tables, wolfing down an egg sandwich and a hashbrown disk. What if the baby's fingers had been forming right at that moment? What if the knuckles were being made, and the only nutrition her body had to work with was junk?

Nicole's smile was rueful. "Yeah, it may be an honor, but it's not going to be easy. We've got no crime scene, no evidence, no clues, no suspects, no ransom note, and no verifiable sightings." She popped another fry into her mouth.

Cassidy shook her head. "I'm like you, Nic, trying to work this thing when there is no new information. This morning I had the cameraman down on his knees so we could get a dog's-eye view. Since you guys found the dog, it was supposed to be like what Jalapeño would have seen when he was with Katie. Did you guys get any clues from it?"

Allison didn't bother asking where Cassidy had come across that little tidbit. She had sources scattered throughout the city. Sometimes she knew things before Allison and Nicole did, which came in handy.

Earlier that day, a woman had been walking her dog near Chapman Elementary when she had spotted the black Lab without a collar. With the help of a dog treat, she coaxed it into her van. She thought it looked like the dog on the Converses' flyers, so she took it to an animal shelter. Luckily, Jalapeño had been chipped.

"There was something dark matted on its flank, but the dog was filthy—fur stuck together, burrs, cuts on its paws," Nicole said. "Everyone got all excited. But it turned out to be canine blood, not human."

"I've been trying for an interview with the woman who found him, but Channel Eight's got her all sewn up." Cassidy took another sip of beer.

"What would you guys have if you didn't have nonstop coverage of this?" Nicole said. "Maybe some actual news?"

Cassidy snorted. "We've talked about this before. Everyone sitting at this table depends upon crime for her livelihood. We don't *make* the bad guys. We catch them!"

Half joking, half not, Allison said, "But the media distort everything."

"Right. Just like all cops are trigger-happy and all lawyers are sharks." Cassidy laughed. Nothing ever seemed to get to her. "The media are not creating the problem. We're reporting it. There's a difference."

As the counter guy set down Cassidy's food, Nicole said, "In about fifteen minutes, could you bring us a black-and-tan brownie and three spoons?"

After he nodded and left, she turned back to Cassidy. "Are you sure there really is a difference?"

"Hey, her parents have begged for coverage. They want everyone to know what Katie looks like, what a good girl she is. They think it will help."

Allison pushed the remains of her salad away. "Sometimes I worry that this much coverage just gives people ideas. Now any sicko who wants his own little piece of the six o'clock news knows that all he needs to do is go out and get his own girl."

Instead of taking offense, Cassidy dropped her eyes and smiled a private smile. "That's what Rick says, too. He says I'm just encouraging them."

Nicole pounced. "Rick! So you've got yourself a new man? You've been holding out on us, girl!"

"This one's a cop. So he understands the hours. He gets that when a story breaks I've got to go."

"Where'd you meet him?" Allison couldn't imagine what it would be like to still be dating. She and Marshall had been together since they were sophomores in college.

"I interviewed him when that 7-Eleven clerk got shot, and afterward we ended up going out for coffee."

Nicole arched an eyebrow. "So is he fine?"

Cassidy licked her lips. "He is very fine. He reminds me of a fox, or maybe a wolf. He's got these pale blue eyes and dark brown hair and a *very* muscular body."

Nicole made a show of fanning herself.

Despite complaining that all the good men were taken or gay, Cassidy managed to find dates every place she went. Dates, yes. Long-term boy-friends, no.

Cassidy was a contradiction. She was always sure of herself when it came to covering a story, but in her personal life she needed constant reassurance. Though she exercised obsessively, she complained about being fat, and worried aloud about growing old—and waited for someone to contradict her. And she twisted herself into a pretzel to gain the approval of whatever guy she was dating.

Three years earlier, she had been a windsurfer for about two weeks when she had a boyfriend who loved windsurfing. Then she had briefly become a vegetarian when she dated someone who abstained. And there was the time she was "seriously considering" converting to Catholicism until she realized the guy she had met on Match.com expected her to stay home and have babies. Lots of babies.

Maybe this Rick guy would be different.

But Cassidy was still the same. Even over dinner with friends, she couldn't stop looking for a story. "Jerry wants a minute-forty-five package about Katie on the news every night. That's an unbelievable amount of time. The world coming to an end would be lucky to get a minute and a half. Normally I would start with the latest update and reverse to the B-roll—but it doesn't seem like there's anything new. Right?" She eyed Nicole closely.

Nicole shot Allison a look, which Allison answered with a little nod. None of this got past Cassidy, who grinned in anticipation.

"I wouldn't say that." Nicole shook a cautionary finger. "But you can't use this, Cassidy. Not yet."

"All right." She nodded so hard that her artfully highlighted hair swung back and forth.

"I mean it. You can't. I'll give you a heads-up when we're ready to release this. But Katie had a MySpace account, and she kept a blog on it."

Cassidy's eyebrows went up. "And her parents didn't take it down?"

"They didn't know anything about it," Nicole said, reaching out to grab some of Cassidy's fries. "It's anonymous, or at least as anonymous as a seventeen-year-old girl can think of how to be."

"In other words," Allison said, "not very." Reading the blog had left her with a residue of sadness. It brought Katie alive for her—and yet as she read her words, Allison grew even more afraid for the girl.

"Right," Nicole agreed. "Like it's called The DC Page, and on the part where people can leave comments, they're all addressed to Katie. There's only one Katie in the Senate page program. What makes it even clearer is that now that she's missing, there are people begging for her to come home, or saying how much they miss her."

"Are there any clues? Like 'Dear Blog, today I intend to disappear . . .' ?"

The counter guy set down their dessert. Cassidy was the first to pick up one of the three spoons.

Nicole shook her head. "No. I wish there were. It's clear she had a boyfriend in the program, but it also sounds like they broke up. It was all very dramatic, very much love one minute and the worst thing that ever happened to her the next. The one thing that gave me pause is that she seemed to have a crush on one of the senators. She called him Senator X, but she also said it was her sponsor. Which would be Senator Fairview."

Allison hadn't known what to make of the blog. Had Fairview returned the girl's feelings? Or had he even been aware of them?

"Fairview." Cassidy rolled her eyes. "I've heard stories about him."

"What do you mean?" Allison asked. Her heart started beating faster. She set down her spoon.

"I've interviewed him before," Cassidy said, taking a bite of dessert that strategically encompassed the brownie, the ice cream, and the caramel sauce. "He's a nonstop flirt who likes it when women are impressed by the fact that he's a senator. His wife—I think her name's Nancy—lives here with their two kids. She's got an upscale children's clothing business. So he spends his time back in DC in a bachelor pad, and maybe comes home once or twice a month. But when the cat's away, he likes to play. . . ."

"So he's like Senator Packwood?" Allison asked.

Bob Packwood, after decades as an Oregon senator, had been forced to resign after dozens of women came forward saying he forcibly kissed or groped them.

"No. As far as I know, all his conquests are willing. But you hear stories about him."

"Like what?" Nicole leaned forward.

"Like him having sex in the back alley with some college girl he met in a bar, while his driver waits in the car."

"That's pretty sick," Nicole said.

"The sick thing is that I heard it from the *driver*. Our honorable senator got a kick out of doing it right in front of him."

Nicole made a face. "A woman in a bar is one thing. A seventeen-year-old girl is another."

Allison was finding it hard to breathe. The food in her stomach had turned into a leaden ball. She remembered another man she had known. *He* had liked to take chances too. The more dangerous it was, the more he got off on it.

It felt like a big piece of the puzzle had just fallen into place.

Allison said, "I don't think the two are that far apart. It sounds like Fairview likes to take risks. What could be riskier—or more tempting— than a seventeen-year-old?"

Making an enemy of a powerful senator was never a good idea. Still, Allison knew it was the right thing to do. She took a deep breath.

"Tomorrow, I'm going to open a grand jury. And I'm going to make sure that the first thing they do is take a good hard look at Senator Fairview."

All the other pages complain about the schedule.

They don't know what they are talking about.

At least here I can make most of my own decisions. If they give me an errand to run, nobody cares how long it takes. If I stop to talk to someone, or to look at a painting, they don't grill me about what I was doing.

Besides, this place is so cool! Like on Sunday evening we all ended up playing Frisbee on the Capitol lawn. I mean, who else gets to do that? We even got one of the Capitol cops to toss it back & forth for a few minutes. And in January we'll hear the State of the Union live. See the president up close & personal. Did you know the pages are the first people to shake the president's hand when he walks in? Look for us on TV!

I've finally made a friend here—this girl E—& sometimes we do crazy things. E & I went on a "guy hunt" the other day, where you take pictures of cute guys with your cell. But they can't catch you doing it or the game is over. We got some pictures of the other pages, bike messengers & a cop. I even took one of Senator X, but I didn't tell E about that one.

When we went through the rotunda, people actually took pictures of us! It must have been because of our uniforms.

Sometimes you do sort of feel important. Some of the senators take time out to talk with you & tell stories in the back lobby. It's awesome when a senator calls you by name or remembers what state you're from.

We're even allowed to get in an elevator with senators, as long as it isn't the senator-only elevator & it isn't crowded.

It's not a big deal to them, but being a page is pretty much scum compared to being a senator. Some senators just ignore pages all together, but a few of them are nice. The coolest is my senator, Senator X. He says he remembers what it was like from when he was a page.

I was talking to him today & some newspaper guy started pointing a camera at us. I noticed how Senator X lifted his chin & started using his hands a lot. I took mental notes for when I'm a politician someday. He looked important. He looked powerful.

And then Senator X caught my eye & winked. With the eye that the camera couldn't see.

Wٖe're talking about destroying the youngest of human lives for research purposes," Senator Fairview said.

He had them all. He could feel it. The Senate galleries were packed. The cameras clicked and whirred. His veins were filled with quicksilver.

He nodded, and Katie set up the metal easel and then put up the poster board. He was in the zone, as he liked to think of it, and even though Katie was very easy on the eyes, he barely saw her. The poster showed a series of photos, starting with a black-and-white collection of cells and ending with a color photo of a little girl.

Stepping out from behind the polished podium, Fairview walked over to the easel. He adjusted a silver cuff link that had caught on the edge of his navy blue blazer, then pointed at the photograph of cells—they looked like a cluster of gray circles—on the left-hand side of the board.

"Even the presiding officer, as handsome as he is"—Fairview paused for the laughter, and got it, feeling a *Yes!* in his gut—"he looked like this at one time, just a little clump of cells. If he had been destroyed at this point, he wouldn't be here before you today. It's important to remember that we all started like this."

He ran his hand from left to right over the series of photographs—a baby sucking its thumb in the womb, a swaddled newborn, a toddler with a teddy bear—that ended with a six-year-old with blonde pigtails and a gap-toothed grin. *Could she be any more perfect?*

"This shows the development taking place that led to Ellie here." He tapped her photograph, then trailed his fingers back to the clump of cells. "If you destroy her here, you don't get Ellie here." Fingers back to tap on the smiling girl. "That's key. If they had destroyed Ellie and used her cells for research, then this little girl wouldn't be alive today. And Ellie knows how important that is. That's why she drew this."

Katie stepped up to take the first poster as he removed it, revealing the second poster, a series of a child's drawings.

Fairview knew that he could be pontificating about unsubstantiated claims of imminent scientific breakthroughs from embryonic stem cell research or rattling on about how adult stem cells or even skin cells had actually been shown to be useful in a variety of cases. *But who would listen to that?* he thought. *Show them a kid. A real live kid. How could they vote to kill a little girl with pigtails and a Band-Aid on her knee?*

He pointed at the circle on the far left, filled with a scrawled happy smile. "Ellie drew this to show herself when she was adopted as a frozen embryo. She is what they call a snowflake. The couple that adopted Ellie had infertility problems. They could not conceive, so they adopted her as an embryo. She was implanted, and now we've got Ellie, and she's already quite the artist.

"She drew these three pictures for me. As the Bible says, out of the mouths of babes comes great wisdom. In this first picture, Ellie is smiling because she got adopted and she got a chance to continue living her life. In the middle is another frozen embryo." He pointed at a circle that showed not a smile, but a straight line for the mouth. "He's sad because he's still sitting in a frozen state. And this one on the end?"

This circle was frowning, with huge tears drawn running down the page.

"As Ellie told me, this one is saying, 'Are you really going to kill me?'

"You see, Ellie knows that this is not just a clump of tissue. This is not just a random group of cells. This is not a hair follicle. This is Ellie. And if nurtured, she grows into this beautiful child who is in our gallery today with her mother and father."

People craned their necks to see. The cameras pivoted. Ellie waved, just as Fairview had asked her to.

"These boys and girls are not spare parts. We absolutely can't use federal money to kill children like Ellie."

As the gallery burst into applause, Fairview dipped his head in acknowledgment. *Today Fox News, tomorrow YouTube. And in the future?* Inside, he smiled.

As she drove back to the office after having briefed the Converses on the total lack of progress in the hunt for their daughter, Nic's cell phone started to buzz on her hip. She gritted her teeth. Her phone rang all the time now. It was starting to feel like a leash she could never be free of.

She lifted it to eye level. The display read LEIF LARSON. Why would he be calling her? She thought of how they had bantered in between answering hotline calls. Something about Leif slipped past her guard.

Flipping open her phone, she said, "Nicole Hedges," sounding efficient and professional. Sounding like she hadn't been wondering about Leif at all.

With no preamble, Leif said, "It's Leif. Meet me over at Twenty-seventh and Vaughn. We've got a twenty-two-year-old guy, Michael Cray, no priors, but his stepsister is saying that on the night Katie disappeared he came home with a swollen eye and what looked like scratch marks on his chest and hands. She also says there's dirt on the floor of the family basement— like someone's been digging. I'm bringing in some of the ERT until we know exactly what we've got."

Leif was the team leader for the FBI's Evidence Recovery Team.

"I'm on my way," Nic said.

Taking the next exit, she went right back on the freeway, doubling back the way she had come. The address was only a few blocks from where the Converses lived—and where Katie had disappeared. Mentally, she began to rehearse how she might break the news to the Converses that their daughter had been found buried in a basement.

There were a half dozen police cars parked in front of the old yellow Victorian house. On the lawn, a young woman with spiky yellow hair hugged herself, a cigarette in one hand. She wasn't wearing a coat, despite the cold—just jeans, a T-shirt, and a brown cardigan sweater.

As Nic got out of the car, she heard the girl say to a cop who was writing down her words, "After I heard about Katie disappearing, I thought back to how he looked that night. And that was the nail in the coffin for me. That's all it took. I knew then and there what he'd done." She took a deep breath. "Because that's the kind of person he is, see? The kind of person who would do something like that."

Her bright blue eyes met Nic's for an instant, but they were blank, unseeing, as if what they saw existed in some other time, some other place.

Nic flashed her badge at the cop guarding the front door. Inside, another cop gestured toward the kitchen, where an open door led to the stairs to the basement. But even before she set foot on them, she could hear people cursing downstairs. When she rounded the corner of the banister, the first person she saw was Leif. His face was twisted with disgust.

"Another waste of time. How could she think Katie was buried down here? You know what we've got? A concrete floor. Concrete! And as old as the house. Hundred-year-old concrete that hasn't been touched."

"What about the dirt?" Nic asked. "Didn't she say there was dirt, like someone had been digging?"

"It's potting soil! There's even a stack of empty plastic pots in the corner. Man, I knew they would come out of the woodwork when the Converses upped the ante to a half million. I just didn't think it would happen so fast."

"They've raised the reward?" This was the first Nic had heard of it.

"Yeah, they told that blonde reporter on Channel Four about it this morning. Five hundred thousand dollars if she's found alive. They got

some of the dad's business friends to kick in, and took out a second mort-
gage on their house. You can imagine what that's going to do to the
volume of tips. I just didn't know some girl would rat out her own brother
just for cash."

"It's her stepbrother," Nic corrected. Thinking of the distance in the
girl's gaze, she added, "And maybe she had her reasons. Maybe she really
thought it was true. Maybe she knows her stepbrother is capable of doing
bad things."

She turned on her heel and went back up the stairs, leaving a startled
Leif gaping after her. The girl was sitting on the porch now, her head in
her hands. As Nic walked past, she squeezed her shoulder.

Later that day, the task force released a statement. "All indications are
that Michael Cray received those injuries at a time well before Katie
Converse's disappearance."

The two grand juries met for two days on alternate weeks in a large room located on the third floor of the federal courthouse. This particular group, twenty-three private citizens from all over Oregon who received a whopping forty dollars a day from Uncle Sam, had already worked through eleven of the eighteen months they would ultimately serve together. Over the past year Allison had watched them become friends and comrades, celebrating birthdays, handing around photos of pets and babies, swapping paperbacks. At breaks they gathered in the kitchen to share snacks and make tea and coffee.

As she hurried into the grand jury room, Allison's nose was assailed with the smell of greasy leftover pizza. Swallowing her queasiness, she put her things on the prosecutor's table and turned toward the grand jurors' expectant faces. The group never knew what they might be asked to investigate—domestic terrorism by extreme environmentalists, hate crimes against a local synagogue, men using the Internet to meet teenagers for sex. By now they had heard over a hundred cases.

The grand jury was Allison's—and any prosecutor's—investigative arm. Even when they weren't in session, in their name Allison could issue a search warrant or a subpoena compelling a witness to testify before them.

"Good morning," Allison said. "Today I'm going to bring you a case about a missing girl. We want to find out if there was foul play. The girl's name is Katie Converse."

As she spoke, she held up the poster of Katie and saw several nods of recognition. Grand jurors weren't banned from watching the media, which meant they often had a passing familiarity with any headline cases she brought them. But now that they knew they would be considering the case, they would have to stay away from any fresh news about it. And no matter how high-profile the case, they were sworn to keep secret what went on inside the grand jury room.

While a grand jury might consider dozens of cases over the course of a year, they never saw a single one through until the end. Instead, they served only to investigate various criminal cases and formally indict any suspects. In some cases, they voted not to indict. Because they weren't asked to determine guilt or innocence, only decide whether charges should be officially filed, their standards were looser than those of a trial jury. And the grand jury didn't even need to be unanimous: only eighteen of the twenty-three needed to agree.

"I'd like to call to the stand FBI Special Agent Nicole Hedges."

After being brought in from the anteroom and sworn in by the court reporter, Nicole explained to the grand jurors who Katie was, how the page program worked, and what steps authorities had already taken in their efforts to find the girl.

"We recovered a computer that belonged to Katie," Nicole said, "and found that Katie had been keeping a blog, which is like an online diary. In the blog, Katie talked about a boy from either the House or Senate page program, but that relationship ended several months before her disappearance. She seemed to be having a tumultuous relationship with someone, but we don't know who. As time went on, she talked more and more about someone she called Senator X. Senator Fairview was Katie's sponsor in the page program. We believe that there is a good chance that he is actually Senator X."

"Do you have any questions for Special Agent Hedges?" Allison asked the jurors. She liked to hear what regular people wanted to ask. If there had been foul play—and she prayed that there hadn't—then the grand jurors' questions could help shape Allison's approach to any future trial. And sometimes the jurors even thought of angles she had missed.

The foreman, a retired hardware store owner, was the first to speak. Allison knew she could always count on Gus Leonard to ask questions. Lots and lots of questions.

"What's this girl's family like?" He tilted his head to the side, looking like a curious old bird regarding a hole that might or might not contain a worm. "Any chance one of them could be involved in this?"

"The dad is a well-known contractor," Nicole told him. "The mom does volunteer work. There's also a younger sister. They are beside themselves with grief."

Gus and a few of the other jurors asked a half dozen more questions. Once they had satisfied their curiosity, Allison excused Nicole and stood to address them again. "There is a chance that Katie may still be alive, but we have so few clues to go on. Given Katie's blogs, I'm asking you to issue a trap and trace on Senator Fairview's phones to see if there is any evidence of a relationship between them."

Unlike a wiretap, which recorded the contents of a conversation, a trap and trace was merely a record of calls made and received. The trap and trace on Katie's phone had turned up little that was suspicious. In fact, it had hardly turned up anything at all. And that in itself had raised Allison's suspicions. A girl that age would be on the phone all the time. Maybe Fairview had called her in her dorm room.

"Are you saying Senator Fairview is a suspect?" a grand juror named Helen asked.

"No. He's a person of interest."

Ever since the Atlanta Olympics bombing debacle, when Richard Jewell had been declared a suspect and turned out to be a hero, law enforcement had shied away from calling anyone a suspect until they were certain.

Allison let her gaze sweep the room, taking a few seconds to look each juror in the eye. "But if the trap and trace comes back with a lot of activity that seems out of line when you consider that he's a senator and Katie's just a kid in high school, then yes. At that point, I will consider Senator Fairview a suspect."

Michael Stone always made it a practice to meet potential clients in his own office, where he was clearly the top dog. No matter who the clients were, no matter how rich or how powerful, he always made them wait at least twenty minutes in the reception area.

He made no exception for Senator Fairview. When his secretary ushered Fairview in, Stone apologized effusively for making him wait.

"I was on a conference call with a client. I can't mention the name, but you might have seen him on the front page of the *New York Times* last week."

In reality, Stone had spent the twenty minutes instant messaging his kids to remind them to do their homework, as well as making a dinner reservation.

"Let me just say, Senator, that I feel honored to be chosen as the attorney for someone I have always admired."

As he spoke, he could see the tension ease from Fairview's shoulders. Stone took a seat behind his desk while his client settled into one of the guest chairs. Stone's chair was six inches higher than anyone else's—a little ploy he had learned from Johnny Cochran.

He sat back in his chair, smiling congenially. "So, Senator, were you making it with this girl or what?"

"What?" Fairview looked too shocked to be angry.

Good. Stone wanted to keep him off-balance. His clients had to know who was boss—and it wasn't the person who was paying the bills.

"I've seen her pictures. She's a cutie. And you're a big shot senator. I'll bet you were like a rock star to her. So were you getting it on with her?"

"No!" Fairview was now light-years away from being relaxed. "I was mentoring her," he said, sounding like he was reading from a tele-prompter. "I often take a special interest in one or two of the pages every year, because that's an integral part of the internship program and—"

"Yeah, yeah, yeah. Look, here's the deal. It's very simple. They've set up a grand jury to investigate her disappearance. Now they're going after your phone records. If you had sex with her or killed her or even sent her that last crappy Paris Hilton YouTube clip, there is no way you should be talking to the feds or any other law enforcement people. Don't worry, I'm not here to judge you. I am here to try and point out the Indians behind the trees. I just want to make sure you even see the trees!"

"But they're dragging my name through the mud. My staff and I agree that this has got to stop. Every time I turn around, someone is ask-ing me about this girl. Not only are they asking me, they're asking my wife." Fairview's eyes teared up. "My kids."

"You're a smart guy," Stone said soothingly. "Hell, you're a senator. Who was that politico who said that the Senate is the most exclusive men's club in the world? Whatever—I understand why you and your 'people' think it is important for you to get out there and say, 'I didn't do anything wrong.' Just stay away from 'I am not a crook,'" he added dryly. "It's been done. But if you talk to the feds, you either tell the truth or you don't talk at all."

"I understand. What else should I know?"

Finally, Fairview was asking an intelligent question.

"Simple. Keep it short and sweet. No speeches, no big explanations. When they ask you a question, answer it in as few words as possible. If they say nothing after that—do *not* start adding to your answer. That's the way you get hung out to dry."

"Okay, okay." Fairview nodded like a bobblehead.

"If you want to sit down with the feds, I will be there. Just don't try to pull the wool over their eyes. My point can be made in two words: Martha Stewart. She went to the can after being convicted of lying about a crime she was never charged with in the first place."

"Well, I haven't been charged with any crime either." Fairview seemed ready to get back on his high horse.

"You really think so?" Sarcasm colored Stone's words. "How long has your cable been out? You might want to call them and get it back on. Because every night I listen to two blonde ex-prosecutors and my fellow defense lawyers debate your innocence. And let me tell you—it's not looking too good for you. The feds may not have charged you, but in the court of public opinion you are already being found guilty."

"Is there anything else?" Fairview sounded irritated.

Stone guessed he was used to being surrounded by yes-men, not someone who gave it to him straight.

"Yeah," Stone said. "Got a check for me?"

SAN FELIPE TAQUERIA
December 23

When will you tell work?" Cassidy asked, biting into a chip loaded with salsa.

A drop splashed into the deep V of her turquoise blouse that exactly matched her eyes. Allison watched as she nonchalantly scooped it up with her index finger and licked it off.

Allison, Cassidy, and Nicole were grabbing a quick meal at San Felipe Taqueria, a little hole-in-the-wall in Southeast Portland that served the best fish tacos in the city. Cassidy had ordered a margarita, Nicole had gotten a beer, and Allison, despite the counterwoman's puzzled look, had ordered a large milk. It arrived in a glass with a beer logo on the side.

Allison said, "I'm not going to tell anyone else until I'm sure everything's going to be okay. When I was working at McGarrity and White, there was an associate who told everyone she was pregnant when she was only a few weeks along. Then she found out the baby had Down syndrome. She took a week off, and when she came back she wasn't pregnant anymore. But everybody knew what had happened." She sighed. "I keep wondering if everything is going okay. This must be how people feel when they find out they have cancer. Like something secret is happening deep inside them, dividing and growing, something you can't see."

"But this is a baby." Cassidy looked startled. "Not a cancer."

Nicole's mouth twisted into something that wasn't quite a smile. "Sometimes it feels like that, though. The baby takes priority, and if there aren't enough nutrients to go around, the mother gets shorted. That's why women used to lose their teeth a hundred years ago."

"Speaking of mothers, what do you think of Katie's?" Cassidy raised her eyebrows.

"Heck, if I were that girl, I might run away just to get away from her." Nicole shook her head. "She's just a tad rigid. And according to her, Katie walked on water. Nobody is that perfect."

"Not even Makayla?" Allison teased. Hidden by the table, she put her hand on her stomach. If this baby was a girl, could she do a better job with it than her own mother had done with her?

"That child can be willful. But she knows I won't stand for any back-talk. She doesn't like the hours I'm working now because of the task force, but I just tell her, 'Honey, how do you expect me to pay for that private school and those ballet lessons?'"

"So how *are* things going with the Katie Converse case?" Cassidy looked at Nicole and Allison expectantly.

"We're getting lots of tips—but 90 percent of them are from crazy people. The big cases bring out the big nuts. I think half the people in the county have had some kind of prophetic dream about her." Nicole popped another chip into her mouth. "We're under orders to treat everything seriously. So we're going on a lot of wild-goose chases, but we haven't found anything. It's like Katie walked that dog out her front door and vanished."

Allison sighed. "The results from the trap and trace on her phone show nothing unusual. Almost all of it is calls back and forth to her parents. A few calls to the senator when the program started, then nothing." For now, she kept to herself the subpoena for Senator Fairview's records.

Cassidy looked disappointed. "What about her blog?"

Behind her, a Mexican soap opera played silently on TV. Allison watched a young woman with flashing dark eyes slap a handsome man in the face. A second later, they were in each other's arms.

"Clearly Katie was having some kind of stormy relationship with somebody," Nicole said. "But whether it was the senator or a boy—or both, or someone else entirely—we don't know. And we checked her e-mail, but there's nothing to go on there."

Cassidy said, "But look at Fairview. He knows the whispers are starting. He's showing up with his wife in tow at any kind of event where there will be cameras. He's always got his arm around her. I think he's acting guilty. And so does Rick." She sighed. "Rick. That man is amazing! I haven't felt this hot for a guy since my first boyfriend!"

"If you say so," Allison said.

Cassidy said defensively, "Well, what was your first time like?"

"The usual." Allison looked away. She picked up a chip. "More his idea than mine."

Nicole raised her head, as if scenting something interesting. "How old were you?"

"Sixteen." Younger even than Katie, she realized. But she hadn't felt young. Her father had just died, and she had felt as old as the world.

"So he went to school with us?" Cassidy asked, licking the salt off the rim of her margarita.

"Kind of." Allison could barely hear her own words.

"What—did he drop out?" Cassidy arched an eyebrow. "You had yourself some kind of rebel boyfriend?" She and Nicole exchanged a grin.

They might not have run in the same circles, but they both knew Allison had been just as buttoned-down in high school as she was now. Part of her just wanted to see the surprise in their eyes.

"No. It was Mr. Engels."

Cassidy set down her glass. "Wait—the AP English teacher? Wasn't he like, fifty or something? And married?"

"He told me we were in love."

"Love? Hello?" Nicole said flatly. "You were just a kid. That's not love. That's some adult manipulating you by using the magic word." She sat back and crossed her arms. "I see that kind of crap every day."

It hadn't seemed like that at the time, Allison thought. *It hadn't seemed like that at all.*

Allison already felt like an adult when she met Mr. Engels. Not only had her father died, but Lindsay was cutting classes and smoking, her downhill slide already well under way. Most mornings when Allison got up, her mom was sprawled on the couch, asleep under the quilt Allison had spread over her the night before, a bottle of brandy on the coffee table.

Mr. Engels had talked to Allison about world and national events. He wanted to know her opinions. He listened respectfully. She began staying after school and helping in his classroom rather than go home and face her mother's retreat, her sister's absence. At least Mr. Engels noticed things about her. Little things, like if she bought new earrings or wore her hair up. He *was* old, forty-six, but after a while Allison was barely aware of that. He was just her friend. He told her about his wife, about how she was so busy with the bakery she was opening that she really didn't have time to talk anymore. That's what he liked about Allison. That he could talk to her, and she really listened.

And that was the exact same thing she liked about him. They were "kindred spirits," that was how he had put it.

"I thought we were kindred souls," she said. Said out loud, the words were ridiculous. And yet at the time they hadn't been.

"The first time was in his office. I stayed after to help him. And I was in the storage room, and he came in and I had to squeeze by." She shivered, remembering what it had been like. "And one thing led to another. For a long time I thought it wasn't really his fault."

"You really believed that?" Nicole asked. "You were the child. He was the responsible adult."

Allison realized that she had asked God's forgiveness years ago, but she had never truly forgiven herself. She felt a flash of pity for the girl she had once been. Pity and tenderness. She sighed. "I was lonely and looking for attention. And he told me he loved me, and I believed him. He said it was true love."

Even Cassidy—who had long ago told both women about losing her virginity when she was fourteen—looked skeptical. "Maybe when you're a teenager you can tell yourself it's true love. But an adult—he knows it's not that simple."

"I'll bet you anything," Nicole said, "that you were one in a long line of girls. You weren't the first. And you weren't the last."

Listening to her friends was like opening the door to a room that had been closed off for years, and filling it with sunlight and fresh air. Looking back, Allison saw how lonely and vulnerable she had been. And how expertly Mr. Engels had manipulated her. Had Senator Fairview done the same thing to Katie?

Allison vowed again to get justice for Katie Converse. No matter what it took.

"Allison Pierce," Allison said in a distracted tone. The office was beginning to empty out as people left early to celebrate Christmas Eve.

But Katie had been missing for eleven days, and Allison felt she couldn't ease up. Line by line, she was still paging through the dozens and dozens of pages from Senator Fairview's trap and trace. They had gotten information for the phones in his Portland home, his DC apartment, and his office on Capitol Hill, as well as for his personal cell. Three months' worth, beginning with the day Katie started as a Senate page and ending now. The resulting stack of paper was nearly four inches thick. Just trying to read the tiny lines of type was giving Allison a headache.

Only silence had answered her greeting, so she repeated, "This is Allison Pierce," in a sharper tone.

"Ally?" The voice was that of a child, but it wasn't really a kid. Just her kid sister.

"Lindsay," she said warily. How long had it been since she had heard from her sister? Two months? Three? "What's wrong?" There was always something wrong.

"I screwed up." Through the phone line she could hear Lindsay gulping back tears.

"What happened?" Pushing down her impatience, she resisted adding *this time.*

When their dad had died and their mother had gone to pieces,

Allison had shouldered the burden of being the adult, even if she was only sixteen. Lindsay had gone a little crazy. It was Marshall who had gently pointed out that, in a way, Allison and her mother had welcomed Lindsay's problems. By focusing on Lindsay, they could temporarily forget that their father and husband was dead.

"I'm in Tennessee, I think," Lindsay said. "Or maybe Alabama."

"What are you doing there?" Allison asked. Exhaustion crashed over her like a wave. She didn't have the energy to deal with Lindsay. Not on top of everything else.

"I met someone new."

On the surface that was good news. Allison hated Chris, Lindsay's most recent boyfriend.

"So how did you end up in Alabama? Or wherever you are?"

"This guy's a long-haul trucker. But it didn't work out. And now, now I don't have anything. All my stuff is still in his truck. And I think I sprained my ankle jumping out of it."

Allison rubbed her temple. "So where are you exactly? Are you some-place safe?"

"I'm at a gas station. Look, could you put some money in my checking account? I just want to come home. Home for Christmas. Wouldn't that be great, Ally? Like old times."

Allison was long past falling for an idea like that. Give Lindsay some money, and it would more than likely go up her nose or down her throat. At least those were the only places Allison hoped it would go. *Please, God, not in her arm.* Lindsay chased after a high so hard that if she used IV drugs it wouldn't be long before she started sharing needles to save time and ended up with hepatitis C or HIV.

"Look, Linds. Get to the nearest airport, figure out what city you're in, give me a call, and I'll arrange a ticket for you."

"Yeah, sure," her sister said sullenly. "I knew you wouldn't help me. I call you on Christmas Eve, *Christmas Eve,* and you turn me away."

"I will help you, Lindsay, but I won't give you cash. We both know why."

"How am I supposed to even get to the airport? I don't have the money for a cab. I don't even have the money for a bus."

Allison sighed. Tomorrow was Christmas, after all. And if Lindsay really did show up, it would make a better present for their mother than the Este Lauder perfume and the book about the Civil War Allison had already bought her.

"I'll put fifty dollars in your account, but that's it. And then you call me as soon as you're at the airport, okay? And I'll buy you a ticket."

"Oh, thank you, Ally! Thank you! I will, I will. Merry Christmas! I'll call you soon, and I'll see you tomorrow!" She hung up before Allison could even say good-bye.

How long would it be before she heard from Lindsay again?

Was it even possible that her sister was, say, not in Alabama or Tennessee, but six blocks away?

With a sigh, Allison turned to the next page of the trap and trace. Everyone, it seemed, had called or been called by Senator Fairview. Other senators, congressmen, a well-known conservative actor, along with dozens and dozens of names she didn't recognize who were probably lobbyists and constituents. But there was one number that was popping up with more and more frequency on his cell phone. Calls to and from the number came in four, five, six times a day, and sometimes lasted twenty or thirty minutes. But the name wasn't one she recognized. K. Page. And then it hit Allison so hard that she actually jerked her head back. How could she have been so blind! No wonder Katie's trap and trace records had only shown phone calls to and from her parents. Katie had gotten a second phone and registered it under the name K. Page. K for Katie, and Page as a little inside joke.

Allison's finger stabbed at the printout. She couldn't wait to hear how Senator Fairview would try to explain this away.

Maybe you should scoot your seat back," Marshall said as they drove to church for the midnight Christmas Eve service. Allison loved the routine of welcoming the Christ Child in the middle of the night. When she was a kid, they would come home from the midnight service, drink hot cocoa, and go to sleep—although Allison and Lindsay often only pretended to, too eager for Christmas morning.

"Why?" Allison stopped typing in her pass code to access the voice mail system at work. Even though she had left the office three hours earlier, her mind still churned. There was no new word on the Converse case. And Lindsay hadn't called back. It seemed that both Allison's fifty dollars and Lindsay had vanished. She just hoped that Lindsay hadn't pulled the same stunt with their mom.

Marshall pointed at the dash. "Maybe you shouldn't be so close to the air bag."

"I think that's the whole *point* of the air bag."

"An air bag is supposed to stop you from breaking your neck. It wasn't designed to protect a baby. I was reading online; the Department of Transportation says pregnant women should sit as far back as possible from the air bag and keep their arms away from the dash area."

"Are you going to be like this the whole time?" Allison patted Marshall's knee. "Remember, women have been having babies for thousands of years. You've seen those diaries pioneer women kept. *Made dozen loaves of bread, plowed back forty, gave birth to son, butchered hog.* They didn't worry about folic acid and air bags, and everything turned out fine."

But even as she was speaking, Allison reached for the lever on the side of the seat and scooted it back as far as it would go. She finished entering her code and put the phone to her ear.

"You have two new voice mails," the woman's pleasant voice announced. The first was a request to change a meeting to a different time. The second was a man's voice, husky, not one she recognized.

"Hey, slut. Listen to me. I know where your fancy house is in the West Hills. I'm going to give you what you've got coming."

Allison gasped. Marshall looked over at her, concerned. With every ounce of will, she forced herself to listen to the man's threats.

"I'm going to tie you down and rape you, and then I'm going to slit your throat." And then he said the same words that had ended the note. "And I'm going to like it."

There was a click.

"End of final message," the woman's voice announced cheerfully.

Allison flipped her phone closed. "This is not what I needed right now," she said, her voice cracking.

Marshall hurriedly pulled into the far end of the church parking lot and turned off the car. He turned to her. "What is it? Did Lindsay call back? Is something wrong?"

"Oh, just a, a message. From someone who's mad at me."

"Allison." Marshall put his hand on her chin and made her look him directly in the eye. "What is it?"

She hesitated, then said, "I've gotten a couple of threats recently. You know the kind of people I put away. It comes with the territory."

"But there's a difference now, Allison. You have to think of the baby."

"These people just like to hear themselves talk," she said, trying to convince herself as much as Marshall. "And I'm taking precautions. There are extra patrols coming by the house. And Rod put a trap and trace on my phone, so I'll be able to find out where it came from."

Marshall sighed. "Maybe with the baby coming you should think about going into a different area of law. One that's less dangerous."

"I'm a third-generation prosecutor, Marshall. It's in my blood." She thought of all her classmates who had gone into white shoe firms. For them, everything was about getting something bigger—the bigger house, the bigger car, the bigger salary. "I think God put me here to make the world less dangerous. I wouldn't be nearly as much use someplace else."

When Marshall still looked doubtful, she added, "Besides, I'm actually safer at work. Anybody who wanted to get to me at my office would have to get past a metal detector, a security gate, and a bunch of law enforcement personnel."

Instead of answering, Marshall pulled her into an awkward hug over the parking brake. Feeling his strong arms around her, Allison finally let herself begin to tremble while he ran a soothing hand over her hair.

After several moments of silence, he said, "I know how important your work is to you. But I want you to promise me that you will take care of yourself. Of our baby. Just once, think of putting yourself first."

"I promise." She gave his hand a squeeze. "The service will start soon. We should go in."

Outside the church, pens had been set up on each side of the main door. A local farmer always brought in newborn animals for the Christmas Eve service. This year it was a lamb and two calves, one so young it could barely stand on shaky legs.

As she looked at them, Allison rubbed her belly. Next year she would be holding a baby in her arms. Two years from now, they would have a toddler like the ones gazing raptly through the bars at the baby animals.

Once they were seated in a pew, Marshall put his arm around her shoulders. Allison closed her eyes and leaned into his warmth. She didn't hear much of the sermon. Instead, she was making a short list of suspects who might be threatening her.

She had prosecuted dozens of people. Why would one of them snap now? Did that mean it was someone she had recently prosecuted—or one of their friends or relatives? Or a guy who had recently gotten out of prison? Or was it merely some random crazy who had seen her name in the paper? If only she had been able to see the face of the man who had seemed to follow her to Katie's vigil. Did this guy really know where she lived—or just the general area?

She only really tuned in when they sang the hymns. "What Child Is This?" made tears spring to her eyes. "O Come, All Ye Faithful" filled her with strength and hope. And "Joy to the World" finally took her out of herself, at least for a moment.

When she shook Pastor Schmitz's hand at the door after the service, he didn't release his grasp. Instead, he leaned closer, and Allison could tell that he saw her, really saw her.

"Are you okay?"

She started to say, "Sure," but her throat closed up. She couldn't speak. Finally, she shook her head.

Marshall said, "There's been a lot going on."

"Would you like to talk?" Pastor Schmitz asked.

They looked at each other and then nodded.

"Why don't you go down to my office, and I'll meet you there in a minute."

Allison and Marshall were silent as they walked back through the lobby, past the smiling people exchanging hugs and small wrapped gifts.

"What's the matter?" Pastor Schmitz asked them five minutes later, as he sat in the brown chair next to the red cloth couch they were sitting on.

"Allison's pregnant," Marshall said.

"That's marvelous news," Pastor Schmitz said, but he didn't smile. "What else?"

"I'm getting death threats at work," Allison said. "And I'm trying to find out what's happened to this missing girl."

"Katie Converse," Pastor Schmitz said. It wasn't a question. Thanks to the nonstop news coverage, everyone knew Katie's name. "Are the death threats related to Katie?"

"I don't think so. But she is my number one priority right now. So you can see that there's a lot going on for us."

"God gives us times like these so that we can turn to His strength," Pastor Schmitz said. "Why don't we talk to Him about it?"

Allison closed her eyes. She felt Pastor Schmitz take one of her hands, and then Marshall take the other. The three of them formed a circle.

"Lord, thank you for this gift, this marvelous gift of a child," the pastor began. He prayed for protection for Allison and the baby, and for Katie, and strength for those searching for her, and peace and comfort for her family. When he was finished, he said, "In Jesus' name . . . ," and the three of them murmured, "Amen."

Allison's fears quieted. But only for a moment.

H e came, Mama! He came! Santa Claus came!"

Makayla was bouncing on the edge of the bed. Nic opened one eye. Everything felt both right and wrong. Wrong because this wasn't her bed, wasn't her house. Right because a long time ago, both things had been hers.

And wrong because it was far too early to get up.

Since Nic had had Makayla, she had spent every Christmas with her parents. For one thing, it just didn't seem like Christmas when you only had two people to celebrate it, and Nic felt that all children deserved a real Christmas. Christmas wasn't Christmas unless you were surrounded by family.

And then there was the matter of food. Lately, Nic's meals had run more to take-out barbecue and cold cereal, but Mama could be counted on to make all the foods that made the holiday special: ham, creamed corn, collard greens, stewed tomatoes, cranberry sauce, sweet potatoes, and pecan pie. This afternoon, the table would be so full there would hardly be room for their plates.

Makayla poked her. "He came, Mama!" she repeated stubbornly.

There was no way Nic was going to be able to stay asleep, no matter how much her body longed for it.

"Get under the covers with me for a second. I'm cold."

She wasn't, but it was the only way she could still get Makayla to cuddle. She no longer let Nic hold her hand, even when they were cross-ing the street.

Nic wrapped her arms around her daughter, her own skin several shades darker than Makayla's coffee with milk. As she held her daughter close, she wondered if the Converses would ever hold Katie again. Nic thought of their shadowed eyes. No matter how hard they pressed the hunt, even Katie's parents already knew it was hopeless. The girl had to be dead. The only thing left was to discover where, how, and why. And to get the creep who had done it.

Makayla squirmed. "You're squeezing too hard!"

Reluctantly, Nic released her. "So did Santa bring you a lot of presents?"

Makayla hadn't believed in Santa Claus since she was six. Still, it was fun for both of them to pretend.

"Lots! And there's one that *has* to be a bike! I touched it, and I could feel the handlebars and the seat and the pedals." She got to her feet again and tugged her mother's arm. "You have to come see."

"Okay, maybe we can go downstairs and open up one present. A small one. But we have to be really quiet—Grandma and Grandpa are still sleeping."

Later in the morning, Nicole's three brothers would bring their fami-lies over, and they would all take turns unwrapping presents.

"No, they're not. At least Grandma isn't. She's in the kitchen making cinnamon rolls."

Cinnamon rolls. That was all Nic needed. With a groan colored by crumbling resistance, she climbed out of bed.

Her daughter danced from one foot to the other, braids bouncing. She already came up to Nic's nose. Makayla was tall for a nine-year-old. People often thought she was older, because of her height. And she had the most unusual green eyes. Even strangers commented on them and sometimes asked where she had gotten them.

No matter how much she tried to pretend Makayla was all hers, there were times when the truth slapped Nic in the face. The green eyes, the height, the pale skin—it all came from Makayla's daddy.

But Nicole had sworn to herself that Makayla would never, ever know that.

Or him.

I've got to get ready for work," Cassidy murmured. She was nestled into the crook of Rick's arm, the sheets tangled around them. Their clothes were scattered all over the room. An empty wine bottle stood on the bureau, and another lay sideways on the floor.

His arm tightened. "You can't go, baby. It's not right. I still can't believe you have to work on Christmas. Especially on a Saturday!"

"I lost the holiday lottery this year. But I get to fill in for Brad, so it's not all bad. Some people think I'm anchor material. This will give me a chance to strut my stuff."

Rick's expression changed. "You'd better not be strutting it for anyone but me."

She pushed his shoulder. "Ha-ha, very funny. When would I have time to see anyone else? I really don't even have time for *you*."

Leaning over, she gave him a peck. Rick turned it into a full-on kiss that threatened to become something more.

Cassidy finally managed to get him to let her up. As she got to her feet, a headache bloomed behind her eyes. What time had they gotten to bed? Had she ever really gone to sleep?

This thing with Rick was crazy and fast. Just the way Cassidy liked it. She liked the way he was watching her now, as she walked around her bedroom naked and pulled clothes from her closet. She didn't even mind that her hair must look like a rat's nest, although she did suck in her stomach. There was something about his ice-blue eyes, always at half-mast, that reminded her of some kind of animal. A wolf, maybe. Something that looked all tame and calm on the outside, but inside was anything but domesticated. He was always watching her, but she never knew what he was thinking. Maybe that came with the territory when you dated a cop.

After a long shower, Cassidy's head felt a little clearer. She didn't remember bringing it in here last night, but there was another bottle of wine in the bathroom. She took a long sip before she brushed her teeth. Surest way to get rid of a hangover, that's what everyone always said.

She came out of the bathroom wearing black pants and a V-neck cranberry red sweater.

"You're not wearing that," Rick said. It wasn't a question. He had propped himself up on the headboard with a couple of pillows.

"Why not? It's a Christmasy color."

"It's too low-cut. I don't want all of Portland ogling you."

Cassidy leaned over the bed. "Oh, so you're the only one who can ogle?"

One second she was leaning over him, the next Rick had flipped her onto her back, holding her arms over her head.

Cassidy laughed in surprise, but she heard how uncertain it sounded. "What are you doing?"

"Making you late for work." He nuzzled the side of her neck.

"No, Rick, don't. I don't want to."

"Don't say that. I know you do." He pulled back and gave her a wolf-ish grin.

"No, seriously, I don't."

Rick's eyes narrowed. His expression changed, hardened somehow.

Something pulsed low in Cassidy's belly. Was it desire—or fear?

"I mean, of course I do. I would love to spend the rest of the day here with you in bed, but I have to go to work. They're counting on me."

For an answer, he grabbed both her wrists with one hand.

Saying you're a Senate page sounds glamorous, but it's not. We're basically gofers. It seems so old-fashioned, all the paper we carry around. Haven't they heard of e-mail? It's probably been the same since Daniel Webster was a page.

This afternoon I ran into Senator X. He asked me what I was doing for dinner tomorrow. When I told him I had a voucher to eat in the Union Station food court, he made his voice break like the kid who works at Krusty Burger on *The Simpsons*. "You want a side of grease with your burger?"

I laughed. The food there does get kind of old. Then he said we should go to that same Japanese restaurant we went to with V. Usually you have to go someplace with another page, but when you're with an adult you can go places by yourself. So I knew it would be just him & me, which is a little weird. But I've heard that every year he picks out a page to mentor.

At the restaurant, he ordered for me. He remembered exactly what I liked from the other time we were there! He said when he was a page it was the same as now—long hours, no glory & bad food. I said he left out the stupid uniform. But tonight I was wearing black pants & my blue cashmere sweater. Everyone always says it makes my eyes look bluer.

He even gave me a present—a beautiful gold bracelet—b/c he had heard I had my birthday. I couldn't believe it! He said I could always look at it & remember my time here.

The night just flew by. When I came home, my roommates were all asleep. They probably had just watched TV in the dayroom & gone to bed. And I had been talking to a senator about my future!

The trap and trace says the threat came from a pay phone," Allison told Nicole. They were in Allison's office, waiting for Senator Fairview and his lawyer.

"Did the voice sound familiar?"

"Maybe. Yes. No." She shrugged. "I don't know. You know how many people I've prosecuted. You've worked most of those cases with me."

Nicole tilted her head. "Then why are they going after you and not me? Or both of us?"

Allison had thought about this. "I'm the one who puts people away. I'm the one they think of when they sit in their jail cells . . . or when they get out."

When Allison's phone rang, both women started.

"Senator Fairview is here," the receptionist said.

Allison looked over at Nicole. "They're here. Let's go pin this jerk to the wall."

As a prosecutor, Allison would never interview a potential witness by herself. If someone told her one thing in an interview and then said something different on the witness stand, she couldn't take the stand herself to rebut him. She needed someone else present to do that.

More than that, she and Nicole made a good team. In an interview, Nicole sat back and listened with all her being, which made some people feel off-balance. They could tell they were being put under a microscope. And with as slick as Senator Fairview and his lawyer were sure to be, her team needed all the advantages they could get.

Michael Stone, Fairview's lawyer, had agreed to the interview only if Fairview was granted "use immunity." Use immunity meant the government couldn't use what was said today against Fairview at any future trial—it was for information only. Even if he broke down and confessed to killing Katie, it would be inadmissible at trial.

Allison had agreed to the stipulation, but mentally she put an asterisk after the agreement. If Fairview bobbed and weaved, if he said anything that put her antennae up, then the interview would be over, and the next time she saw Fairview would be in front of the grand jury. And if he said anything at all different to the grand jury, she would know he was lying. While technically she wouldn't be able to use that knowledge, it would still make all the difference.

She knew that Stone knew this as well. Most lawyers took the safe route and just said no thanks to an interview, even with use immunity. But Stone was a risk taker. He practiced law expertly, but often very close to the edge. Of course, he would also turn around and not only tell the media that his client was cooperating, but hint that Fairview was actually helping to track the real killer down.

The two men were waiting in the lobby.

Dapper and neat, with black hair silvering at the temples, Senator Fairview wore a perfectly tailored black suit and an appropriately concerned expression. He shook Allison's hand with just the right amount of firmness. In her two-inch heels, she was eye to eye with him.

Michael Stone was as famous for his expensive suits as he was for his high-profile clients. Today he wore a charcoal gray suit with a subtle pinstripe, which had probably cost more than Allison's car, as well as shiny Prada shoes with the little red stripe up the back of the heel.

"Hi. I'm Mike Stone. How you folks doin'?" Stone also shook their hands, his teeth gleaming in his tan face.

"We appreciate you coming in during the holidays," Allison said. "I'm sorry to have to take you away from your families."

"This is a matter of life and death," Fairview said portentously. "I will do everything in my power to help you find that girl."

Allison ushered them into a conference room that overlooked the Willamette River. Senator Fairview smoothed the front of his jacket before sitting down. He reminded her of some kind of smooth, self-contained animal, a cat maybe, or an otter. She knew every word out of his mouth would have been rehearsed with Stone many times over.

"Now, Senator Fairview," Allison began.

He cleared his throat. "Please, call me James."

"I understand Katie Converse was your page," she said, careful not to call him anything at all. "How many pages do you have at one time?"

Fairview's shoulders seemed to relax. "That's not how the page system works. She wasn't 'my' page. There are only thirty Senate pages per program, and two programs per year. I usually only sponsor a page every two or three years. But they don't work for me. They work for the whole Senate."

As he spoke, Nicole took notes. Later she would write up a report and send it to Allison.

Stone was pecking away on his Mac PowerBook. He was either taking copious notes or playing solitaire. Either way, he seemed to be distancing himself from the interview, giving Allison and Nicole a free hand. If it was a ploy, it was one that worked for Allison.

"How many applicants did you have for the slot Katie took?" Allison asked.

He shrugged. "I think five or six. My staff narrowed it down for me. I only spoke with the top three finalists."

"So you first met Katie . . . ?"

"Last spring when I interviewed her."

"Was anyone else present?"

"Her stepmother—Valerie—was there, but I asked her to stay in the waiting area. Valerie and her husband have donated to my campaign, and I've met her at a few fund-raising events." Fairview allowed himself a small smile. "But frankly, she seems like a bit of a helicopter parent—do you know the term?"

"A parent who hovers?" Allison asked.

"Exactly. I want to hear from the student applying to be sponsored by me, not from some parent who interrupts everything they say to explain, 'What Jonathan really meant was . . .'"

"You said the Converses had donated to your campaign. Is that a prerequisite to being a page?"

"Of course not," Fairview said in a disappointed tone. "Katie was chosen on her own merits. She was bright, well-spoken, and had glowing references from her teachers. The other candidates had those things too. But what made Katie stand out was how much she loved politics. She wasn't just thinking that a stint as a Senate page would look good on her college transcript. She truly cared. Her parents could even have been Democrats and I still would have wanted to sponsor her—although I'll admit it's not likely liberals would have asked me to sponsor their kid."

He smiled disarmingly. Allison caught herself starting to smile back.

"And what was your impression of Katie?"

Fairview made a show of looking at Stone, who said, "Just tell them what you know, James, like we talked about. Just tell them the truth."

It was all Allison could do not to roll her eyes. Stone's words reminded her that the whole thing was an act from start to finish.

Fairview cleared his throat. "At that time, I thought Katie was bright and very capable."

"At that time?" Allison echoed, drawn in despite herself. "Did your opinion change?"

He pursed his lips and then said, "Shortly after the program started, I met Katie in a hallway when she was running an errand. She started telling me how lonely she was. Of course, I was completely sympathetic. It's a bit of a shock to the system being away from home and family and friends for the first time. Plus, being a Senate page is hard work. I understand, you know. I was one years ago. It's like having two full-time jobs: student and Senate worker. It's extremely stressful."

"Did you talk more after that?" Allison asked.

"Katie had a lot of questions about politics. And she wanted to discuss the issues. She's a political junkie, as I am. She wanted to know about the ins and outs, the horse trading, how bills get made, the work of the committees." Fairview's voice rose with unfeigned passion. "You know how few people care about those things, even though they affect everything in their lives?"

"Did you ever call her?" Allison watched him closely. This was her chance to see how far he would go with his lies.

He did not seem concerned. "A few times. I felt I should check to see how things were going. I was worried about her, frankly. I even talked to my wife about it."

A few times? Is that what he calls a couple of hundred conversations?

Allison concealed her glee. "What were you worried about?"

"Katie's emotions were very volatile. Everything was either the best thing that ever happened to her or the end of the world. She was seeing a boy, one of the House or Senate pages, but it wasn't going well. It was a rocky relationship. Very volatile."

Nicole looked up from her notes.

Allison said, "Who was it?"

"I don't know his name. She never told me."

"Did you ever see him? Can you describe him?"

Is he inventing the boy for his own purposes? There were some blog entries about a boy, but they didn't sound as full of turmoil as Fairview was making out.

Fairview shrugged. "Between the House and the Senate, there are dozens of pages. She never pointed him out to me, and I never saw her with one particular boy."

"Did she tell you where he was from?"

"No." His voice finally showed strain. "I don't know anything about him. All I know is that I told Katie if it was causing her that much turmoil, maybe she should just break it off. Maybe I was wrong." His eyes welled with tears. "Maybe she needed all the friends she could get, and I took one away from her."

"Katie was clearly lonely." Allison put on an expression of sympathy. "Look, sometimes kids don't realize the signals they send out. It wouldn't be unheard of for her to come on to you. Is that what happened? And then the relationship got too complicated . . ."

"It wasn't like that at all," he said flatly.

"So are you saying you were flattered by how she confided in you?"

Instead of being insulted, Fairview shook his head. "Frankly, no. I didn't need some clingy girl who thought her problems were the whole world."

Could he be telling the truth?

"We've heard that you took Katie out to dinner."

His expression remained innocent and open. "Her parents, who, as I've said, are also campaign contributors, made a point of asking me to watch out for her. As the program went on, I noticed that Katie started to lose weight. To be honest, she reminded me of my daughter, who's also had some food issues. I occasionally took Katie out for meals so I could monitor her eating."

"How were you able to take her out?" Allison asked. "Don't pages need to be accompanied by another page at all times away from their job?"

Fairview shook his head. "Not when they are in the company of an adult."

Nicole spoke for the first time. "Didn't you worry about how that would appear?" She gave him a skeptical look.

Fairview straightened up. "I'm her mentor. Katie views me as a father figure. She's troubled, and I tried to help her. And now I'm being crucified for that." His jaw jutted forward like a bulldog's. "Every time I open my front door, reporters yell questions in my face. They're hounding my family."

"Then why didn't you get Katie some help?" Allison asked. "Shouldn't you have reported her to her proctor?"

"I knew what would happen. They would just ship her home to get the problem off their hands. And I knew that would completely crush Katie. Being a Senate page was her dream. She saw it as the first step toward a career in politics. If I reported her, her dream would die." He put his palm over his heart. "And I would have been the one to kill it."

It was time to show him that there was a fist inside the velvet glove. "So you ignored Katie's problems," Allison said.

Fairview straightened up. "I did not ignore them. I tried to help her." His face showed a trace of annoyance. "Are you saying I should have forced a troubled girl to give up the one thing that gave her life meaning?"

"You yourself said she was troubled. But you just let that go?"

"I did talk to her about it. Many times. I wanted her to see a counselor. But she would have had to do it through the page program's providers, and she was afraid they would report back. She said I was the only one she could talk to."

"So did you ever wish there was a way you could just—get rid of her?" Allison asked softly. "It's understandable, really."

His face flushed. "Are you saying I did something to her? I did not. I'll take a lie detector test. I'll do whatever you want to prove to you that I didn't do anything to that girl." He took a deep breath and calmed himself. "As we got closer to Christmas break, I was worried she might do something rash. She was depressed that she had to go home and live with her stepmother again. Valerie has strict standards, and Katie's gotten used to being on her own."

"When was the last time you saw her?"

Fairview seemed to be holding himself carefully, choosing his words with care. "Actually, it was December thirteenth. A few hours before she went missing. I was Christmas shopping with my wife in Nordstrom when I ran into Katie. She was looking for something for her stepmother. Our conversation lasted only a few seconds."

"What time was this?"

"The lunch hour. Around noon or so."

"Did she seem upset or troubled?"

"Not really, no. She seemed fine. I've been over and over those few sentences in my memory, but I can't think of any clues. As I said, our conversation was very brief."

"So was this the last conversation you had with her?" Allison held her breath.

"Yes, I believe it was."

"You believe it? Or do you know it?"

Fairview's eyes widened. He was caught, and he knew it.

"She also called you repeatedly on that date. Correct?" Allison said.

"Well, no, that's not true."

"Your phone records show that. Your phone records show that a phone belonging to Katie called your cell phone repeatedly the day she went missing. Five times."

"Well, that . . ." Fairview hesitated.

Stone seemed to be trying to look as if this wasn't news to him. He was doing a lousy job. This was clearly a body blow.

"I mean, she might have left a message. She might have reached my voice machine, my uh . . . uh, phone company voice answering machine. She may have called and left a message."

"Her parents are in hell, Senator," Nicole said. There was zero sympathy on her face. "Imagine one of your own children missing."

"I do, every day. I feel so badly for the Converses." Tears welled in Fairview's eyes. "Day after day, not knowing. But sometimes you wonder if not knowing is perhaps easier on them. I mean, the longer this goes on, the more likely that they are never going to see Katie alive again. Is it better for them to cling to a little hope than to be crushed by certainty?"

That was the moment when Allison knew in her gut that Fairview knew where Katie was. He knew what had happened to her.

He knew because he had been there.

Cassidy was scheduled for a live hit at 12:03. Never before had she had a story that led newscast after newscast. But with the Katie Converse story, it was like she had jumped on the back of a tiger.

Only sometimes she wasn't sure if she was riding the tiger or the tiger was riding her.

Out in the field there was no teleprompter, of course, so Cassidy had to memorize everything she was going to say on camera. The voice-overs were recorded earlier in the studio, but there were still a lot of long sentences that she had to recite verbatim during the stand-up.

Andy gave her the signal. Cassidy took a deep breath and said, "On the left side of your screen, you are looking at a live picture of the front door of the Converse household. We've been following this developing story over the last fourteen days: the missing Senate page Katie Converse. Today the parents of Katie Converse—whose disappearance has attracted national attention because of her friendship with her hometown senator—urged legislator Senator James Fairview of Portland, Oregon, to tell what he knows."

As she was speaking, Cassidy knew they had cut to the B-roll footage of the Converses, wearing buttons with Katie's picture, looking dazed and tired as they faced dozens of reporters. Cassidy pressed the plastic IFB earpiece—she had no idea what the initials stood for—deeper into her ear to make sure it was in securely. It had been cast for her ear, so in theory it was supposed to fit exactly, but sometimes she found she had to wiggle it. The IFB allowed her to hear instructions from the producer, questions from the anchor, and all the other sounds of the newscast. The curly cord—a light brown color that was more or less skin tone—ran down from her ear and was clipped to her back.

This part of the package had been put together earlier in the studio, so all Cassidy had to do was listen. On the IFB she heard Valerie say, "I am heartbroken, but I still remain optimistic. I believe, and I continue to hope and pray, that Katie will come back to us alive. But if Senator Fairview can shed any light on what has happened to her, we need him to." The B-roll footage would be switching to the now ubiquitous shot of Katie handing materials to Senator Fairview as he spoke to the Senate.

Next Cassidy heard her own voice, recorded earlier in the studio. "The couple's news conference came just after Mr. Fairview, who is married and has described Katie Converse simply as 'a young woman he mentored,' met with authorities. The fifty-two-year-old Republican has donated $10,000 of surplus campaign money to a reward fund for the return of Ms. Converse, who is seventeen. In a written statement issued today, he said he shared her parents' worry and concern and offered his continued cooperation. The authorities say there is no evidence connecting him to Katie's disappearance.

"But by some news accounts, there are records showing that Katie telephoned Mr. Fairview repeatedly. Katie also confided to friends that she had a boyfriend whose identity she did not disclose. Senator Fairview himself refuses to grant interviews. In a statement today, he attacked the 'tabloidization' of the case."

Andy signaled that Cassidy was live on camera again.

She said, "Katie, who is scheduled to return to Portland next month to resume classes at Lincoln High School, has spent the fall as a Senate page in Washington DC." She gestured to the house behind her, with the huge photo of Katie on the front door. "She returned here for Christmas break.

"Across America, there are hundreds of missing people. What makes Katie Converse different is her rumored romantic involvement with the senator from her district." An hour earlier, the station's lawyer had agreed, reluctantly, that this statement would probably not cause them to be sued for libel.

Brad, the anchor, said into her ear, "Cassidy, just to put a small piece of it in perspective, can you describe to us the media scene in front of the Converses' home?"

As Andy panned the crowd of other reporters—the shot a sure sign of a news story that had no "new news"—Cassidy said, "There are literally dozens of media people here, but we work carefully not to intrude upon the Converses. We have regular conversations with the family to make sure that we don't interfere with what they have to do and yet maintain a presence so that if they want to speak, we are here at a moment's notice. And the Converses have been extremely willing to talk to us when they have something to say. Obviously, all the media attention benefits the case of their missing daughter.

"Now we are hearing that there is a negotiation going on. Fairview's lawyer, Michael Stone, says he is willing to discuss the possibility of a polygraph. The negotiation has been stuck on the scope of the questioning. Stone says there have to be some limitations, but federal prosecuting attorney Allison Pierce has said that the authorities will decide what the questions are, and there will be no limitations. So it's a bit of a stalemate."

In her IFB, Brad said, "How is the hunt for Katie going? Have there been any new leads?"

"No, Brad, but not for lack of trying. Police are continuing to search outbuildings, sheds, garages, that sort of thing, in the area where Katie disappeared. There are also plans to take cadaver dogs—which are exactly like they sound: dogs that look for bodies—to take these dogs out to the landfills.

"Authorities have thoroughly searched Fairview's home, car, and local office for signs of a struggle. The material that they got from that was apparently fairly minimal. But we're told that the police are having their evidence technicians go over it. The experts say that they can find signs of blood, body fluids, hair, and other signs of a struggle, even if there has been some attempt to cover them up. They also say that Fairview is one of nearly one hundred people they have interviewed. Even so, they still have not been able to answer the most important question, and that is—what happened to Katie Converse? Until authorities are able to answer that question, they still have a long way to go in this investigation."

Her face serious, Cassidy added, "Back to you, Brad."

FAIRVIEW RESIDENCE
December 28

The Portland cop slumped in front of the video monitor watched as absolutely nothing happened on the screen, which showed the Fairviews' driveway and front door. The video camera providing the feed had been installed across the street from the Fairviews by a guy wearing the uniform of a local cable company.

The monitor was in a house a few blocks from the Fairview home, which the task force had rented and converted into a small watching post. Anyone coming out of the house or pulling up the driveway or running across the front yard was seen immediately.

Whenever Fairview left, he was followed. Two unmarked cars were assigned to track his movements. To avoid alerting Fairview to their presence—"getting burned," as the surveillance people called it—they rotated the ground units so that the vehicles were never the same from one day to the next.

The FBI had donated the use of one of the bureau's single-engine Cessnas to assist the ground units. All day it stayed high above Fairview's house, sliding in and out of the clouds, circling endlessly. If Fairview pulled out of the driveway, the air unit would follow. A spotter seated next to the pilot would watch Fairview's movements, making sure they stayed with him.

"Okay," the spotter would say, speaking over the radio to the units on the ground, "Eagle has the eyeball."

Their only hope was that Fairview would lead them to Katie. Dead or alive.

Between the pregnancy and the Katie Converse case, Allison was having trouble sleeping. Could Katie still be alive? Could Senator Fairview have hidden her away so that she wouldn't talk with the press? Certain passages in her blog had shown her turmoil and depression. Could she have committed suicide? Could she have run away?

One by one, the reports came in from the various FBI offices where the young pages had scattered over the holiday break. One of Katie's roommates reported that the senator did seem to spend more time with Katie than any other page. A second hadn't noticed anything out of the ordinary. The third roommate said she was good friends with Katie and that absolutely nothing was going on, that the senator was friendly with everyone. She did yield the name of the Senate page Katie had been involved with: Dylan Roessler, who lived in Nashville.

An FBI agent from Tennessee called Allison, speaking in a drawl so slow that she found herself gritting her teeth.

"I interviewed that Dylan kid your missing girl used to date. Although 'dating' might be too strong a word. It was more like they spent a week or so doing some heavy necking in the common room at the page residence. When she quote, 'broke up,' end quote, with him, he thought at first it was because he wanted to take things further. But later he realized it was because there was someone else."

Allison wanted to crawl down the phone line and shake the agent. Why couldn't he have led with this information? "And who was that?"

"He said it couldn't be one of the pages, because they all lived so close together and he would have known. He thought it was an adult. Quote, 'And not like someone going to college. A real adult.' End quote."

"Where was Dylan the day Katie went missing?"

"Home. Three thousand miles away. And they weren't really on speaking terms before break."

"Did he think she was suicidal?"

"He wouldn't go as far as that. All he would say was that she was moody."

Every lead petered out. With a shallow pretense of cordiality, the interview with Fairview had ended in a draw. Even once his lie about Katie's phone calls was unmasked, Fairview continued to maintain that he had told the truth. What did it matter which phone she called him on? He hadn't known she had gotten a second phone, and he certainly hadn't suggested it to her. Katie was a troubled girl. He had tried to help her. And that was all. The only relationship between them had been platonic.

To prove it, Fairview's wife, Nancy, had agreed to being interviewed by Nicole and Allison. The law protected communication in certain relationships—between a doctor and patient, priest and penitent, attorney and client. And between husband and wife. But Fairview had waived that right and agreed for Nancy to come in and talk to Allison and Nicole.

Since Michael Stone couldn't represent both the senator and his wife—it was a conflict of interest—Nancy came in with her own lawyer, a quiet, corporate type named Joel Rickert. Nancy was a tall, thin woman, probably eye to eye with her husband, with a long face, big teeth, and a wide swathe of gums. She reminded Allison unfortunately of a horse.

They met in the same conference room in which Allison and Nicole had met with her husband.

"Have you ever met Katie Converse?" Allison asked after the preliminaries were out of the way.

"Actually, James introduced me when we ran into her while we were Christmas shopping at Nordstrom. We had a very brief conversation."

"This was the same day Katie disappeared, correct?"

Nancy shrugged. "I guess so. I didn't really think about the date until later."

"And did she seem upset about anything?" Allison asked. "Did she share any of her plans for the rest of the day?"

"Our conversation only lasted a minute or two, if that. It was about the weather, if they were both enjoying the break, things like that."

"And what did you think of her?"

Nancy pursed her lips, looked down at her hands, looked back up at Allison again. "I think she was head over heels about James."

Allison was surprised by her honesty. She cut her eyes to Rickert, but his expression betrayed nothing. "What makes you think that?"

"She would barely look at me, but she was all over him. Giving him a hug. Complimenting his tie, of all things. His tie! I pick out all of James's clothes."

"Do you think your husband was having an affair with her?" Allison asked.

"I don't know. And frankly, I don't want to know. But after twenty-some years of marriage, you know when something might be going on. James is a gregarious man. He gets lonely sometimes, living three thousand miles away. But his little flirtations don't mean anything. They don't mean anything to our marriage. And I understand that. It's always some young thing who will look up to him. He likes that. Some simpering little nothing who—" Nancy stopped abruptly.

Allison wondered if her lawyer had touched her knee under the table. Warned her to shut up. *Simpering little nothing*—either Nancy or her lawyer must have remembered she was speaking ill of a girl who was more than likely dead.

"And what happened after that? Did you talk to him about it?"

"Talk?" Nancy snorted. "There was no point in talking. As soon as we left Nordstrom, I told him he was not going back to the office, he was coming home with me. And then I spent the rest of the afternoon reminding James exactly how I'm not like any of those silly girls he likes to flirt with. I'm not some naïve, virginal little nothing who doesn't know which end is up." Nancy's head was up, her eyes were narrowed, and her breathing audible. "Because I love my husband, and I will do what needs to be done to help him. Even if it means, like now, being forced to share my private life with strangers."

"**W**hat do you think?" Allison asked after Nancy and her lawyer had left.

Nancy had walked out of the interview room with her head held high, as if daring them to try to picture her teaching her husband a lesson.

"I think she's lying," said Nicole. "Only I'm not sure about what. You?"

"I think you're right. Nancy's not telling us the truth, at least not the whole truth, no matter how embarrassed she claimed to be." Allison looked back at the empty chair where Nancy had been sitting and ran the woman's words through her mind again. "But the thing is, maybe she's not lying to save her husband's skin."

Nicole looked up from the report on which she was putting the finishing touches. "What do you mean?"

"Maybe Nancy's lying to save her own skin. That alibi gets both her husband and her off the hook. She clearly hates Katie. Maybe she hated her enough to kill her."

Nicole didn't answer, just tapped her pen against her teeth and looked thoughtful.

By the time Allison left the office, it was well after eight o'clock, and she hadn't eaten since lunch—which couldn't be good for the baby. In the car, she turned on the radio. It was still set on the station she listened to in the morning for its frequent traffic updates. Outside of drive time, it was a series of conservative talk shows. Allison heard enough one-sided arguments in court that she didn't like to hear them in her car as well. She was reaching out her finger to push the off button when she recognized the topic: Senator Fairview.

A sonorous voice she recognized as belonging to this particular show's host, Jim Fate, was saying with disgust, "Isn't lying in a criminal investigation enough? Isn't that enough, Senator Schneider?" Fate's radio show, *The Hand of Fate*, had started out small, but Allison had heard enough promotion for it in between traffic and weather reports to know that it was now syndicated nationally.

"If you're under oath, of course it is. It's perjury."

Fate said, "It wasn't under oath. But you know, sources say that Fairview has just refused to tell authorities about his affair with a minor. He just wouldn't tell them. First he denied it, and then he clammed up. Isn't that enough to get him impeached?"

Schneider said mildly, "I would think not."

Fate's voice dripped with disgust. "Really? If you, Luke Schneider, were on the Senate Ethics Committee, which you're not, and evidence came in that a senator lied to the authorities in what could well be a murder investigation—are you saying that wouldn't be enough to get him out of there?"

"But Senator Fairview's been charged with nothing."

"All right, so if someone from the FBI would stand up and say, 'This guy impeded the investigation . . .'"

"Of course that would be enough," Schneider said.

Fate echoed, "That's enough to get him out?"

"Well, it's enough to take to the Ethics Committee. They can move to expel, censure, or admonish him."

"So what would it take for you guys to get rid of this creep?" Fate demanded. "I mean, it has reached critical mass. Wouldn't you say that most decent human beings would have resigned by now, with all the stuff that we know about him? We're talking corruption of a minor, statutory rape, and crossing state lines to have sex with the girl."

Schneider said, "Right now those things are only rumors. They have not been substantiated. If someone came forward with proof, then we could deal with it. We don't make decisions based on what people are saying on TV. There's a process. There's the Constitution. You can't just get annoyed with someone and kick him out."

"What about Katie Converse?" Fate demanded. "Did she have any rights in the matter? Who sticks up for her rights, Senator?"

There was a half-second pause. Schneider had just begun to answer when Fate overrode him. "I'm afraid we are out of time, Senator. Senator Schneider, thank you for joining *The Hand of Fate*."

Dryly, Schneider said, "The pleasure has been all mine, Jim."

At my regular high school, I was always the smart one. It would be a lot harder to be the smart one in this group. But sometimes I think that maybe I don't have to be the smart one here. I could be the funny one. Or maybe the pretty one.

Since there are only thirty Senate pages, you get to know everybody on a very personal level. You work together all day long & live in the same dorm. You do pretty much everything together. So certain people that you would rather not see any more, you see every single day—at meals, in class, at work & on weekend trips. Some people just don't understand that there's real love & then there's things that aren't real love, but more just fooling around.

The funny thing is, I think I might have found real love. Maybe some people would say I'm too young to know what real love is. But how do they know what I'm feeling? How can they see the thoughts swirling around in my head? Just b/c I've never been in love before doesn't mean I can't find real love now. It doesn't mean I have to wait until I'm older, like in college.

What if I've already met my true love?

Cassidy, I've got some news." It was Jerry, the station manager.

"Huh?" Cassidy barely heard him. On her computer, she was rearranging the order of the questions she would ask tonight. Senator Fairview and his wife had agreed to be interviewed by her. By Cassidy Shaw. Live. On prime-time TV. The interview would be carried nationally. This was it at last—her big break.

Everyone in the station was rushing around madly. They had been running a promo nonstop for the last three days, one that showed the by-now infamous clip of Katie Converse handing Senator Fairview a poster board at a Senate hearing. Over it, the graphic designer had laid a specially designed logo—WHERE IS KATIE? in jagged-edge type.

Jerry hesitated so long that Cassidy finally looked up.

He gave her an anxious twist of a smile. "Madeline is flying in. The Katie Converse story just keeps growing. It's national news now, not just local. It's going to be on the cover of *People*. So Madeline wants in on the action."

Cassidy's head jerked up. "Oh no. I will not be bigfooted."

Madeline McCormick anchored the nightly news for the network that owned Channel Four.

Despite Cassidy's words, she and Jerry knew that bigfooting happened all the time. A junior reporter would get a lead, do all the work, and then before it could go to air, the more senior reporter would take the story and claim it as his—or in this case, her—own.

"You don't have a choice," Jerry said, twisting his hands. "We can't afford to make Madeline angry."

"You can't do this to me. This is my story. I broke it, and I'm the one making it happen."

"And Maddy appreciates that," Jerry said, as if he and "Mad Maddy" were now best buddies.

Cassidy was sure he had probably spoken only to the woman's assistant.

"No, you don't understand. You know all the good leads I've been getting? Well, the sources I have inside this investigation are *my* sources, and my sources only. How do you think I broke the story about Katie's blog? How do you think I knew before anyone else that the blood on Jalapeño was the dog's and not Katie's? You give this story to Madeline and that will be the last we hear from any of my sources, I can promise you that."

Jerry stared at her. They both knew Cassidy was telling the truth.

She allowed herself a small smile. "Tell you what. Madeline can do the intro and bring viewers up to date. But this is my interview. And mine alone."

That evening, a calm descended over Cassidy as she waited for a signal that they were on air. Until then, it seemed that the senator and his wife were in no mood for small talk. They sat together on a blue love seat, facing her, but not looking at her or each other. They both wore pained expressions. It was clear that the only reason Senator Fairview was here was to make a last-ditch effort to save his reputation.

What they didn't know was that Cassidy had instructed one of the cameras always to be on them, even now, before the program officially began. You never knew when an outtake might be the most valuable piece of film you shot. Senator Fairview looking bored, or shifting his eyes from side to side, or ignoring his wife—all of it could be used to make a point in later coverage.

The story had gotten so big that it was now drawing crackpots. Twice now Cassidy had gotten voice mails ordering her to stop asking so many questions about Katie, warning her that it was none of her business. She was hoping that the next call would be even juicier so she could play it on the air.

The cameraman counted down with his fingers, and they were on.

Cassidy took a deep breath. TV viewers sometimes complained that women couldn't do serious news, not with their tendency to half smile even when announcing horrendous death tolls. Not with their singsong, high-pitched voices. She was careful to keep any hint of a smile from her lips as she spoke in a low-pitched, even voice.

"Senator Fairview, Mrs. Fairview, thank you so much for joining us tonight. Senator, I would like to ask you what everyone in Oregon—and in the nation—is wondering. Do you know what happened to Katie Converse?"

Even as the words left Cassidy's mouth, Fairview was already answering. "No, I do not."

Now he looked at her steadily. Next to him on the navy blue love seat, Nancy held her husband's hand. Her expression had changed to one of concern.

"What was your relationship with Katie, Senator?"

He looked up and to the right, as if he were searching his memory instead of trotting out another carefully rehearsed answer. Cassidy was sure Fairview had practiced every word, every expression, every turn of phrase. Just as she had.

"Well, I met Katie Converse last spring when she applied to be sponsored by me as a Senate page. Which I agreed to do. And then in September she became one of dozens of young people who work as pages in the House and the Senate."

"Did you have anything to do with Katie's disappearance?" Cassidy kept her pacing quick. She wanted to get to the good stuff, to the topics that might knock Fairview off balance.

"No, I didn't." His answer was smooth. Concern with just a hint of anger.

"Did you kill Katie Converse?"

"I did not."

She decided to switch it up a bit and project sympathy. "Have all the rumors and speculation been hard on you and your family?"

Fairview turned to Nancy, and they exchanged a glance that appeared private and that Cassidy bet had also been rehearsed a dozen times.

Then he turned back to her. "The media have tried to go through my wife's medical records, and the tabloids have chased my children. But the fact of the matter is, this is not about the Fairviews. This is about the Converses. And what we've experienced is minor pain compared to what Mr. and Mrs. Converse are going through. Our hearts go out to them."

"Nancy, how are you coping with the media onslaught?" Cassidy asked. "Do you read everything? Do you listen to everything? Or are you tempted to put your hands over your ears and not take it in?"

Nancy's mouth crimped. "They have completely lost sight of Katie. Instead, they want to make it about innuendos and half-truths and out-right lies about my husband."

Fairview shook his head. "It's ridiculous that we are even being asked these questions. Katie is a troubled young woman, and I have tried to help her. And this is the payback I receive? To be accused of her murder?"

Was this the first crack in the façade? Cassidy felt like she could levi-tate out of her seat. "Troubled? What do you mean by troubled?"

He sighed. "When you first meet Katie, she seems older than her years. I mean, how many people her age want to talk about how bills are made? But the longer you know her, the more you can see how lonely and inse-cure she is."

Cassidy shook her head. "But Katie has gotten straight A's, she was president of several clubs at her high school, and she got into this competitive page program that takes only a handful of students from across the nation. By every account, Katie is a success."

Fairview made a gesture with his hands as if he were brushing all that aside. "A lot of these young people look successful on the surface. But inside they're hollow. Inside they are filled with turmoil and weakness and self-loathing."

Cassidy suddenly *knew* that Fairview was talking about himself as much as he was Katie. Nothing was hidden from her, there were no shadows, everything sparkled. And it wasn't just the studio lights. She was in the zone.

"So you are saying—what? That Katie was . . . depressed?"

"Katie was a very troubled young woman. And seeing a friendly face from home, she reached out to me. I was afraid to turn her away. Afraid if I did, she might do something rash."

"Rash? What do you mean by rash? Do you mean you were worried she might run away? Do you think that's what's happened?"

"I have no idea what's happened to Katie. But yes, Cassidy, I was worried that she might run away." Fairview's Adam's apple bobbed as he swallowed. "Even that she might possibly go further and choose the ultimate method of running away."

Cassidy let her eyes widen. Her mind and her mouth were operating on two separate planes now. She was weighing her next words, searching through her mental data banks, anticipating the senator's response, while her mouth and tongue simultaneously shaped the words she had chosen a second earlier. "Are you saying Katie was suicidal?"

"I'm not a professional counselor. All I know is that Katie is a very troubled young woman. She can be in tears one moment and then bouncing with happiness the next."

"But doesn't that describe a typical teenager? You yourself have a fifteen-year-old son and a thirteen-year-old daughter." Cassidy watched the skin around Fairview's eyes tighten. She only hoped it showed on camera. "As a father, don't you feel that these types of mood swings are common to every teen?"

She hoped the viewers caught the unspoken corollary: *As a father, can't you see that you wouldn't want an old guy like you hanging out with his daughter?*

"These moods of Katie's were more than that. A few times, she talked about how she didn't feel like she could go on. I tried to get her to go to a counselor, but she adamantly refused. She said I was the only one she could talk to. And I was afraid if I forced her, she might act on her threats. Frankly, I got caught up in the intensity of it."

"Senator, excuse me, but I have to address this." Cassidy drew a deep breath. "There are rumors that your relationship with Katie was sexual."

It was clearly the question Fairview had been waiting for. His practiced answer flowed out of him as if she had just pulled a cork from a bottle.

"Well, Cassidy, I have not been a perfect man, and I've made my share of mistakes. But I've been married for twenty-four years, and I intend to stay married to this woman as long as she'll have me."

He and Nancy looked at each other, and Nancy even managed to squeeze out a smile for the cameras.

Fairview turned back to Cassidy. "But out of respect for my family, and out of a specific request from the Converse family, I think it's best that I not get into those details. That's not what matters now. What matters is that Katie is missing."

"So you are denying that you had an affair with Katie Converse?"

"Let me just say this. I may have made some errors in judgment, but I have done nothing illegal. I never touched a hair on Katie's head. But the fact of the matter is this. I've been married twenty-four years, I've made some mistakes in my life, and I'm not a perfect man. But out of respect for my family, and out of a request, a specific request from the Converses, I will not go into the details of my relationship with Katie Converse."

There they were. All the messages in one breath. *Again*. Practically word for word.

"What exactly did the Converses ask you to do?" Cassidy hadn't heard anything about it. In fact, as far as she knew, the Converses and the Fairviews were no longer speaking to each other.

He shifted. "A couple of nights ago on one of the TV shows, uh, they said they did not want to hear about the details of the relationship, how I feel about Katie, or how she feels about me. So I'm trying to honor that. I think the American people understand that people are entitled to some privacy. I'm entitled to try to retain as much privacy as I can. The Converses are entitled to retain as much privacy on behalf of their daughter as they can. So I'm going to honor that."

That was the best his lawyer and the media coach could come up with? That the Converses had made some offhand remark on TV that Fairview was now treating as a specific request made directly to him?

Cassidy put on a stern look. "But, Senator, you are protecting your privacy at the expense of a young woman who is missing."

A hint of anger crept into his voice. "Well, that's not correct. That's not correct at all. Because I have cooperated with law enforcement. I mean, I have not been part of the media circus if, if that's your point. No, I haven't held a news conference, and no, I don't do talk shows. But I have cooperated. I have worked with law enforcement at every step and given up a lot of my civil liberties to make sure that they have all the information that they need."

"Don't the people of Oregon deserve the truth? The people who elected you to this office?"

Fairview jutted his chin. "They deserve the truth. And the truth is that I have done everything asked of me by the people who are responsible to find Katie Converse. It's not the news media's responsibility to find Katie Converse. It's law enforcement's. And I have worked with the authorities to do just that."

Maybe Nancy was the weaker link.

Cassidy softened her tone. "What toll does this take, Nancy? I mean, when you're the wife of a public official and you hear these whispers and you have law enforcement coming to you and asking you questions about your most intimate relationship, how do you handle that as a wife?"

Nancy managed a half smile. "I don't listen to rumors. I know James Fairview. I know about our relationship, and I feel very secure in it. And I don't need other people to tell me what they think about it." She put on a sad expression. "Instead of focusing on finding Katie, or talking about the good things my husband has accomplished, the media are trying to make something out of nothing."

Out of nothing? Either this lady was in denial, or she was completely heartless. Cassidy couldn't wait to see how they reacted to what she said next.

The words hurried off her tongue. "I'm going to turn to another area. A young woman, a cook at the Senate cafeteria named Luisa Helprin, has told me that she had a relationship with you, Senator. And that you asked her to lie about it. True?"

For a second, Fairview and his wife exchanged a glance. Cassidy wished she could read that glance. Did Nancy already know? Guess? Choose not to know?

"I didn't ask anyone to lie about anything," Fairview stuttered. "I did not ask Luisa not to cooperate with law enforcement. That's an absolute lie."

Just the way Fairview said *Luisa* confirmed the whole thing. Obviously, his lawyer and his media coach had not prepared him for this. Cassidy would bet that the two of them were watching this on TV and having a heart attack—and that Allison would be on the phone as soon as the program was over, demanding Luisa's contact info.

Inside, Cassidy was grinning, but she kept her expression grave. "We have a statement that your lawyers gave to Luisa, and it says, 'I do not and have not had a romantic relationship with Senator Fairview.'"

He shifted. She could see the sweat shining on his forehead. Nancy was no longer smiling. Her mouth was half open, her expression stunned and frozen.

"Well, uh," Fairview stuttered, "that's a statement that a lawyer sent to another lawyer. I did not have anything to do with that."

"But why would your lawyer write up the draft of something without your authorization? Why would you want her to say that she didn't have a relationship with you?"

Fairview found his footing. "Because she didn't."

He managed to sound like he meant it. How good was he at compartmentalizing? Had he told so many lies that he sometimes believed them himself? Or was he one of those people who could parse a sentence ("I did not have sex with that woman" came to mind) so narrowly that he sincerely believed it was true?

"Why would this young woman make it up?" Cassidy emphasized the word *young*.

Fairview pursed his lips and nodded as if he was agreeing with something she had said. "You know, Cassidy, I'm puzzled by people who take advantage of tragedy."

"Are you saying that Luisa completely fabricated this?"

"She's taking advantage of this tragedy. She didn't know Katie Converse. So she gets to have her moment of publicity, of financial gain. And I'm puzzled by that."

As far as Cassidy knew, Luisa had only told her story to her. And at Channel Four, they never paid for interviews. Of course, that didn't mean a paid-for interview with Luisa wouldn't run in one of the tabloids tomorrow. Or that Fairview wouldn't cast as many aspersions on Luisa as he could.

"Do you think Katie Converse's disappearance has made you less effective as a senator?"

"No."

She waited, but it was clear Fairview was determined not to say any-thing more. "But don't the people of Oregon deserve a senator who is not distracted by this type of allegation? Have you considered resigning?"

Fairview reared back as if Cassidy had slapped him. "No. I won't resign. I will finish out my term. Let me tell you—"

Nancy laid her hand on her husband's thigh and leaned forward. "Because there are so many, many more who don't want James to resign."

He nodded emphatically. "My dad taught me when I started a job to work hard and finish it, no matter how tough it got."

"But with all due respect, Senator, your father never envisioned a miss-ing girl and a Senate Ethics Committee investigation."

Fairview narrowed his eyes. "I think the principle applies to anything you do in life. And that's the easy way out. People know my history and my record. People know I'm a fighter. And this is the toughest fight of my political life. Which is why I want to thank you for giving me this oppor-tunity to set the record straight."

"Thank you so much, Senator and Mrs. Fairview."

"Thank you," they chorused. Looking daggers at her.

MARK O. HATFIELD UNITED STATES COURTHOUSE
December 31

Unable to sleep after watching Fairview's interview, Allison had gone to work ninety minutes early. Just as she was putting her key into the lock, the phone began to ring inside her office. She quickly unlocked the door and lunged for the receiver, catching it right before the call went to voice mail.

"Allison Pierce."

"It's Greg." Greg worked down the hall from Allison. The connection was bad, and she had to strain to hear him. "I forgot my security card. Come down and let me in."

Before Allison could say anything, she heard a click. He had hung up. With a sigh, she dropped her purse and coat on her chair and then started for the elevator. When the doors opened, she got on and pressed the button for the ground floor.

But something about the request nagged at her. Greg was nearing retirement, quiet, polite, and very responsible. He and Allison seldom talked unless they happened to be standing in front of the office coffeepot together. He always made a point of pouring her the first cup, letting her enter the elevator first, and holding the door for her or any other female.

That was what bothered her, Allison thought, as the floors ticked by. Greg wouldn't order her to come down and get him. He would apologize for putting her out and then politely wait for her to offer to help. Or he would explain himself to security and not bother her at all. Really, there was no reason for him to involve her. Security must have a procedure for when someone had lost or forgotten his badge.

Allison shivered. It felt like something cold had touched the back of her neck. So why *had* Greg called her? And how had he known she was in her office so early?

She replayed the conversation in her head, focusing not on the words, but on the voice. A hoarse voice, made even rougher by the poor connection. It could have been Greg—but it could just as easily *not* have been Greg. Had the voice sounded anything like the man who had left the message on her voice mail?

Her arms prickled as the hair rose. What if the person waiting for her in the deserted lobby wasn't Greg?

What if it was the man who had made it clear he wanted to kill her?

The building was wrapped in darkness; it was at least an hour until daylight. Normally she wouldn't even be here. Had someone been watching her, following her, ready to seize any opportunity to get her alone? Allison remembered the words on the note, on her voice mail. *"I'm going to kill you. And I'm going to like it."*

The doors slid open. The elevator lobby was empty. Its very emptiness seemed expectant, menacing, as if someone was on the verge of jumping out at her. Allison hesitated, her hand on the black rubber edge of the open elevator door. All she had to do was walk around the corner, go out through the security gate, and she would be in the main lobby.

But once she walked through the security gate, who would be waiting for her?

Finally, Allison stepped out of the elevator and pressed her back against the wall, too frightened to pray. Her ears were alert to the slightest sound. She heard nothing but her own speeded-up breathing. She unclipped her cell phone from her belt and dialed.

"Security."

She recognized the voice. It was Tommy, who worked the midnight-to-eight shift. During the afternoon and evening, he ran a barbecue joint in Northeast Portland. Despite the fact that he must never get any sleep, Tommy always wore a smile.

"This is Allison Pierce," she said in a low voice. "I'm in the elevator lobby on the main floor. I just received a call in my office from a man claiming to be Greg Keplar. He said he lost his badge and needed me to come down and let him in." As she spoke, she could feel her pulse beating in her throat.

There was a pause. "And you don't think it's Greg," Tommy said matter-of-factly.

"No, I don't. Can you check it out for me?"

As she waited, Allison's breath came faster and faster. *This can't be good for the baby,* she thought, consciously trying to slow her breathing down, but her fear was nearly overwhelming.

It was so quiet that she could even hear soft footsteps on the carpet in the main lobby. Someone was walking toward her. Any second the person would come around the corner. And she had no place to hide. Panicked, she stabbed the elevator button repeatedly. Why hadn't she gone back upstairs to wait?

Then Tommy turned the corner. His gun was in his hand. His face was grim.

"There was somebody, but it sure wasn't Greg. He started running as soon as he saw me, but I lost him." He shook his head, defeated. "Some guy in a blue parka."

On the big-screen TV in the FBI gym, Fox's Shepard Smith leaned toward Valerie Converse. The volume was turned up loud enough that Nicole could hear even over the sound of her jump rope slapping the mat.

"Do you want Senator Fairview to take a lie-detector test?"

Valerie nodded vigorously. "Of course, Shepard. We want the comfort of knowing that the people who are closest to Katie are giving complete and truthful information to investigators. Has he disclosed everything? We honestly don't know."

Smith nodded thoughtfully. "Excuse me if this question is painful, Valerie, but were you surprised or shocked by the news that Senator Fairview may have had an inappropriate relationship with your daughter? A man who has children near your daughter's age?"

"Nothing surprises me anymore, Shepard, and everything shocks me." Valerie's cheekbones were sharp on her newly hollowed face. "All of this seems surreal. What matters most to me is to see Katie again."

Dropping her jump rope, Nic bent over, put her hands on her knees, and tried to catch her breath. Far from hiding from the media, the Converses had embraced it. Wayne, Valerie, or both had appeared on every morning TV show, every radio talk show, and now were even showing up with increasing frequency on Fox and CNN. They were determined to keep the media's eye focused on their daughter. As a result, interest in

Katie grew every day. The number of tips flooding into the hotline was exponential.

But they still had no real leads. This morning Nic had heard from an FBI agent in DC who had interviewed Luisa Helprin. The young woman was now making her own rounds of the talk shows, milking her past relationship with Senator Fairview for what it was worth. Which wasn't much. They had gotten together six or seven times over the course of a month. Luisa had been eighteen when it started, so she wasn't underage. All that the interview with Luisa had substantiated was that Senator Fairview was a horndog—and they already knew that.

The lack of progress filled Nic with frustration and gave her no place to put it. Which was why she was here. She moved to the corner, put on her hand wraps and gloves, and began to work the heavy bag, drowning out Valerie's sorrow, Smith's sympathy.

Nic had learned the joy of boxing at Quantico. The first physical test—which involved sit-ups, push-ups, and running—took place on the second day, and the results sent some would-be agents packing. Taking the tests was as much a mental as a physical battle, as Quantico class instructors, counselors, and general staff liked to turn out to see who was up to snuff. The new recruits were also instructed in defensive techniques, including grappling, handcuffing, disarming, and boxing.

At Quantico, Nic had discovered that she loved boxing. Loved it because she lost herself in it. It was one of the few times that her brain just completely shut off. After leaving the academy, she no longer fought against an opponent, but she worked out with a heavy bag two or three times a week.

Sometimes when new agents saw Nic putting on her pink hand wraps, the pink boxing gloves lying on the ground waiting for her, they would smile. Like she was some silly little thing who would give the bag a few light taps.

Then they saw her in action and stopped smiling.

Today her punches were as fast as lightning strikes, each one fueled by frustration. She knew the backs of her fingers would ache the next morning, that all the muscles of her upper arms and shoulders would be sore. But it was worth it. She put her stress behind every jab, uppercut, and hook, grunting with each punch. Then it was on to combinations, left hook, right uppercut, double left jab. The thing about boxing was that you put your whole body into it. It wasn't just your arm. You punched with your leg, hips, and back. You punched with your mind and your heart.

When she stepped close to the bag for a series of uppercuts, Nic imagined she was driving her fist into Fairview's soft gut.

SENATOR FAIRVIEW'S OFFICE
December 31

It was a media circus—and exactly the kind of thing that Cassidy reveled in. The city of Portland had gotten smart and started renting sidewalk space in front of Senator Fairview's office to the various networks that wanted to cover the Fairview story. And that's what it was gradually becoming—the Fairview story. Not so much the Katie Converse story. Because every day brought a half dozen new developments related to Fairview, as reporters started digging up his past.

Station management, sensing that the senator himself was the new news, had switched many of its resources to Fairview. Conventional newsroom wisdom held that no station ever got to be number one unless it owned whatever the big breaking news story of the day was. The rule was to throw everything at a potential story, then pull back if need be.

As for Katie Converse? Katie was still missing, but there were no new sightings, no new clues. And how many times could you plow the same ground?

But each story about Fairview spawned a half dozen new ones. Anyone with an old grudge or a new desire to swing the evenly divided Senate was coming forward with tawdry tales. And some of them were even true.

Now each small square of space on the sidewalk in front of Fairview's office was covered by a tentlike structure stuffed with hundreds of thousands of dollars in equipment. Inside each tent was also what they called the "soapbox"—a box that lifted the reporter above the crowd when each filmed his or her live hits.

Word had come down that there was going to be some kind of statement handed out this morning. They'd had to scramble so fast that Cassidy's hair was still wet in the back—but the camera would only get a front shot.

Everyone thought TV makeup and helmet hair were about chasing after beautiful perfection. Instead, it was all about eliminating distractions. Sweaty foreheads, five o'clock shadows, and hair hanging in your eyes made viewers stop paying attention to your storytelling. It wasn't about looking pretty—it was about looking professional.

Cassidy's adrenaline was pumping as she stepped up on the box. There was nothing like being on air live. Nothing. Factually, you could never be wrong. You also had to go quickly with what you knew. You needed to be able to speak coherently and to organize and write the story even as you were still telling it.

The cameraman gave her the signal, and Cassidy said, "Reporting to you live outside Senator Fairview's Oregon office. Yesterday, transcripts of what are purported to be Fairview's instant messages—or IMs—to a Senate page who served the year before Katie Converse were leaked to the media. The content is too graphic to discuss on air, but you can go to our Web site and read them. You should be warned, though, that they are, as I said, graphic and disturbing. It is not clear whether Fairview had a sexual relationship with this second girl. What is clear is that it is no longer simply a question of Fairview's political career. This investigation has now shifted into the legal arena."

All around Cassidy, she could hear the babble of other reporters doing their stand-ups. It was so noisy that she had to resist the urge to shout. She knew the microphone picked up her voice above the crowd behind her. "The FBI has announced that it is looking into whether Fairview broke federal law by sending these inappropriate e-mails and instant messages to underage girls."

Being above the crowd meant Cassidy could see past them. The main door to the building opened, and out came Michael Stone. She almost felt sorry for him. No matter what Fairview was paying him, surely today it didn't seem enough. Then again, this story was pumping his career up too.

"Okay, it looks like Fairview's lawyer is going to make a statement," she said as the camera cut away from her. She got off the soapbox and elbowed her way toward the front. Other reporters gave Cassidy dirty looks as she stepped on toes and squeezed through nonexistent spaces, but she had covered this story from the beginning. She was the one who had *made* it a story.

Michael Stone didn't look the least bit nervous as he slowly walked to the knot of microphones that looked like Medusa's head of snakes. Like Cassidy, he seemed to be one of those people who loved the media blitz. In his hand was a single sheet of paper.

"I am Mike Stone, and I represent Senator Fairview. I would like to read a brief statement from the senator."

Stone waited until the sound guys had their boom mikes properly hung over the crowd and the camera guys stopped shuffling for their best angle. Speaking slowly and clearly, he said, "Senator Fairview's statement is as follows: 'I am an alcoholic, and through the benefit of counseling and therapy, I have come to recognize and accept the fact that alcoholism is a disease and needs to be treated like any other disease. Recent events have crystallized my recognition of my long-standing problem with alcohol and the emotional difficulties attendant to such an addiction. I deeply regret and accept full responsibility for my inappropriate conduct while under the influence of alcohol.

"'On Saturday, with the loving support of my family and friends, I entered an in-patient facility to address my disease and related issues. I am grateful beyond words for the prayers and encouragement I have received. However, my greatest fear is that the media has turned its attention toward me and away from the search for Katie Converse. I have asked my attorney to fully and completely cooperate regarding any inquiries that may arise during my treatment. It is vital that there be no distractions while Katie is still missing. My only wish is that Katie will be found or come forward.'"

Even before Stone had finished folding the paper in half, reporters were shouting questions at him.

"What is the name of this facility?" yelled a reporter with some kind of Eastern European accent. The tangled story of the underage page and the senator had begun to attract worldwide interest.

"To maintain the privacy of Senator Fairview and the other patients, we are not at liberty to disclose that," Stone said.

"Was Fairview ever drunk in the Senate?" a reporter from Channel Two shouted.

"Senator Fairview has conducted himself totally appropriately and has been 100 percent sober at all times when he was discharging his duties and responsibilities as a United States senator," Stone said. "That has never been in question."

"What about those new instant messages?" Cassidy shouted. "The ones that show him having a sexual conversation with a page while participating in a Senate roll-call vote?"

Stone visibly flinched. Being drunk was Fairview's only excuse for his behavior. But if Stone said Fairview was drunk when he created those IMs, then the lawyer had just repudiated the other part of the assertion he had made only seconds earlier. He settled for a statement that answered nothing and everything.

"I'm not aware of those reports and cannot comment on them. Look," Stone continued, his voice finally showing the strain, "while Senator Fairview may have exchanged some inappropriate joking instant messages with a page, he has never, ever had inappropriate sexual contact with a minor in his life. He certainly regrets the silly but harmless communications that he made while under the influence of alcohol, but they are meaningless. He is contrite, remorseful, and devastated by the harm that his actions have caused others." Stone took a deep breath as his gaze swept over the dozens of reporters. "We ask you—we beg you—to keep focused on the real problem here. A bright young woman is missing and needs to be found. Let's not forget that Katie Converse is the *only* thing of importance."

Then Stone turned and walked back toward the building, ignoring the cacophony of dozens of reporters hollering out questions to which he had no good answer. The show was over . . . at least for now.

Four security guards blocked anyone from following.

Allison Pierce," Allison said after picking up the ringing phone.

"Safe Harbor Shelter is on line one."

"Thanks." There was no way she had time for this. She pressed the blinking button. "This is Allison."

"She's here again. Sonika. I think it's bad. Can you come? She says she'll only talk to you."

"I really ca—"

"Please? I think she needs to get to a hospital, but she refuses to let us take her. She's so scared. I'm afraid she might bolt."

Allison took one more look at her desk, which was so covered with papers that she couldn't see the surface. She sighed. "I'll come."

Twenty minutes later she walked into the children's playroom. Still wearing a dark brown coat, Sonika was crouched on her heels, her face pressed against her knees. She lifted her head, and Allison gasped.

"You see. He make me ugly."

Her eyes were slits surrounded by puffy red skin. From swollen lips, a slow trickle of blood ran down her chin. Gingerly, she wiped it on her coat. Allison saw the cloth was already sodden.

Allison reached out her hand.

Sonika flinched, nearly toppling over.

"I'm sorry," Allison said. She knelt beside her, careful to keep some distance. "What happened?"

Without a word, the young woman reached out her hand. Her fingertips grazed Allison's belly, then touched her own.

Allison didn't bother asking how Sonika knew. "You're pregnant?"

Getting pregnant and trying to leave were the two most dangerous times for an abused woman.

"Maybe." Sonika hesitated. "Maybe not anymore."

And then Allison saw what she hadn't before—the blood on the floor between Sonika's heels. She yanked her cell phone from her belt. Within minutes, the sirens sounded.

As the paramedics flung open the ambulance doors to buck the gurney inside, Sonika grabbed hold of Allison's hand. The other women at the shelter peeped from their windows, some looking stoic, others frightened. How many of them had been in a similar situation? Hurt if they didn't fight back, hurt if they did. One of Allison's clients had been sentenced to ten years after she killed her husband, her self-defense argument laughed out of the courtroom. Too many people—including cops and judges—still thought domestic violence should never be discussed outside the family.

"He told me I shame him if I leave," Sonika said before the paramedic shoved the gurney inside the double doors.

As Allison drove back to her office, she passed the animal shelter where Jalapeño had originally been taken. Squeezing the wheel to keep her hands from shaking, she thought, *In this country, there are more animal shelters than women's shelters.*

EMERICK RESIDENCE
December 31

Leif Larson was standing next to the fireplace at Rod Emerick's New Year's Eve party when he caught sight of the most beautiful woman.

And then it was like adjusting the focus on a microscope. It was Nicole. Nine months earlier, Leif had been transferred to the Portland office from Oklahoma. In that whole time, he had always seen Nicole dressed in variations of the same outfit: dark, well-cut pantsuits worn with flats and small gold earrings.

Tonight she was almost unrecognizable in a long, sleeveless black dress. Its wide straps crisscrossed in the back, revealing the strong muscles of her shoulders. She laughed at something Rod had said, her large silver hoop earrings swinging back and forth.

Leif couldn't take his eyes off her.

Nicole was the smartest woman he knew, and the most aloof. She was like a cat, he thought, and not just because of her tip-tilted eyes.

Some people were like cats and some people were like dogs. Dog people liked everyone. They came when they were called, could be taught lots of tricks, and begged for affection and treats.

You had to wait for cat people.

Leif decided he was willing to wait. .

Brad Buffet leaned down and kissed Cassidy's cheek at the party he was hosting for everyone for Channel Four. She giggled as his five o'clock shadow grazed her skin. He might as well have kissed her ring. Brad had been the king of the station for the last three years, ever since he showed up from Sante Fe. Now it was clear her star was the one in ascendance.

A second later, Rick hissed in her ear, "Come outside. Now!" He yanked her arm. In the hallway, he said, "I saw you. I saw you flirting with that guy."

Rick's eyes were crazy, as if he had caught her having sex instead of getting what was practically an air kiss from a colleague. Cassidy felt shocked and yet oddly guilty. She had been laughing and flirting, sure. But that was just who she was. Wasn't it?

"I was just having fun," she said. "It doesn't mean anything."

Rick's hand snaked under her silver-sequined top and pinched her waist hard enough that she sobered up instantly. She knew it would leave a tiny nip of a bruise.

"Listen to me," he said urgently. "Listen."

She could smell the whiskey on his breath.

"You're acting like a slut."

The word was a punch to the gut. It was the word her father had used when he caught Cassidy with Tommy Malto in the backyard one summer night when they thought everyone was asleep. She was fourteen. Her parents had made it clear that she was used goods, of value to no one.

"No, I'm not," she said, her voice not angry but pleading.

"You talk to guys like you're ready to go to bed with them." Rick was so close she could feel his spit flecking her face. "You should be ashamed of yourself."

Something inside Cassidy broke. It felt like her head was filling up with liquid. Tears and the beginnings of nausea.

She and Rick left a minute later.

The next morning, Rick somehow bought two dozen red roses. He didn't know what had gotten into him, he told Cassidy, tears sparkling in his eyes. He was jealous, that was all. Just jealous. And, he added, it was only because he loved her.

The first day of the new year was a lazy one for Allison. She slept for nearly eleven hours. When she finally got up, she and Marshall went out for a long, leisurely brunch.

They spent the day catching up on chores and looking online at cribs, changing tables, rocking chairs, and the million other things you supposedly needed when you had a baby.

In a few weeks, Allison would be in her second trimester and they would make it official. Tell coworkers and relatives. She would buy maternity clothes and stop trying to button her pants by looping a rubber band through the buttonhole and over the button.

And whenever she started to think about Katie, Allison pushed the thought away. Just for today, her life was her own.

PIZZICATO PIZZA
January 3

But if Katie's body never turns up, how could you prosecute someone for murder?"

Cassidy leaned over her plate and took a big bite of pepperoni and cheese pizza. It always amazed Allison that her friend could eat the messiest foods while somehow managing not to drip on her clothes or smear her lipstick.

Pizzicato Pizza was Portland's local version of a chain, and a great place to grab a quick slice. Allison, Cassidy, and Nicole were sitting in the back of the hole-in-the-wall downtown branch, which catered to everyone from businessmen to tourists to street kids who had managed to panhandle enough change to buy a cheese slice.

"Obviously, it's a lot easier with a body, but it's not impossible without one."

Trying not to enviously watch the other two women devour their pizza, Allison dipped her fork in a little cup of balsamic dressing and then speared another bite of her arugula pear salad.

"I prosecuted a case six years ago where a woman had gone missing. Her car turned up at the airport. Wiped clean of prints, so it was pretty hard to believe she had just hopped a plane. Her credit cards and bank account hadn't been touched. All we found were a few spots of blood in her driveway."

"I wasn't living in Portland then, but I remember that case," Nicole said. "That's the one where her husband was seen hosing down the drive-way the night after she disappeared."

"Right," Allison said. "So we took him to court. At the trial, his defense lawyer said that Darcy had probably run off with some mysterious guy she might have met. In his closing arguments he says, 'Because her body has not been found, it's possible that Darcy is still alive. In fact, ladies and gentleman, Darcy might walk through that door right now.' And he turns and points dramatically to the door. *Everyone* in that room—the judge, the jury, the gallery—they all turned and looked. But I didn't. I was watching the defendant. And *he* was the only other person who didn't look."

Cassidy said, "Because he knew Darcy wasn't coming back."

"Exactly. But even without a body, I still got him sentenced to twenty-five years."

"Did her body ever turn up?" Cassidy asked.

"No."

At night, Allison used to lie awake next to Marshall, thinking of places they might search—a patch of woods near the guy's house, a friend's farm, under a nearby overpass. Even after Darcy's husband was convicted, he refused to say where her body was, or even to admit that she was dead. But Allison had sensed it from the moment Darcy's mother had handed her a photograph of her daughter.

Just as part of Allison had known when she first saw Katie's picture on TV.

"Men!" Nicole said with a snort. "If a woman kills her husband, an hour later you're going to find her still standing over his body holding the gun and crying. If a guy does it, the next minute he'll be figuring out how to hide it. Women don't kill their spouses unless the guy gives them a darn good reason. Women don't go online and try to talk some eleven-year-old coming over to their house to play doctor. It's men who rape and rob and steal."

"And start wars," Cassidy added helpfully.

Allison straightened up. "Hey," she objected. "Don't let a few bad examples let you write off half the human race. Not all men are serial-killing robbers slash rapists slash warmongers. Look at Marshall. Look at your dad, Nic, or your brothers. They're all good guys."

"Maybe." Nicole shrugged. "But sometimes I think they are the exception to the rule."

"Until recently you were spending all your days chatting with pervs," Cassidy said. "That tends to make you jaded."

Nicole nodded, but Allison could tell she wasn't fully convinced.

Allison was the only one in a steady, solid relationship. Cassidy changed men about as often as she changed shoes. And Nicole never dated.

Privately, Allison felt that whoever Makayla's dad was, he must have been very bad news. By the time the three women had gotten re-acquainted, there hadn't been a daddy in the picture, just bright-eyed, pigtailed Makayla. Nicole never talked about who Makayla's father was, and even Cassidy's skilled probing had run into a brick wall. A brick wall fortified with steel.

"Darcy should have gotten out earlier," Nicole said now. Her voice was matter-of-fact, not judgmental. "I remember reading about her husband. He was charming but manipulative when he first started dating her, then he moved on to yelling at her—the neighbors heard him—and then by the end he was beating her. With guys like that, it always escalates."

"But," Cassidy said, "it's not like they all go from being charming and manipulative to hosing their wife's blood off the driveway."

Nicole shrugged. "Yeah, but too many women make excuses when the guy gets violent. Too many think he means it when he says he's sorry and gives them flowers and kisses." She wiped her face with her napkin, balled it up, and dropped it on top of her plate. "And by the time they figure out he isn't all that sorry, it's too late."

Her words were distorted as she reapplied her lipstick. At work, Nicole always dressed conservatively, but Allison thought her secret side was revealed by the ever-present lipstick that played up her full lips. Today it was a dark wine red, a good contrast to her navy blue pantsuit.

"Maybe after this Katie Converse thing is over, I should do a feature on domestic abuse," Cassidy said, looking uncharacteristically subdued. She broke off a chunk of the huge chocolate-chocolate chip cookie they were all sharing. "You know, what to watch out for, how to help your friends, what to do if you're being abused. What are some of the things they tell women who call Safe Harbor?"

Allison ticked them off on her fingers. "We say they should always know where the nearest phone is. And we tell them to have a cell phone, if possible. We tell them that the kitchen and the bedroom are the two most dangerous places. And that they should keep all their essentials—their ID and prescriptions—in one place, ready to go. Oh, and that they should use a code sentence when they are on the phone and he can hear them."

"What is it?" Nicole broke off a piece of cookie and popped it into her mouth.

"We tell women to use the phrase 'I heard it might rain this weekend.' Then they tell a friend or relative who already knows that she's in danger," Allison explained. "So if she says the phrase, the friend knows she's in trouble and should call 911."

Too bad, Allison thought, that Katie had never had the chance to call 911.

Something about Cassidy was bugging Nic, but as she walked back to work, she couldn't figure out what it was. Something about her had seemed out of place—but what was it? Nic was still trying to put her finger on it when her phone rang.

It was Wayne Converse. "Someone who was at the vigil has her!"

"What?" Nic said. "Wayne, what are you talking about?"

"The school secretary called us and asked if we wanted all the things people left in front of Katie's photo at the vigil." He was speaking so fast that his words ran together. "It didn't feel right to tell her just to toss them. They sent over a big box, but I didn't look through it until today. But there were some flowers in there that were starting to rot, so I opened up the box to throw them out. And her necklace is in there! Katie's! I gave it to her for her birthday, and she told me she wore it every day."

Nic felt her heart begin to race. She picked up her pace until she was almost running. "Did you touch it?"

"No. Thank goodness, no. I reached out and I almost did, but something stopped me at the last minute."

"We'll need to find out from the school who handled things there." She hoped people hadn't stopped, picked things up, examined them, put them back. That they had been more respectful. Like mourners. Not like people at a garage sale.

Twenty minutes later, she was in the Converses' living room. "Valerie's with Whitney at a movie," Wayne said while Nic stared at the jumble that filled an old cardboard box. "We're trying to take her mind off what's happening."

Inside the box, a brown stuffed bear leaned against a purple plush monkey and a green stuffed frog. They were surrounded by two dozen votive candles burned down to puddles of wax inside their glass enclosures, as well as a drawing of a dove, a ceramic angel, two smaller photographs of Katie, and other offerings.

"That's it," Wade said, pointing at a delicate silver chain with a teardrop-shaped purple amethyst tucked into a corner of the box. "It belonged to her mom."

Nic doubted they could even get a partial off it, but she couldn't take any chances, not with a case gone as cold as this one. "Do you have a pencil?"

"Why—?" And then he caught on and ran into the kitchen.

She could hear him rummaging through a drawer.

After he handed her the pencil, Nic managed to catch the tip in one of the links. She held up the long line of chain, with the stone set about a third of the way down. Wayne sucked in his breath. The clasp was still fastened, but one of the silver links had been snapped. It had been one thing to imagine that Katie had taken it off herself, or even that someone had demanded she hand it over. But this—this implied violence to Katie's person.

Wayne's face was white. "Some sicko put his hands around her neck and tore it off. And now he's taunting us."

"Look," Nic said, "it still tells us something very important that we didn't know before. Now we know that whatever happened to her, a person did it. Katie didn't fall into a river or a manhole or something. Somebody took her."

Clearly, they were looking at a kidnapping. Or more likely, a kidnapping and a murder.

Or, Nic thought to herself, were they? What if Katie had dropped out herself? And this was her clue. Her clue that she was still alive.

Jeff Lowe was running on the Wildwood Trail when he caught a glimpse of a dog ahead of him.

Limping.

"Here, boy," he called, but it didn't stop. Then the trail twisted, and he lost sight of the dog.

There was no one else around in Forest Park. Early January, cold rain slanting down—it wasn't exactly a day to entice anyone outside. But Jeff Lowe had just moved to Portland, and he was getting to know the city the way he liked best—through the soles of his running shoes. He had grown up in a housing project in Cleveland, and the idea of a five-thousand-acre forest in the middle of a city amazed him.

There was no way to get lost on the Wildwood Trail—everything he had read said so. Still, Jeff Lowe was a city boy, and to him it felt like he had stepped into a fairy tale. Dark, thick trunks, furred with bright green moss, surrounded him. He had seen no one for forty-five minutes. The only sounds were the rain and his feet thudding and his breath echoing inside the hood of his jacket.

Catching a glimpse of the dog's reddish-brown fur through the trees, he veered off the trail and into the emerald ferns and jade-colored rhododendrons. Even in January, everything was green here. He slowed to a walk, not wanting to scare the animal. Maybe he could coax it out of the underbrush. Grab it by the collar. It didn't look that big. Maybe fifty, sixty pounds, with a low bushy tail. He had never owned a dog, and he didn't know what breed it was. Some kind of German shepherd mix?

Jeff Lowe imagined calling the owner on his cell phone. Carrying the dog back to his car. In his imagination, it lay quietly in his arms, grateful for the attention. And he wrapped it in a towel and laid it on the passenger seat and then drove to the owner's home, and she—of course it was a she, this was *his* daydream—she—

The dog burst out of the bushes ahead of him. It turned and looked at him over its shoulder.

Jeff Lowe thought several things at once.

The dog wasn't a dog. It was a wolf or something.

With yellow eyes.

And with something pale in its mouth.

And that something was a woman's hand.

So I'm not sure how to deal with my life right now.

Pretty much, today sucked. Or just lately . . . everything sucks.

I'm sick of everything right now. Everything & everyone, as a matter of fact. I'm angry, too. With the entire world. The way some people act, the choices I make & the things people do because "it's complicated." Well, news flash—I'm done. I'm done with feeling miserable over someone who doesn't seem to care anymore.

I've done enough for everyone else. I deserve to be happy. And I'm sick of crying my eyes out because I've been lied to. Because I cared too much for everyone else. Including that one person who doesn't care enough back.

Jeff Lowe's hands were shaking so badly that he had trouble pulling his cell phone from the pocket of his rain jacket. Finally, he yanked it free, flipped it open, and pressed 9-1-1. His eyes went back to the thing lying ten feet in front of him. At the angle it was right now, he could almost pretend it was a piece of trash.

The wolf or coyote or whatever the hell it was had looked at him for a long time with its yellow eyes before letting that thing fall from its mouth. Then it had turned and run off.

Leaving him alone with it. The thing that might be a piece of trash. Or a paper bag. Or some kind of strange flower or fruit that only grew on the floor of the Oregon forest.

Except that didn't explain the pink nail polish.

The phone was still pressed to his head, but he couldn't hear a thing. Jeff pulled it away to look at the display.

No Signal.

His teeth were chattering. The woods were absolutely silent except for the rain, which was beginning to taper off.

Okay, if that thing was a hand—and he had to admit that it must be one—then where was the rest of it? The rest of the body it had come from?

The thought jolted him like an electric shock. Frantic, he spun in a circle, his eyes darting from rocks to roots to dripping ferns. The hand was already more than he could deal with. He couldn't deal with a whole body. He couldn't deal with some dead woman. What if she was cut up? What if she was all in pieces scattered around him?

And what was that noise? It ratcheted up his fear to the point it was nearly unbearable.

And then Jeff realized it was moaning—and that it was coming from him.

Jeff wanted to be inside. He wanted to be warm and dry and with nothing around him that wasn't man-made. No wild animals, no dead people, no parts of dead people, no dark wet shadows under bushes. Everything clean and neat and tidy.

But first he had to tell the police what he had found. Let them take care of it. That was their job, to deal with the things that weren't clean and neat and tidy.

About twenty feet behind him lay a clearing. He hurried over to it, holding his phone in front of him but taking frequent glances back at the hand, as if it were capable of scurrying off on its own. He lifted the phone up to the clear spot of sky. For a second, the display flickered. But even as he felt a surge of hope, it went back to reading No SIGNAL.

Jeff had to get out of here. Get out of the woods. Get back to civilization so that he could call the police. But if he left, could he bring the police back here? To this exact same spot? What if he couldn't find this place again? What if the animal came back for its lunch?

With dawning horror, Jeff realized there was only one solution.

He would have to take the hand with him.

FOREST PARK

January 4

Allison got the news from Nicole. A hand had been found in Forest Park.

A woman's hand.

The more time that had passed, the more Allison had known this was the only likely outcome. Katie dead, not off in some alternate universe. Not hidden away by Fairview. Not hitchhiking to San Francisco. Not wandering the streets of Seattle with no memory of how she got there or who she was. Forest Park was only a mile from Katie's house, but it was five thousand acres, nearly all of it old-growth forest.

After checking Allison's ID, a police officer waved her into the parking lot at the base of Forest Park. It was already nearly full. Nicole's car was near the entrance. A mobile command post—which looked more like an extra-large RV or a tour bus—took up one corner of the lot. Allison nosed into a spot at the far end. Most of the cars in the lot belonged to the FBI.

Agents were clustered in small groups, all dressed alike in khaki cargo pants and blue long-sleeved shirts with yellow lettering on the back that read FBI EVIDENCE RESPONSE TEAM. Allison knew that the entire sixteen-member ERT was always called out when there was a body scene.

Only so far there wasn't a body. Just a hand.

Until now, Allison hadn't realized how much she wanted one of her half-imagined alternatives for Katie to be true. She put one hand on her cross and the other on her belly and sent up a wordless prayer for Katie's parents. Their hearts would be broken tonight. Allison knew that God still offered a peace that surpassed all understanding. She prayed that Wayne and Valerie could find that peace, at least in time.

Finally, Allison sighed and got out of her car, her eyes on the towering centuries-old cedars and Douglas firs that covered the hills ahead of her. Katie must be somewhere up there, but it wasn't surprising she hadn't been found until now. There were parts of Forest Park where no one ventured, isolated and inaccessible areas that held bobcats, elk, great blue herons, and black-tailed deer. There were even reports of black bear sightings.

As she looked up, a slight breeze rattled the last of the season's brittle leaves from the hardwoods scattered among the evergreens. With a little imagination, this could be the forest of a thousand fairy tales. A fairy-tale forest where evil lurked and witches lured young girls. Where wolves hunted their prey.

"Hey, girlfriend," Nicole said from behind her. "You look lost in thought."

Allison turned. "Just feeling a little sad. I knew this was how it would end, but I still kind of hoped it wouldn't, you know?"

"You and me both. Once we locate the body and get some idea of what happened, I'll have to tell the Converses."

Allison looked past Nicole at a man in his early twenties who was leaning against the back bumper of the mobile command post. He was wearing workout gear but no jacket, even though the temperature felt like it was dropping below freezing.

She jerked her chin in his direction. "Is that the guy who found it?"

The young man clutched a paper cup, the steam rising in the air. A dark gray blanket was wrapped around his shoulders, but Allison could hear his teeth chattering thirty feet away.

"The citizen's pretty upset," Nicole said. "He's not certain where he was on the trail when he found the hand. Or maybe I should say where he was when he found the coyote that found the hand. Unfortunately, he didn't leave it there. Since he was having trouble getting a cell signal, he wrapped it up in his jacket and brought it back here."

"And you're sure it's a woman's hand?"

"It's smaller, with no calluses, no age spots—and it's got pink nail polish. The only missing person we have that matches it is Katie. A couple of the fingertips are intact. If we're lucky she scratched whoever did this."

Allison's stomach rose up and pressed against the bottom of her throat. "So was it cut off? Is this a dismemberment?" With difficulty she managed to swallow, bile bitter on her tongue.

"No. The medical examiner has already said that it looks consistent with animal predation. Now our goal is to find the body as fast as we can and get the crime scene roped off. All we need is to have the media show up and muck up the evidence worse than it's already going to be." Nicole looked past Allison. "That's why we brought in a cadaver dog."

A plump woman in her midfifties was coming out of the mobile command post. A tan dog with dark ears and a muzzle scrambled down the steps behind her. They walked over to a man Allison recognized as Leif Larson, the ERT team leader. He was solidly built, over six-foot-two, with reddish-blonde hair that always reminded Allison of a Viking. He was a quiet man who kept his own counsel, but when he said something it was worth listening to.

Allison followed Nicole over to the two of them, and Nicole introduced her to Belinda, the trainer.

"German shepherd?" Allison hazarded. She hadn't grown up around dogs.

"Belgian Malinois," Belinda said with pride. "AKC registered. And certified cadaver dog."

She leaned down to stroke the dog's head. It whined, low and eager.

"Most dogs can only stick with an odor on the ground. So for a tracking dog to find your missing young lady, she would have to have walked up here on her own power, leaving traces on the bushes and the ground. But Toby's different. Cadaver dogs can scent in the air, too. So if that girl's

body is up here, no matter how she got here, Toby will find her. Even if
someone carried her or brought her by car." She stroked the dog again.
"Are your people ready?" she asked Leif.

"Yeah. We want to be able to find her while there is still some light."

Belinda leaned over and unclipped the leash. "Find, Toby. Find!"

With an eager whine, Toby raced up the path. In a few seconds he was
out of sight.

"How do we know when he's found something?" Allison asked.

"You'll hear it." Belinda tucked the leash into her jacket pocket. "The
more excited his bark, the stronger the odor. Cadaver dogs are like good
hunting dogs. A big bird excites the dog more than a small one. And for a
cadaver dog, a good strong smell is more exciting than a weak one. Dogs
are honest. They can't contain their excitement if the smell's really good."

"If he finds her, he won't disturb her, will he?" Allison had her own
disturbing thought. Animals had already been eating at Katie. "The dog
would still know Katie is a person, right?" She swallowed, trying to push
down a sudden rush of nausea. "Toby wouldn't see her as a meal, would
he?"

Belinda shook her head sharply. "Don't worry. Toby's trained. He
knows he can only possess the scent, not the object. As soon as he's located the body, he'll go down well away from it. By going prone, he
controls himself. And he'll wait for us to come."

They waited, mostly in silence. Five minutes passed. Ten. Twenty.

In the distance, a bark. Allison froze. The ERT members raised their
heads, listening with all their beings. A minute later, there was another
bark. Triumphant.

Standing about twenty feet away from Katie Converse's body, Leif Larson was making a list of everything that needed to be done to process the scene. Half hidden by a rhododendron, the body lay sprawled on its belly, head turned to one side. The right arm stretched overhead. The right hand was gone. The left hand, which still wore a black knit glove, was curled near what was left of her face. The glove had saved the hand from predation, but it also meant there would likely be nothing under the nails. Leif just had to hope they had better luck with the scavenged hand.

And around the neck, looped tight, was a bright red dog's leash, with ten feet of lead lying on the ground next to the body.

He returned to where his team waited, taking care to step from stone to root so he wouldn't leave any footprints. His team members were putting on shoe coverings, hairnets, and white Tyvek suits. The suits served a twofold purpose: to keep them from accidentally leaving trace evidence at the scene and to protect them from any biohazards they might encounter.

Leif assigned some of his team to set up the high-tech lighting system and others to mark a way in and out with pin flags. To the rest, he pointed out four trees that would serve as the rough square for the interior perimeter. Leif's back-pocket rule was to rope off at least one hundred feet from the farthest item of visible evidence.

He settled for setting the first boundary two hundred and fifty feet from the body. It was easier to decrease the size of an area than to increase it, and he didn't need the press and onlookers destroying any evidence.

Because this was such a high-profile case, he also asked them to set up a second perimeter about a hundred feet back from the first. The nearer one would still not contaminate the crime scene—if that was what this was—but it could be offered to any VIPs who wanted closer access than the general public. The second perimeter was for everyone else. Along it, Leif stationed local officers and special agents who weren't part of the ERT to make sure no one trespassed. Privately, the ERT called the yellow crime scene tape "flypaper" for its ability to attract gawkers. But for the moment the only people on-site belonged here. Portland police had stationed officers at all the formal entrances to the park, but that wouldn't keep the media and the simply curious out for long. Not once they heard that Katie Converse had been found.

And they would hear, even though officials were keeping it off the scanners. With the amount of police presence alone, there was no hope of keeping it a secret. A few minutes earlier Leif had heard a helicopter buzz overhead, but the trees made too thick a canopy for them to see anything.

While they were getting ready, he saw Nicole Hedges taking a quick look at the body. She came back to Leif as he was pulling on a second pair of latex gloves. She wore a single pair, which she was already stripping off and stuffing into the pockets of her parka.

"It's her. It's Katie Converse," she said grimly as Leif began to apply duct tape where his left glove and the suit met.

"The hair, the height, the build, the clothes—they all match. There's even a gold bracelet we were told she owned, although now it's just loose. Must have been on the hand the coyote took." She pointed at the roll of tape. "Need help with your other hand?"

"Sure."

Leif held out his wrists, and she began to wrap the duct tape where his suit and gloves met. He watched her without seeming to, her face intent as she carefully pressed it into place. Her slanted eyes, her comfort with silence, how she had looked on New Year's Eve—it all intrigued him. Nicole was a cipher.

And Leif liked ciphers.

He had only gone on a couple of dates since he'd moved to Portland. Nice enough girls, he supposed, but neither of them had been the kind he could imagine discussing his day with. They liked that he was in the FBI, but didn't want to know the details. Details like those that would consume him today.

When Nicole had finished, she gave his gloved hand a pat. "All done." She sighed. "I'm going to go back and tell the parents."

"How do you think they'll take it?" Leif knew the question was stupid even as it left his mouth. Shoot, he knew Nicole had a kid. Could a parent even recover from such a thing?

"I'll come back afterward and let you know." She said it flatly, no sarcasm, and it was worse for that.

Pushing aside his embarrassment, Leif picked up his camera and re-entered the crime scene. Within the ERT he had a dual role: team leader and photographer. Before the team began work, he took entry photographs to show how the scene looked when they arrived. Next he would take evidence photos. And once his team was done processing the scene, he would take exit photographs to show what it looked like when they had finished.

Being the ERT's photographer meant you had to get up close and personal with the body in order to document exactly what had been done to it. It meant struggling to retain a clinical detachment as you photographed maggots on a corpse.

Or in this case, it meant documenting the evidence of what coyotes and crows and perhaps rats could do when presented with a nice fresh body. Only this one wasn't so fresh anymore. The smell of death coated the inside of Leif's nose and filled the back of his throat. It was sweet and rotten, acidic, like nothing else. No wonder the dog had found her so quickly.

Using a Canon SLR, Leif took establishing photographs of the body, then midrange photos, close-ups, and finally close-ups with a paper ruler laid down for scale. It was easier when he was focusing through the camera. It put some distance between him and what he was seeing, as if it were already two-dimensional. He took dozens of pictures, looking for abrasions, bruising, bite marks or impression evidence, bloodstain patterns, defensive wounds—and finding precious little.

Still, Leif had been taught to photograph everything. Evidence disappeared. Processing went awry. A photograph might offer the only clues they would ever have. How much evidence had already disappeared or degraded, washed away by the rain or dried up by the faint sun that had shown intermittently since Katie's disappearance?

As the shutter opened and closed, Leif asked himself the four questions he did at every crime scene: What was the cause of death? Could the victim have caused her own death? Were there any signs of a struggle? And what object had caused the injuries?

So was this murder—or suicide? Leif wondered as he bent over the body and snapped another photo. Someone had fashioned a simple noose by threading the end of the leash through the hand loop, forming a second loop that was now buried in the swollen purpled flesh of the girl's neck. The rest of the leash trailed on the ground next to her. Right now it looked like suicide, but looks could be deceiving. He remembered another case, a man's body found in a crashed car. It had seemed open and shut: a single-car accident. Then the autopsy had turned up five stab wounds to the chest.

Besides, if it was suicide, why wasn't she still hanging? He looked up but didn't see any broken branches.

Leif held his breath as he bent closer to the girl. Only she wasn't a girl anymore. She was a husk, a shell, a life-sized rag doll. It was easier to think of her that way. Not as a girl who might have been wondering what she might get for Christmas.

Normally he paid particular attention to the victim's eyes, hands, and feet and the soles of their shoes, but for the first two he had to be content with photographing where each had been.

Seasoned veteran of the ERT, Rod Emerick, kept the photo log. As Leif worked, Rod carefully noted the pertinent facts of each photograph: its number, a description of the object or scene, its location, and the time and date. Every evidence tech had heard the cautionary story of what had happened when the FBI took photos of JFK but neglected to note whether the photos were of entrance or exit wounds. The pictures had wound up being useless.

Leif took another photograph, this one of the head. Hanks of dark blonde hair clung wetly to the skull, but most of the face had been eaten away. What was left of her visible skin looked brown and stiff. She had been out here long enough that she had begun to mummify.

He straightened up and stretched, pressing his fists into the middle of his back. It gave him a chance to check in on his team without being obvious. Even the seasoned agents looked upset. A young kid like this, chewed up by animals—it was a hard scene for anyone. Leif decided to organize a trauma debrief in the next week, get a chaplain to come in. It was a good way to check in with everyone while underlining that the ERT was a team in every sense of the word, a team that looked after each other.

He leaned over again and snapped photos of the red leash. Some of Katie's hair was caught underneath.

Leif imagined how it had gone down. She could have looped the leash around her own neck, tied the other end around a branch, let her weight sag forward. It was a lot easier than most people thought to hang yourself. Your feet didn't even need to leave the ground. Over the past few years he had been called to scenes where people had died with a noose around their neck leaning, kneeling, sitting, or even lying down. The noose didn't even need to be tight to be effective. The heart and the lungs failed, although the brain probably eked out a horrible minute or two.

Alternatively, someone could have looped the leash around Katie's neck and strangled her.

What had happened to Katie Converse—and why? The why was the most important thing. Her navy blue parka seemed to be zipped all the way. Her coat covered her butt, but her pants looked like they were in their proper place. But just because her pants weren't down around her ankles didn't mean she hadn't been raped up here. Throw her down on a bed of leaves and there would be no one around to hear. But Leif saw no signs of a fight—no defensive injuries, no broken branches or scuffed earth. Could she have been killed someplace else and then dumped here? But this area would only be accessible by ATV, and he hadn't seen any tracks. And it was hard to picture someone carrying her all the way up here. So whatever had happened had probably taken place here.

Had the girl fled here from one of the popular trails, chased down by a killer? Or had someone stuck a gun in her back and forced her up here?

Or had Katie come up here to solve her problems in her own sad way?

I know I haven't written much lately. A lot has been going on, but I can't say most of it.

The Senate worked until 2:00 a.m. last night. Senator X had a whole bunch of pizzas delivered, just for us. Everybody likes him. And there I am thinking that I know him on a whole different level.

We got excused from school today, but not from work. I feel terrible. I'm so exhausted. I keep drinking coffee, but all it does is make me feel like I want to throw up.

Channel Four had gotten a tip from a woman who lived near a parking lot for Forest Park. She reported a lot of police activity, including some kind of search dog.

Cassidy and Andy had had to park their car three blocks away. Once they made it to the parking lot, the policewoman stationed at the entrance would let them come no farther. And, she said, no one was available to speak on camera about what was going on.

They began to set up for a live shot in the yard of the woman who had tipped them, with Andy's camera pointed in the direction of the parking lot full of marked and unmarked cars, as well as a mobile command post.

In her head, Cassidy was putting together the story—as sketchy as it was—when she spotted Nicole walking to her car. She hurried across the street.

The policewoman sighed when she saw Cassidy tick-tocking toward her again in her high heels and short skirt. "I already told you, you're not allowed in the lot."

"But I know her," Cassidy said, and called and waved. "Nic! Nic! Can I talk to you for a second?"

Nicole stopped, turned, and finally—reluctantly, Cassidy was sure—nodded assent. With a huffy grunt, the policewoman let Cassidy past.

"So have they found Katie?" she begged. "Is that what happened?"

"Come on, you know I can't say," Nicole said, her expression unreadable. "Notifications have to be made."

"Is that what you're doing?" she guessed, remembering that Nicole was the liaison to the Converse family. "Come on, Nicole," Cassidy begged. "You've got to give me something here. I'm the one who told you guys about the rumors about Fairview. And I'm the one who turned up Luisa."

Nicole stared at her without answering, without twitching a muscle, without any kind of expression on her face. Typical Nicole, with her typical poker face.

When it was the three of them—Nicole, Allison, and Cassidy—the relationship worked. They laughed, they shared tips, they shared gossip, they shared desserts. They were the real Triple Threat Club. But when Allison wasn't around, it was out of balance. Cassidy was painfully aware that, compared to Nicole, she talked too fast, shared too much, laughed too loud.

"Please?" Cassidy begged. "They're threatening to let Madeline McCormick take over the story if I don't keep on bringing it home. The only reason I haven't been bigfooted yet is that they know I have sources nobody else does. But I've got to give them a reason for keeping me on!"

Finally, Nicole sighed, and Cassidy knew she had won.

"That's the guy who found the hand," she said, pointing to a man in his twenties with a blanket wrapped around his shoulders, standing at the far end of the lot. He stared down at the paper coffee cup in his hand, but it was clear he didn't really see it. "His name's Jeff. He might be willing to be interviewed."

"Thanks! Thanks a lot!"

Nicole gave Cassidy one of her thousand-yard stares. "Don't thank me. We never even had this conversation." She opened her car door.

Cassidy scurried over to the guy, glad that Andy was still down on the street, out of sight. Stick a camera in a guy's face first thing and you could lose the whole interview. Cameras made most people leery. So she often did a bit of a bait and switch. By the time she talked this guy into the interview and he figured out it was on camera, not for the newspaper, it would be too late.

"Hey, Jeff, I'm Cassidy Shaw. I'm a reporter. One of the FBI agents suggested I talk to you."

Jeff still looked shell-shocked, as if he wasn't totally in touch with reality. Well, at least this wouldn't be as bad as some of the interviews she had done over the years. Sticking her microphone into the faces of grieving parents and saying, "Your son just died. How do you feel?" all the while hating herself. But give this Jeff guy a day or two, and he would probably be glad for his newfound celebrity status. After all, he hadn't known the girl. He had never even seen her—just her hand. That was a pretty small price to pay for your fifteen minutes of fame. People would ask for his autograph, take his picture, buy him drinks. All the good stuff.

Ten minutes later, Andy gave Cassidy the go signal on the tipster's lawn while curious neighbors gathered to watch. Jeff was starting to look a little wobbly, so Cassidy grabbed his elbow.

She said rapidly, "We are here at Forest Park where human remains have been found. It is possible that they are those of Katie Converse. And here with us to tell us what he found is runner Jeff Lowe."

If anything, the crowds had grown outside the Converses' house. And it wasn't just the media anymore. The media circus had attracted its own onlookers, as if they hoped to see real tigers leaping through flaming hoops, or at least catch a glimpse of a weeping family member or a famous talking head. It was as big an attraction as Portland's Peacock Lane had been only a few days before, where neighbors vied with each other for the most over-the-top Christmas lights and decorations.

As soon as Nic—accompanied by the Bureau's victim witness specialist and a police chaplain—turned up the walk, the crowd surged forward. The three of them ignored the shouts and the clicks of hundreds of cameras.

"Why are you here?"

"Is there something new on the Katie Converse case?"

"What's happened?"

They kept walking, never looking around. Valerie answered the bell. She was wearing a white apron and holding a potato peeler.

They did not wait for an invitation before stepping inside. Nic closed the door behind them. The vultures didn't need to film this.

"Is your husband here?" she asked gently. "We need to talk to both of you."

Valerie sagged against the wall. "No!" The cry was ripped from her. "No, no, no." Instead of getting louder, her words got softer.

Wayne hurried around the corner, drying his hands on a dish towel.

Nic made herself meet their pleading eyes. "Mr. and Mrs. Converse, I'd like you to meet Denise Anderson, our victim witness specialist, and Bob Greenfield, a Portland police chaplain." She turned to Katie's parents. "Could we please go into the living room and sit down?"

"I'm not going anywhere until you tell me why you're here," Wayne said. He stood as straight as a fireplace poker, but Nic knew a single touch could knock him over. "Tell us now."

She took a deep breath. "I'm afraid we have bad news. Human remains have been found in Forest Park. They appear to be Katie's."

With a wail, Valerie fell to her knees. "Did, did she suffer?" she gasped out. The potato peeler was still clasped in her hand, forgotten.

"There are no signs of a struggle." This was true, as far as it went. But even after the oxygen was cut off, the brain still functioned for several minutes. And who was to know what those minutes were like?

"You said it *appeared* to be Katie," Wayne said. He let the dish towel fall to the floor. "So you don't know for sure."

Opening the hall closet, he pulled out a coat. Nic saw how his shirt hung slack over his arms, how his pants sagged on his hips. He must have lost fifteen pounds in the three weeks since Katie's disappearance.

"Maybe it's not her. I have to see for myself. There's probably been some mistake."

"I'm afraid you can't," Denise said.

No parents should ever have to witness their child reduced to a piece of discarded carrion.

"The scene is still being investigated," Nic said. "And then we'll need to take the body to the medical examiners so that we can determine what happened."

Nic would rather be dead than have to answer the next question about her own daughter. She asked, "Does Katie have any identifying marks— scars, tattoos, birthmarks, moles?"

Despite what was shown on TV or in books, in Oregon it was the medical examiner's job to identify the body—never the family's.

"She has a two-inch scar on her knee," Wayne said. "Her right knee. From when she was seven and went ice skating. Why? Have you looked? I told you, it's probably not her. That's why I have to go. I could take one look and tell you right away that it's not her."

She hated having to kill his hope. "The body is dressed in the same clothing Katie was wearing. And judging by the girl's age and the color of the hair and how long the body appears to have been there—it's her. It's Katie."

Nic had a flash of Katie's face—or what was left of it—and pushed the memory aside.

"Why are you saying all those things about scars and moles?" Still on her knees, Valerie looked up at her with desperate eyes. She was trembling, the potato peeler shaking back and forth. "We gave you her photo. You should be able to take one look at this body and know if it's Katie's."

Wayne slipped his arms into the sleeves of his coat. "And since you are not sure, then it's probably not her. That's why I have to go there myself."

"You have to remember, this body has been outside for some time," Denise said softly. "There has been some . . ." She hesitated. "Some predation."

"Predation—what does that—you mean like predators?" Valerie's voice arced higher in horror. "Do you mean animals? Animals have eaten my daughter?"

Nic nodded, her misery complete. "There's been some damage to the face." She cleared her throat. "Could you tell me what color your dog's leash was?"

"Red," Wayne said. "Why? Did you find it, too? Just because you found it in the park doesn't mean it's Jalapeño's. Do you know how many people walk their dogs there? Probably hundreds. And most of them off leash, too. A leash—a leash could be anyone's."

"Did you find her holding it?" Valerie finally remembered the potato peeler. She put it down on the entrance table next to her and wiped her hands on her apron. And kept wiping them.

"Not exactly." Nic wished she didn't have to say the next words. "The leash was around her neck."

"Oh no!" Valerie choked out. "You're saying she killed herself. I knew she was in pain, but I never—"

"We don't know what happened, Mrs. Converse," Denise said. "We don't know anything for sure. That's why the medical examiner needs to do an autopsy."

"I'm going out there," Wayne repeated stubbornly. "Even if it's not Katie, you can't leave this girl lying out there. It's freezing. You can't just leave her out there in the cold."

"The body will be removed from the scene as soon as possible," Bob said. "And I can assure you, she will never be alone."

Something inside Wayne seemed to crack. "But I am her father! I need to be there. I didn't protect her when she was alive. At least I can do it now that she's dead!"

Nic felt the hairs lift on the back of her neck. She stepped forward and touched him lightly on the arm. "What do you mean, Mr. Converse? About not protecting Katie?"

He bit his lip and looked down. "This creep took her, didn't he? Some creep took my baby. And I wasn't there to stop him." He lifted his head again. "But it can't be Katie. I would know if it was my daughter. I would know right here." He thumped his fist over his chest. "And I don't feel it. I don't know it. So it can't be true. It can't."

His eyes were lost. "Because if it is Katie, how am I supposed to live? How am I supposed to live?"

FOREST PARK
January 4

As Leif took photographs, the rest of the evidence response team was collecting any potential evidence, tagging it, logging it, and packaging it so that it remained intact on its way to the lab. The chain of evidence couldn't be broken, or they risked a killer going free.

If there was a killer. Leif's mind kept going back to that thought.

The team also gathered soil, fauna, and insect samples. Later they would be compared with anything found on the body to see if it might have been dumped here. But Leif was pretty sure they were just going through the motions. He would bet anything that Katie had died here in Forest Park.

They found the dog collar about twenty feet from Katie's body. Unfastened and undamaged. It went into its own evidence bag, as did the gold bracelet and every windblown candy and chip wrapper.

The ERT members also looked for signs of a struggle—tufts of pulled-out hair, trampled leaves, torn-up moss, a scrap of cloth caught on a branch, footprints in a place someone would normally avoid.

Karl Zehner waved Leif over to where he had found two footprints about fifteen feet away from the body, both, to the naked eye at least, belonging to the same set of shoes—and far too big to be from Katie's feet. In a fight, footprints were often made at an angle as people fought for purchase, but these footprints looked flat. To make it easy to sort out which footprints belonged and which didn't, all of the ERT members were issued the same high black Danner boots with steel toes. Everyone else who had been on the scene—the runner who had found the hand, the dog handler, Nic—would have their shoes photographed and documented as to make, model, and size.

But were these prints meaningful? Would footprints really have survived two weeks or more, including days where there had been rain or snow? Or were they much newer than that?

Leif took photographs and then told Karl to cast the prints. Someone had stood here and looked at her. Why? When? The footprints would never give that away. But who—*that* they might be able to figure out.

As Leif returned to the body, Karl set about making a cast, kneading water and casting material in a plastic bag until the texture was like pancake batter. The dental stone would pull up not only the footprint but an additional inch of dirt. And in that dirt there could be trace evidence that had been carried in on the wearer's shoes: hairs, fibers, maybe a different type of soil. Leif sent up a prayer for carpet fiber. After the casts had set, Karl would carefully lift them free and put them in paper bags to take them back to the lab.

Thinking of trace evidence that might have been carried here made Leif think of evidence that might have been carried away. Blowing on his hands in a vain attempt to warm them, he walked over to one of the Portland police officers stationed at the perimeter.

"Can you get someone to find out where all the trash cans in the park are and when they were last emptied? Someone could have dumped something."

The cop nodded. Leif was turning to go back to the body when Tony Sardella, the medical examiner, said, "Aren't you guys done yet? How long until I can take custody?"

Leif had done this difficult dance before. Before releasing the body, the ERT had to be sure that they had gotten all necessary information from it. But MEs typically got impatient with the painstaking process.

"I should be done in about twenty minutes," he said, pretending not to hear Tony's sigh.

He had to be sure he wasn't missing anything. People thought they could remove all traces of a crime scene, but it couldn't be done, not really. With the help of luminol, Leif had seen blood fluoresce on a kitchen floor even after it had been scrubbed with bleach, observed bloody handprints glow under fresh paint. Killers missed the blood spatter on the ceiling as they pulled the knife back to stab again, or the super-fine blood mist left by a shotgun. But with this body, if you didn't count the chewed face and hand, there were no signs of blood.

Finally, he got to his feet and signaled to Tony that he was ready. His heart lifted when he saw Nic standing behind Tony. He raised his eyebrows to ask how it had gone, and she gave him a twist of the lips to let him know the answer was about as well—or as badly—as could be expected.

He waited while Tony bagged the hands and feet, tying them securely at wrist and ankle. Given the glove, Leif thought it was probably a wasted effort, but you never knew. Then Tony spread out a clean sheet for the body. Next, they would wrap it around her to catch any trace evidence, and then Katie's body—still facedown—would be placed in a body bag and then on a stretcher. Leif didn't envy the two guys who would carry the stretcher. It was going to be a long, rough walk.

As they lifted the girl, Leif looked for any wounds on the front of the body, or any evidence underneath it. He saw nothing and was about to tell Tony to wrap her up when Nic said, "Wait."

She knelt beside the body, focusing on a long smear of mud on the front of Katie's coat. With her gloved hand, Nic lifted the edge of a horizontal crease almost obscured by the mud. Inside the fold, the fabric was clean.

"Somebody dragged her," Leif said, embarrassed that he hadn't noticed it himself.

"Before or after she was dead?" Nic asked, although he thought she probably knew the answer as well as he did. Maybe she was just trying to help him save face.

"It's too regular. Whenever it happened, she wasn't struggling."

Leif took a photograph, then pinned the fold in place. Then he and Tony finished transferring Katie to the stretcher so that the girl could begin her long journey out of the forest.

"Do you think it's suicide?" Nic asked.

"It's hard to say. No note, but no signs of a struggle. The problem is there's no sign of where the leash was fastened. There's nothing on this tree to show that she hung herself—no snapped branches, no moss or bark that looks disturbed."

"Hey!" Karl called. "Look at this!"

Leif and Nic turned, as did the rest of the ERT. Karl's flashlight was pointed up into the tree he was standing under. It lit up the white, splintered end of a broken branch about six feet off the ground.

Six feet off the ground—and thirty feet from where they had found Katie's body.

It was so quiet up here in the woods that Nic could hear the sound of a nearby creek babbling over stones. Scarves of mist wrapped around the trees. The scene was still lit up by the generator-powered lighting system. If anything, the light just made the blackness around them darker. Overhead, the stars were sparkling pinpoints. Each time Nic took a breath, it felt like the cold air was pulling her lungs inside out. She was marching in place just outside the perimeter, stamping her feet in a futile effort to get some feeling back in her toes.

Leif was taking exit photos to show what the scene looked like after it had been processed. Other than Leif, the ERT had left. The team would be back tomorrow to do a final line search in the daylight. On hands and knees, each agent an arm's length from the next, they would make sure they hadn't missed anything.

The two Portland cops who had been assigned to keep out any trespassers were talking quietly at the far corner of the perimeter. Nic was waiting for Leif.

She was here because Leif had asked her to stay behind. He had offered no explanation, and she had asked for none. To her surprise—and she thought to Leif's as well—she had agreed.

So what would they talk about during their long hike back? And what would happen once they got there? Nic's senses were still heightened, her body still keyed up, first from viewing the body, then from speaking to the Converses. Saying yes to Leif was the scariest thing she had done in years—and she didn't even know what she was saying yes to.

Leif snapped one last picture and then began to walk slowly toward her, stowing his camera gear. As he did, Nic thought she heard a noise on her left. She whipped her head around. It was just the faintest of sounds, a crackle, a pause, another crackle. Like someone moving slowly and cautiously toward them.

Leif shot her a puzzled look. His mouth opened as he started to ask a question, but she put her finger to her lips.

Putting her left palm out flat, Nic walked the fingers of her right hand on it. Then she pointed in the direction of the noise. She took her gun from its holster and turned on her flashlight, although she shone it at her feet, not in the direction of the noise.

Leif froze, and they both listened for a long time, perfectly silent, barely breathing. Nic was about to dismiss the idea that she had heard something, but then the sound came again. And this time she was sure of what it was: slow, stealthy footsteps.

Leif and Nic ran toward the sound. Brambles snagged their clothes and branches scratched their faces. To their right, Nic heard the two cops shout as they realized that something was going on. Then she caught a glimpse of a white-haired figure.

Leif, with his longer legs, was already well ahead of her. "Halt, FBI!" he yelled.

Instead of stopping, the man turned and tackled Leif at the knees, knocking him over.

Intent on getting to Leif as fast as possible, Nic caught her toe on a tree root and went sprawling. She managed to hold on to her gun, but the flashlight flew from her hand and went out. She heard the explosive sounds of a scuffle. Shouts, a curse word, branches snapping.

No time to find her flashlight, not when Leif needed her. Nic got to her feet and ran blindly. About fifty yards behind her, she could hear the two cops. Their flashlights sliced through the dark, lighting up two men rolling around on the ground: Leif and a man with thick white hair, who looked like a transient.

"Hands up in the air or I'll shoot!" Nic was ready to, adrenaline ramping through her body. Time had slowed down. She caught a glimpse of Leif's gun and kicked it away.

The two cops ran up and dragged the man off Leif. The man bucked, struggled, shouted incoherently. Something about the stars shining.

"Cuff him," one of the cops yelled.

The cops were half dragging, half carrying him away when Nic yelled, "Wait!" She ran in front of them and turned to face the man. His eyes were rolling, as wild as a bucking horse's. "What are you trying to say?"

"Starshine!" he said urgently. "Starshine!"

The cops sighed, exasperated by his nonsense, but Nic held his gaze. And then he said, "My daughter! I can't leave her!"

"Your daughter," Nic echoed. "Where is she?"

"In the cabin."

Cabin? What cabin? He was probably delusional. Starshine would turn out to be a naked plastic baby doll, the cabin a cardboard box.

He pointed. Leif swung his flashlight back. Nic looked and didn't see anything. Just as she was about to turn back, something took shape right in front of her.

Hidden beneath tall fir trees was a wood-framed shelter. Covered by a green tarp, it blended in with the ferns and undergrowth around it.

"Your daughter's in there?"

He nodded, still panting.

"How old is she?"

"Ten."

Just a year older than Makayla.

"I'm Tim Chambers. My daughter's name is Starshine." His breath came in gasps. With his white hair and lined face, he looked too old to have a ten-year-old daughter. "Let me loose and I'll go get her."

Leif shook his head. "Sorry, no can do. Nicole can go get her."

"Starshine," Nic called out as she picked her way to the shelter. "Starshine, please come out. I promise we won't hurt you."

Even to her own ears, the words didn't sound reassuring. After all, this kid had just spent five minutes listening to four cops taking down her father. Trying to imagine how Makayla might react, Nicole found her mom-voice, reassuring but no-nonsense.

"Starshine?" The door didn't have a handle, just a hole. There were no windows. The whole cabin was probably ten by ten. "Starshine—please come out."

Slowly, the cabin door opened and a girl appeared, moving as lightly and carefully as a deer in hunting season. Skinny, with blonde hair in two crooked braids, eyes so wide that Nic could see the whites on each side. She was clearly frightened, but so brave that it nearly broke Nic's heart.

After making sure the child's hands were empty, Nic bent down to look into her face. "Hi, my name's Nicole. We need to talk to your father about something, but we can't leave you here alone. That means we need to take you with us."

The only answer was the sound of Starshine's too-fast breathing.

Leif radioed ahead. The police would take the man to jail. He could be held for up to forty-eight hours without charge while they determined exactly what he had to do with Katie's death. Starshine would be put in the custody of Children's Services until that could be determined.

They left behind one of the cops, and then the five of them made their way back to the main part of the park. Nic, Leif, and the other cop, who were all wearing boots, had difficulty navigating the trail. Chambers and his daughter, wearing only street shoes, were as nimble as mountain goats—even though the father's hands were handcuffed behind his back.

The first words Nic heard Starshine speak were a protest when they put her father in a cruiser.

"Please, please don't take my father away! No!" She tried to run to him, but Nic caught her and wrapped her arms around her.

"We just need to check on a few things," she told the girl, her heart aching for her. "If everything is okay, you can go back to your father."

It was such a big *if* it might as well have been a lie.

Can you hear me okay?" Medical examiner Tony Sardella looked up over the edge of his surgical mask at Nic and Owen Simmons from the Multnomah County sheriff's office.

Nic and Owen were seated in the special observation room that overlooked the autopsy suite. Below them were the dead girl, Tony, Leif, and a pathology assistant.

"Coming in loud and clear," Owen said, combing one hand through his black hair, which Nic was pretty sure was dyed.

"Have you seen an autopsy before?" Tony asked.

Owen nodded, and Nic said, "Lots of dead bodies, but no autopsies."

"You guys should be glad you're behind the glass," Tony said. "It's a little ripe in here."

Nic was glad of the window in another way. It gave her the illusion that the girl on the metal table was as artificial as an image on TV or a movie screen. She could pretend that when this was done, the girl would pull the special-effects moulage off her face and sit up with a smile.

Still wearing the clothes she had been found in, Katie lay faceup on the waist-high, stainless steel autopsy table. Slanted, it had raised edges to keep blood and fluids from spilling onto the floor. Nic was grotesquely reminded of the carving platter at her folks' house, with the channel that ran around the edge to catch the juices.

Tony put his hand on one of Katie's knees and wiggled it back and forth, then did the same thing with her other knee and then her elbows. "Her joints move freely," he announced. "There's no rigor mortis, and the body is cold. That means she's at least thirty hours dead."

"Do you think she died the same day she went missing?" Nic asked. "That was December thirteenth."

"We'll see. With luck, I'll be able to narrow it down for you to a day or two."

Tony pressed a pedal on the floor and began to dictate into the transcribing machine. He reeled off the facts of the husk that had once been Katie Converse: her race, sex, age, hair color.

"Eye color unknown; eyes are missing," he said before continuing. "A red leash is found looped around her neck. Decedent is wearing a hip-length dark blue Columbia parka, a black V-necked sweater, jeans, and Nike sneakers. No signs of disturbance to her clothing."

Tony tapped the foot pedal again to turn off the transcription. As his gloved fingers teased the noose away from the puffy discolored flesh, he said, "If we get lucky, you guys might find fingerprints on this."

Leif snapped pictures as Tony worked.

After the leash was bagged for evidence, Tony leaned down, examining the indentation on Katie's neck more closely. "What will help is figuring out whether we are looking at a hanging groove or a strangulation groove."

"What's the difference?" Nic asked.

"A hanging groove will be deepest opposite the suspension point. So in a typical hanging, that would be here." Straightening up, Tony pointed to his Adam's apple. "Then it fades away as it approaches the back of the neck. Now if someone strangled her, the groove should be more marked—and it won't disappear at the back of the neck."

He squinted, lifted Katie's shoulder, peered closer, walked around the table to look at the other side, and finally sighed. "It's hard to tell. Even though it's been cold, there's too much decomposition. Hopefully it will be more clear when I open her up."

Next he tugged off Katie's single glove and slipped it into a paper bag for the evidence lab. Her exposed hand looked like a cleverly fashioned wax replica.

He inspected it carefully before looking up at Owen and Nic. "No defensive marks and nothing under her nails."

Leif snapped a photo of Katie's hand. He was so quiet that, between flashes, he faded into the background. But his eyes didn't miss anything. Including Nic watching him. He lifted his head to look directly into her eyes, and Nic felt her cheeks heat up.

"What about her other hand?" Owen asked.

"I already examined it, but it's a chewed-up mess. Two of her fingertips are gone, and there's nothing under the remaining three nails. About the best we'll be able to do is match it up to her."

"Let's keep that out of the media," Nic suggested. "If we need to, we can bluff a suspect by saying we found DNA."

Owen and Leif nodded.

Tony and the pathology assistant began to remove Katie's clothes. They unzipped her coat and then rolled her from side to side to take it off. It reminded Nic uncomfortably of undressing a sleeping Makayla. Next the assistant lifted up Katie's legs while Tony tugged off her pants. The pathology assistant put each item of clothing in its own paper bag, stapled it closed, and labeled it with the case number. They would be shipped off to the lab to be examined for trace evidence—bodily fluids, soil, glass, paint residue, chemicals, illicit drugs.

They were pulling her arms overhead when Nic remembered Wayne's certainty that this couldn't be his daughter. She leaned forward. "Is there a scar on her right knee?" Maybe there was some tiny chance that he was right. Maybe this girl had borrowed Katie's clothes, or simply dressed liked her. Heck, didn't all the kids dress alike these days?

Tony moved down the table and leaned over her knee. "Yup. A little over six centimeters long. Does that match what the parents told you?"

"Yes," Nic said in a soft voice.

Owen shot her a curious look. Of course she had already known the answer, just as Wayne and Valerie had. Still, it was hard to let go of hope.

The girl was completely naked now under the merciless fluorescent lights. Nic felt embarrassed on her behalf. But nakedness also restored Katie as a human, offset some of the strangeness and horror of her mauled face and missing hand. Three weeks ago, she had been living, moving, dreaming. Nic pushed the thought away.

But it wouldn't stay gone. This damaged body had once been somebody's daughter. With an effort of will, Nic could sit in this room and not have it affect her—but only if she didn't imagine it was Makayla lying on that slab. If she ever lost her child, then all bets were off. She would howl at the moon, try to throw herself into her daughter's grave, slit her own throat.

But first she would hunt down whoever was responsible and make them pay.

Of course, this girl wasn't Makayla. Still, Nic knew that before she fell asleep tonight, she would let herself imagine for a few seconds what it would be like. A secret part of her believed that imagining Makayla in various horrible scenarios—leukemia, bike accident, child molester—somehow magically protected her. If Nic walked herself through the horror, then it could never happen. She knew it was illogical, but a tiny part of her still believed it might help. And another part of her was ashamed that after everything that had happened, she still held on to such an irrational belief.

As for herself, she knew that nothing could help her. Religion, faith, prayers—they were all useless. You didn't need them to be a good person. You didn't need them to keep you doing what was right. And they wouldn't help you when you were desperate, when you needed a miracle. Ten years ago, she had screamed in desperation for God to help her, and what had He done? Nothing.

Now she was no longer blinded by faith, unlike her two friends. Nic could tell that Allison, with her steady churchgoing, thought of herself as more grounded than Cassidy, who flitted from belief to belief. But in Nic's eyes the two women were basically the same. Imagining God—or the universe or karma or whatever—could offer them solace and comfort. Imagining they could influence events with their thoughts and prayers, when nothing could help them and they were powerless. You were on your own in this world, and when your life ended, that was it.

Tony's voice interrupted her thoughts. "I'm not seeing any injuries other than the postmortem animal feeding." He lifted the shoulder farthest away from the viewing room, rolled Katie on her side, and inspected her back. "Huh," he said, his voice so low it seemed pitched for his own ears. "That's interesting."

Leif bent down and began to snap pictures.

Owen and Nic leaned closer to the window. "What?" Owen asked.

Tony looked up. "You know about lividity, right?"

Nicole said, "It's when blood settles into the lower part of the body after death and changes the color of the skin."

"Right. Lividity is like if I put a wet sponge down on the counter. After a few hours, the top would be dry and the bottom would be wet, because the water would drain to the bottom. Same with the blood in a dead body. Once the heart stops pumping, the blood settles and stains the skin. It won't show anyplace the capillaries are compressed, like areas that are pressed against the ground."

Nic still didn't see what he was getting at. "Yeah?"

Katie's skin was stained reddish-purple on the edges of her chest, under the tops of her shoulders, and on the sides of her abdomen—just the way it should be, since she had been found facedown.

"Katie has lividity in two different places."

"What do you mean?" Owen asked.

Then Nic guessed the answer. "Is it because she was hanging, and eventually the branch broke, and she fell?"

"No. If that was the case, you would expect to see staining on the bottom of her feet."

They all looked at her waxy yellow-white soles.

"But look at this." He tugged at Katie's shoulder, shifted the body until Nic and Owen could see what he already had—the fainter purple-red stains between the girl's shoulder blades and on the small of her back.

"First she was on her back long enough for lividity to set in, and then later she was put in the position you found her in. But not all the blood migrated from her back to her front."

"That fits with what we found at the scene," Leif said. "We found a broken branch that might have been used for hanging, but it was thirty feet away from the body."

"Can you tell when she was moved?" Nic asked. "How soon after death?"

Tony said, "My best guess is three or four hours. For lividity, you've got about a twelve-hour window. After that, you can move the body all you want, but it won't cause any more staining. The question is—why did someone move her after she'd already been dead for a while?"

Suddenly Nic knew. "Her body was half under a bush. Someone killed her, panicked, and left, then returned to the scene and tried to hide her. That would explain the mud on the front of her coat."

"Or it could be that she died and someone found her, maybe tried to help her, and then realized she was dead and dropped her," Leif said. "This still doesn't rule out suicide."

As Tony and the assistant opened up the body, and Leif documented every step, Nic tried to watch them as she might a documentary. Keep her distance. Not think that a few weeks ago, this had been a girl with dreams and hopes and fears. On the pretense of shifting position, she shot a sideways glance at Owen and was heartened to see that he looked like he was having a hard time too.

Tony looked up at them. "Basically, what we're looking for is trauma or other indications of the cause of death. For example, heart disease might turn out to be the real cause of death for a middle-aged man."

"Not in Katie's case, though," Nic said.

"No. Not likely in this girl's case," Tony agreed. "I'll run some more tests, of course, but so far everything looks normal. Now I'm going to expose the neck structures to see if I can figure out what happened."

He spent a long time examining what he found. Then he raised his eyebrows and murmured, "That's it."

Leif started snapping photos.

Nic had no idea what they were looking at, but she leaned forward anyway.

"We're lucky she was facedown, or her neck might have gotten chewed up, too, and I would never have seen this."

"Seen what?" Owen asked.

"This is the cause of death right there. She has a fractured larynx—and that obstructed the trachea. She died from asphyxia, since the air couldn't reach her lungs."

"But could that come from hanging?" Owen asked.

"It's very unlikely. This was caused by a blow to the throat." Against his own throat, Tony made a chopping motion with the side of his gloved hand.

Nic said, "How long would it have taken for her to die?"

"Not long. She would have tried to scream, even just tried to breathe, but since no air could pass through, it wouldn't be possible. Every time she tried to breathe, her lungs would have collapsed. She might have been able to fight back for a minute or two, but as the oxygen content of the blood dropped, she would have become more frantic and confused. In twenty to thirty seconds—two minutes on the outside—she would become so weak that she collapsed. Death would come pretty quickly afterward."

That didn't sound quick at all to Nic. "Could Katie have survived if she had been brought to a hospital right away?"

"She wouldn't have made it to a hospital. If someone had performed a tracheotomy on her right there in the park, maybe she could have made it. But that's very much a maybe."

"Okay," Nic said. "She died from a blow to the throat. Then that means there's only one reason she has a leash around her neck."

"Right," Tony said. "Someone wanted this to look like a suicide. But Katie Converse was definitely murdered."

MYSPACE.COM/THEDCPAGE

Trouble

November 24

think I have a problem. If I'm right, it's a big, big problem. All I want
to do is sleep & not deal with it.

   I can't deal with it.

   I mean, what would I do?

What kind of shape is the girl in?" Allison asked Dr. Sally Murdoch. They were in her cramped office, tucked into a corner of Good Samaritan Medical Center.

Dr. Murdoch's dishwater blonde hair had once been caught back in a bun. Most of it had escaped to curl in tendrils that framed her gray-blue eyes.

"I'd have to say excellent. No evidence of sexual molestation, no scars, no bruises, healthy weight, very fit." As Dr. Murdoch spoke, she tucked pieces of hair behind her ears. "The girl's even fairly clean, especially when you consider she says they bathe in water from a creek. A creek! That can't be any fun this time of year. Heck, even her teeth are in great shape. She's never had a cavity. Starshine says she's ten, and I see no reason to doubt it." The doctor flashed Allison a tired smile. "Honestly, the kid's in better shape than a lot of the ones I see in my private practice."

"Did she say anything to you about the dead girl? We found her body not far from where Starshine was living."

"No. And I didn't ask. I figure that's your purview. I did talk to her about her father." Dr. Murdoch's hands stilled. "The two are obviously each other's whole world." She held Allison's gaze. "If you separate them, it would break this girl's heart, her spirit."

Allison sighed. "I wish I could promise you that we could keep them together, but that's going to depend on what the father tells us. And whether we think he's telling the truth. Right now, he's definitely a suspect." She looked at her watch. "This is really bad timing, but I have a doctor's appointment myself in twenty minutes. Could you ask Children's Services to bring Starshine over to my office in two hours?"

"Sure." Dr. Murdoch looked at Allison more closely. "Is everything okay?"

The two women had known each other for years. "Better than okay," Allison said, and left it at that.

Allison lay back on the crinkly white paper that covered the exam table. Marshall, who was standing at the head of the table, smiled at her and squeezed her hand. It was still hard for Allison to believe this was happening after all these years. The one good thing about the Katie Converse case was that it kept her from obsessively ruminating about the baby. At least some of the time.

Dr. Dubruski said, "Now if we don't hear anything today, don't worry." She was a tall, thin woman with close-cropped blonde hair. "This is about as early as we can expect to hear fetal heart tones."

She squirted jelly on Allison's belly, then picked up the black Doppler wand. Pressing lightly, Dr. Dubruski began to run it back and forth in the area just under Allison's navel.

There was silence for a few seconds, long enough for Allison to begin to get anxious.

Then they could all hear the sounds magnified through the microphone. *Clomp, clomp, clomp, clomp,* so fast the thumps were barely separated. Every few seconds there was a burst of static.

A delighted laugh spurted from Allison's lips. Marshall was squeezing her hand so hard that it hurt, but her mind was on what she was hearing.

The doctor looked down at the readout. "One hundred fifty-eight beats per minute."

"That's so fast!" Marshall said, sounding a little panicked.

Dr. Dubruski smiled. "Right in the middle of the normal range."

"What's that staticky sound?" Allison asked. She realized she was grinning.

"Fetal movement."

Marshall's fingers tentatively grazed the edge of Allison's belly. "Alive and kicking?"

Dr. Dubruski nodded. "Alive and kicking." She lifted the monitor. "You probably won't be able to feel it yourself for another six weeks or so."

Allison looked down at her still flat stomach. There was something inside of her that was moving around on its own, that had its own heart-beat. It was real. The baby was really real. Tears pricked her eyes.

As she pulled on her stockings after the visit, Allison said to Marshall, "It's hard to believe there's a baby inside me. I mean, I know this happens to women every minute of every day, but it feels like such a miracle."

"I can hardly believe it's happening myself." He leaned forward in his chair, put his hands on her hips, and gently kissed her belly.

For the rest of the day, Allison kept a smile tucked away inside. It wasn't appropriate to smile, not now, not when they were trying to figure out how a girl had died.

In the midst of death, we are in life.

In the lobby of her office, Allison introduced herself to Starshine and to Jennifer Tate, the Children's Services worker, a plump woman in her midtwenties. Both of them shook her hand, although the girl didn't meet Allison's eyes. While Allison would do the questioning, Jennifer would be on hand to serve as a second witness to Starshine's words.

Thin as a stick, the girl wore her blonde hair in two crooked braids. She was dressed in brown polyester pants, blue sneakers, and a gray sweatshirt layered over a green turtleneck. Nothing brand name, nothing new—but no holes, either. And no obvious dirt.

Allison rejected the idea of taking the girl into one of the conference rooms. Her office was homier, less impersonal and imposing. She led them down the hall, and the three of them sat down around the small round table where Allison sometimes held meetings. She saw Starshine taking in Marshall's framed black-and-white photos and the plaque on the wall that a group of FBI agents had given her at the conclusion of a particularly difficult case. It read CAN'T SEW, CAN'T COOK, SURE CAN LITIGATE.

Allison decided to approach this obliquely. "How long have you and your dad been living in the woods, Starshine? Do you know?"

Starshine spoke to her hands, folded neatly on the table. "Since my mother took sick. I couldn't live with her anymore, so my father took me."

The girl had a formal, old-fashioned way of speaking. What was it like, Allison wondered, living in the woods like some pioneer child, with no running water, no heat, no electric lights? Had she ever played Nintendo, gone to a movie, listened to an iPod? Did she care that her life was so different from that of other kids?

"How long ago was that? When you started living with your father?"

"I'm not certain. Perhaps three years ago."

"And what's it like living outside?" Allison asked. "Do you like it?"

Starshine looked up for just a moment. A flash of blue eyes as bright as a summer sky. "But we don't live outside. We have a house."

Nicole had described it as a jury-rigged lean-to, but Allison decided not to argue. "Don't you get cold?"

A shrug. "You wear layers. And no cotton. Father says cotton kills. Once it gets wet, you never get warm."

"Where do you go to school, Starshine?"

"My father teaches me. And we get books from Goodwill that I read."

"Could you read something for me?"

"Yes."

Before Allison could find her a magazine, Starshine turned and plucked a heavy law book from the shelves, opened a page at random, and began to read in a steady voice.

"Causation. Establishing that the defendant's conduct caused the proscribed result ordinarily is not difficult. If a professional killer shoots the victim in the head and the victim dies, a pathologist can conduct an autopsy and then testify at trial that the bullet fired by the defendant brought about the victim's death by producing massive injury to the victim's brain."

"That's enough," Allison said hastily. She and Jennifer exchanged a quick glance.

Starshine replaced the book, lining it up neatly with the others on the shelf. If she realized that the topic of the paragraph in question might possibly apply to her father, not a flicker of emotion betrayed her. She folded her hands again.

"How often do you see people around where you live?"

"Once every couple of months." Starshine was still not meeting her eyes. "Maybe less. People hiking or running. Less often now, because it's colder. If we don't come out, they don't see us. Even if we are outside, we know how to blend in and stay very still. No one knows we're there. Father says that no one *can* know."

One quick glance up. Her teeth pressed against her lower lip. "He says if anyone were to find out we lived in the woods, I would be taken away. I guess he was right."

Allison said carefully, "If you answer my questions truthfully, I'll see if we can get you back there."

It wasn't a lie, but it wasn't the truth either. Even if Starshine's father was innocent, too many people now knew that the two of them were living in the middle of what was a public park, no matter how wild it might seem. It wasn't like everyone could look the other way and pretend it wasn't happening.

She reached across the table and touched the girl's folded hands. Starshine looked up, startled, and Allison pulled her hand back.

"This is an important question, Starshine, so I want you to think about it seriously. Has anything bad happened recently?"

Allison phrased it broadly enough that it could apply to Starshine's father beating or molesting her. And it could also apply to the dead girl and how she got that way.

Starshine pressed her lips together and looked back down at her hands. "No."

"There was a girl in the woods, Starshine. Not far from your camp. She was wearing a navy blue coat. She probably came there with a dog, a black Lab. About three weeks ago. She had blonde hair down to her shoulders. She was seventeen. Her name was Katie Converse."

Getting up, Allison went to her desk and found the photo of Katie and Jalapeño. She held it out. After a moment's hesitation, Starshine took it. She stared at it, expressionless.

"Have you seen her before?"

Starshine tilted her head to one side. "That photograph is stapled to most of the telephone poles when we go into town."

"That's not what I mean, and I think you know that. Have you seen her in real life?"

There was a long pause. Allison waited. Her face was calm, but her pulse was racing.

Finally, Starshine nodded, a nod so slight that it was nearly imperceptible.

"Where?"

"She's dead. Her body's under a rhodie by a tamarack tree."

Jennifer sucked in her breath.

Allison had to take the girl's word for it. Forest Park was filled with trees, but that's all they were to Allison. Trees, not cedars and spruces and tamaracks.

"This is very important, Starshine. I need you to tell me the truth about what happened to her. How did this girl die?"

"I don't know." She looked up at Allison with pleading eyes. "Father says I have to stay in the cabin. He told me not to ever come out no matter what."

"Did your father have anything to do with this?" Allison asked softly. "Maybe there was some kind of accident?"

Starshine's eyes grew wide with shock. "Father didn't kill her. He just found her body. That's all. He didn't kill her! Don't take him from me, don't!" She blinked, but the tears that brimmed in her blue eyes remained unshed.

Where's my daughter?" Tim Chambers demanded when Nicole and Allison walked into the interview room.

His impatient words overrode Allison introducing herself. His left eye was nearly swollen shut and his words were distorted by a fat lip.

"Where is Starshine? Is she okay? She's not used to being away from me. She's probably freaking out."

Chambers had not requested a lawyer, which Allison had been glad to hear. Questioning was always easier when there was no one making objections.

"I understand your concern, but she's fine," she said. "Right now, she's eating lunch."

When Nicole had told her that the autopsy had shown that Katie had definitely been murdered, Allison's sympathies had shifted away from Chambers. Clearly, he had done a good job raising Starshine. And just as clearly, he would have had the motive, means, and opportunity to kill Katie.

"We just need to clear some things up," she continued, pulling out a chair and sitting down. "So why don't you start by telling us why you're living out there in the woods, Tim."

"Is that really any kind of life for a child?" Nicole interjected, turning around the chair next to Allison and straddling it.

"Hold on," Allison said, raising a cautioning hand. "Let Tim tell us his side of the story. I'm sure he has his reasons."

With a sigh, Chambers sat down on the other side of the table. "Starshine's mother is in Dammasch."

Dammasch was the state mental hospital.

"We never got married to each other, but we lived together until Starshine was two. We were fighting a lot, so I took off. I'm not proud of it, but I only saw Starshine about twice a year, because my ex made it clear that she didn't want me coming by. Then two years ago her sister-in-law sent a letter to my PO box saying my ex had attacked another boyfriend and been committed. She told me that if I didn't take Starshine off their hands, they would put her in foster care. Of course I couldn't have that. Starshine's my flesh and blood."

"But why live in the woods?" Allison asked.

"I get a $400-a-month disability check. There's no way to live on that." His tone was matter-of-fact.

Allison nodded. "What about a shelter?"

Chambers made a face. "I've done that before, but they're not set up for men with kids. A woman with kids, yeah, maybe she could find a place. But a man with a kid—there's no place for him to go, not really. They would have split us up. I won't risk having my daughter taken from me. I'm the only family she's got. And I won't live on the streets and expose her to what she would see there—alcohol, drugs, kids her age selling themselves. So one day we hiked into the park, got off the trails, and just kept going until we were in a part that looked completely wild. It's beautiful there. We're surrounded by God's creation, not by concrete and garbage and junkies. We started out in a tent. Then I built a little cabin. Once or twice a week we go through the trash bins in the park and look for recyclable cans and bottles we can take back to the store. You'd be surprised what some people throw away."

Allison nodded agreement, hoping he was referring only to cans and bottles. It was one thing to think of a grown man eating someone's discarded half-eaten sandwich. It was another to think of a child eating out of garbage cans.

"And on Sundays," Chambers continued, "we go to church."

"Church?" Allison echoed in surprise. "Which one?"

"First Congregational."

"Do the people there know you're homeless?"

The church, with its downtown location, was known for its outreach to the down-and-out.

"We're not there for charity." Chambers looked affronted. "We're there so Starshine can learn about Jesus."

Nicole cleared her throat, and Allison realized that they had wandered off track. She wasn't here to solve Chambers's problems. She was here to find out whether he had killed Katie.

Taking over the questioning, Nicole crossed her arms and slouched. "Do you know why you're here, Tim? Why we want to talk to you?"

He didn't bother to pretend that he didn't know what she was talking about. "Because of that poor dead girl."

"She's got a name," Nicole said. "It's Katie Converse. She's not just some dead girl. This was someone's daughter."

"You think I don't know that?" Chambers said. "I pray for her soul every night. She must have been in terrible turmoil to do what she did."

Allison watched him closely, wondering if the reason he was praying was to ask forgiveness for what he had done.

"We need to find out what happened to her," she said. "If you're completely honest with us, we can help you and Starshine get into a subsidized apartment, get you on food stamps."

Nicole glared at Allison, but it was all for show. At least Allison thought it was. Nicole had been in a bad mood ever since she had come back from the autopsy. And Nic was always better at playing bad cop than Allison was at playing good.

"Don't lead him on." Nicole turned back to Chambers. "You've got a dead girl a couple hundred yards from where you camp out, and you expect us to believe you had nothing to do with it, and just let you go on your merry way? Tell us what happened. And don't lie to us, because we already have the forensic evidence."

"It must have been hard keeping it a secret," Allison said sympathetically. "No one to talk to."

Chambers sighed. "What happened is, Starshine and I, we were down at the grocery store turning in our cans. It was getting dark. We were almost home when I saw this girl sprawled on the ground. Not moving. I yelled at Starshine to get in the cabin and stay there. I knew that she didn't need to see it."

"What day was this?" Nicole asked.

"I don't know." Chambers shrugged. "A school day, that's all I remember. When we go into town on a weekday, I have to make sure we do it late enough in the day that no one will ask me why Starshine's not in school."

"Did you pass anyone on your way back?" Allison asked.

"No. But the girl had obviously killed herself. There was a leash around her neck and a broken branch overhead. Poor kid." His eyes misted at the memory. "She didn't look that much older than Starshine. I didn't know what to do with her. I figured if I told anybody, they would start asking questions about us and then take Starshine away. I thought about trying to carry her closer to the main trails so she could be found right away, but I was afraid someone would see and get the wrong idea. So I yelled at Starshine to stay in the cabin. Then I pulled the girl underneath a bush and away from the path we use to get to town. I didn't want my daughter to have to see her every time we went someplace. And then I said a prayer over her."

"Look, Tim—do you love your daughter?" Nicole demanded. "If you tell us what really happened—and I mean the full truth—then I guarantee Starshine will go to a good home. With loving parents who can give her everything, even send her to college when the time comes. Otherwise she'll be left to the mercies of the foster care system, bouncing from home to home. And you've heard what those places are like. Children's Services pulls a kid out of one home because they're getting beat up, then sticks them in the next home where they get sexually abused."

As Nicole spoke, tears gathered in the corners of Chambers's eyes.

"You can't take her away from me. Starshine and me, we've only got each other."

"Then tell the truth," Nicole said. "Because you know where I was this morning? At that girl's autopsy. And she didn't kill herself. So I already know you're lying to me. Somebody did that to her. And I think that somebody was you."

To Allison's eyes, Chambers looked genuinely bewildered. "No, I didn't. Why would I do that? I saw enough death in Vietnam. I would never do that. I tell you, she was already dead when I got there."

Allison leaned closer. "But is that what really happened, Tim? I mean, if it went down another way, it's completely understandable. You're living out there in privacy, not bothering anyone, and then this girl comes blundering in. Did she see your camp? Or worse—did she see your daughter? You had to stop her, didn't you, before she ran off and told. Was there some kind of accident?"

"What are you saying?" Chambers looked shocked by Allison's words. "She was dead when I got there. She was *already* dead. That's not how it happened at all."

"Isn't it, Tim?" Nicole's face was all planes and edges, no softness at all. "Tell us the truth now, while you still can. Because we have that leash—and the prints on it are being analyzed right now."

This was a total bluff, as far as Allison knew. Nicole had said there weren't any prints. But then there was a knock at the door. A Portland police officer stuck his head in.

"Nicole, I need to talk to you."

Chambers watched her go, biting his lip.

Allison figured Nicole must have arranged for this. "Tim, I'm a Christian like you. And we both know that Christ offers us forgiveness if we confess our sins. Now is the time to get this off your chest. It will look a lot better for you if you confess than if you keep lying."

"But I'm not lying." He was calmer now. "When I found her, her spirit had already fled. If someone did that to her, I didn't see them." His faded blue eyes fastened on her, and he leaned forward and patted her hand. "God's laid a heavy burden on you about this girl, hasn't He? She's become as much your responsibility as Starshine is mine. But the Psalms say, 'Cast your burden upon the Lord and He will sustain you; He will never allow the righteous to be shaken.'"

Allison looked at him in astonishment. What had just happened? How could some homeless guy who lived in the woods be offering her solace and comfort?

When Nicole opened the door, she was holding something behind her back, her face incandescent with rage. "Oh, you're just some poor disabled vet, forced to live in the woods because you don't make enough on the government dole? Then how do you explain this?"

Her hand whipped out. In it was a fresh-picked marijuana leaf.

"There was a cultivated patch of pot less than a half mile from where you lived. Don't deny it—I know it's yours."

Chambers's eyes widened—and Allison's did too. This put a whole new spin on things. Chambers, with all of his talk of God, must have been trying to pull the wool over her eyes.

"They tell me there are five hundred plants there, with a street value of a half million dollars. Now you tell me, Tim—would someone kill to keep half a million dollars safe?" Nicole answered her own question. "Hell, yeah. So Katie blundered into your little agricultural operation, and you caught her. Did she run from you? Is that what happened? She ran from you and you tackled her, and then you hit her in the throat?" She slashed her hand sideways for emphasis. "Did you watch her die? Did you?"

Nicole's face was inches from his. "They said she wouldn't have been able to scream, wouldn't have even been able to talk. But she would have been able to think. And she would have been able to feel her body shutting down. Do you know what it feels like to have no air, Tim? It's supposed to be the most terrible feeling in the world."

"I didn't!" Chambers's eyes were despairing. "I tell you, I didn't kill her! That's not my pot, and I didn't kill her!"

Cassidy was not the kind of woman who belonged on an ATV. She realized this as they bounced and jutted over roots and stones. She had one arm around Andy's waist, and with the other she held tight to his camera. More equipment was strapped on behind her.

As they cut through the forest, following a faint path only Andy could see, wet bushes slapped at her denim-covered legs. Mud flecked her face. So much for her carefully applied makeup. Overhead, she heard the sound of a helicopter. Whatever channel it was, they were going to be kicking themselves when they saw that Cassidy had gotten the story first—again.

Twenty minutes later, she was doing her stand-up. They had to hurry to get the tape back to the studio in time for the noon news. More than that, Cassidy had to show Jerry that she was still bringing him scoop after scoop. There was no way she was just going to lie down and let Madeline McCormick walk all over her.

"It was a lonely life," Cassidy told the camera lens, "but a simple one. And for a fifty-five-year-old Vietnam vet named Tim Chambers, it was the only life he thought he could have and still keep his daughter with him.

"Portland police say Chambers and his ten-year-old daughter have lived here, deep in Forest Park, for years. Not in a tent, but in an elaborate camp dug into a steep hillside."

She swept out her arm as Andy panned the camp. "They had a shelter, a rope swing, and a tilled vegetable garden. And this creek was where they got the water to clean and cook with."

Leaning down, she dipped her fingers into the water, which was bone-chillingly cold. "They placed rocks around this small pool to collect water and store perishable foods."

Straightening up, Cassidy gestured behind her. "They lived inside this shelter."

As Andy followed her, she walked over and pulled open the door.

"The father taught his daughter using the encyclopedia you see here." She pointed at a red plastic shopping basket that held a stack of old World Book encyclopedias. "They slept in sleeping bags on these two cots."

Despite her puffy down coat, it was only through force of will that Cassidy was keeping her teeth from chattering.

The camera panned around the tiny space. In addition to the cots, there were a makeshift table, a large metal pot, a handsaw, and an old wooden apple crate that now held canned goods.

"Authorities say the two went into the city once a week to stop by the bank, attend church, buy groceries, and pick up a few odds and ends at Goodwill."

Cassidy could not imagine it. Nicole had said something about a "pit toilet," whatever that was, and she just hoped they didn't stumble over it.

"Police were amazed to find them clean, well fed, and healthy. To be certain the girl was not being maltreated, authorities split up the two and questioned them separately. They say the girl is well-spoken beyond her years. They were also examined by a doctor and evaluated by state welfare workers. They fingerprinted both of them and did a thorough national background check. Everything was negative. Tim Chambers receives only a small disability check for post-traumatic stress disorder related to his service in Vietnam. He told authorities he chose to bring his daughter to the woods rather than subject her to the streets or risk being separated from her if he went to social services.

"Chambers has reportedly told authorities that he knew Katie

Converse's body was nearby, but was worried that if he alerted anyone about it, he would lose his home—as he has. Is he a suspect? Authorities aren't saying, but they haven't charged him with anything and have released him from custody. They do say they aren't sure what will happen to them next, but there is some speculation that Tim's fears could come true—and that he and his daughter will end up separated."

She looked into the camera, her expression serious and determined. "I'm Cassidy Shaw, reporting from deep inside Forest Park."

The Lincoln High School auditorium looked like it had been decorated for the prom, not for a girl's funeral. Bunches of purple balloons trailing purple crepe paper streamers hung from the walls. Nic remembered the Converses telling her that purple was Katie's favorite color. The closed casket sitting on stage, however, was white and gold, draped in white roses.

When Wayne had told Nic about the plans for the funeral, he said, "Valerie chose not to see the body."

She and Allison had tried to talk him out of viewing his daughter's remains too, but Nic had heard that he had disregarded their advice.

"She said she wanted to remember Katie the way she was. And she's right. Because whatever is in that casket isn't Katie. My baby isn't in there anymore. But we're going to give her one hell of a send-off. This is going to be every party Katie will never get to have. This will be all her birthdays, her prom, and her wedding all rolled into one."

Now neighbors, students, teachers, businesspeople, and strangers sat shoulder to shoulder, stood in the stairwell, crowded the balcony, and filled the lobby. Scattered among them were FBI agents and cops, looking for clues, looking for suspects, looking for answers—and finding only anguish. Nic had been given a place near the front, where, if she half turned, she could see most of the audience. Twenty feet from her, Wayne, Valerie, and Whitney sat surrounded by aunts and cousins, grandparents and friends—but alone in some fundamental way.

The service began with a slide show projected on two ten-foot screens set at each side of the stage. Between the screens sat a grand piano and fifty-person choir, with the casket on a dias behind them. Accompanied by classical piano music, photo after photo of Katie flashed by.

An infant Katie on her belly, head raised, wearing nothing but a diaper and a triumphal smile. A five- or six-year-old Katie in a Tigger costume, grinning, with her hands held in mock claws. Katie behind a podium, but still so young that only her eyes were visible. The photo of her with George Bush that Nic had seen in her room. Katie holding aloft a trophy. And finally the photo from the vigil: Katie with eyes as blue as the sky behind her.

In every photo Katie was smiling, but Nic began to wonder just how real those smiles had been. Was it her imagination, or was Katie's expression a mask that hid a deeper sadness in her eyes?

After the slide show, a friend of Katie's recited a rap poem he had written. Another played the trumpet, but halfway through lost his breath to emotion. After trying and failing to start again, he let his trumpet fall to his side and began to weep softly, his head bowed, his shoulders shaking. Finally, the officiating pastor led the boy away, but by that time the crowd was undone by grief and drama.

Girls wailed with their arms around each other. Boys with reddened eyes awkwardly wiped their noses on the sleeves of their ill-fitting suits. Still other kids snapped photos with their cell phones. Nic just hoped they didn't leave the service, go across the street to where the hundreds of reporters had gathered, and offer to sell the photos to the highest bidder.

Then the pastor—who did not seem to know Katie well, if at all—read a letter from Portland's mayor. The letter quoted a biblical passage: "The righteous are taken away to be spared from evil."

Spared? Nic thought cynically. She remembered Tony saying Katie could have lived for minutes after the blow that shattered her larynx. How she would have tried to speak or scream, but nothing would have emerged but the faintest of sounds. What could be more evil than that?

As the service drew to a close, Wayne got up and began to enumerate Katie's virtues, pawing through note cards, naming off awards and honors, frequently losing his place. Finally, he set the cards down. When he looked out at the audience, his eyes were wild, his face wet and red.

"Why? Why? Why?" Wayne shouted. The mic whined with feedback. He pounded his fist on the podium. It sounded like the beating of a giant heart. "I accept dying, I know we all have to die. But this way, the way Katie died! Why?"

At the sight of Wayne's anger, the standing-room-only audience grew silent.

"God took my first wife from me, and now He's taken my baby girl. For no reason!"

Nothing but muffled sobs answered him. Nic looked at Valerie. Her head was high, her expression blank. Whitney's mouth gaped wide as she wept, her face crimson and swollen.

Finally, the pastor touched Wayne on the elbow and murmured something in his ear. Wayne, his head hanging, shuffled back to his seat beside his wife and remaining daughter.

It's over. I can't stop crying.

He tells me to hold on to the future.

I think the future is a long way away & it never really gets here.

W hen Cassidy answered Allison's knock, she was dressed in an old terry cloth robe and not wearing any makeup. Her eyes looked small and tired. In one hand she held a remote control and in the other a water glass half filled with what Allison thought was red wine.

Nicole pushed impatiently past them both. "Okay, we're here," she said, turning to face Cassidy. "What's so important you needed us both to drop everything and come over?"

Cassidy closed the door behind them. "You know that feature we do called 'Nasty Neighbors'? It's all people who steal their neighbor's papers or collect junker cars. Because of the whole Katie Converse thing, I've got a huge backlog of submissions, so I was trying to get caught up today. I was logging tapes when I found this."

She pointed the controller, and the big-screen TV at the far end of the living room came to life.

What appeared on the screen was the corner of someone's lawn. The scene was unwavering, as if the camera were on a tripod. There was nothing else on-screen besides the yard—no people, no clues, not even any other houses. Just a lawn and a hedge, a sidewalk, and beyond that a little slice of street. At the edge of the screen, a curtain. Viewed through a window. A lawn and nothing moving.

So why was it so important?

Allison squinted at the date in the corner. It read 12/13.

The day Katie disappeared.

The back of her neck tingled. It was like watching a movie, waiting for the killer to jump out of his hiding place. Allison half expected to see Katie appear, walking Jalapeño, or maybe being hustled into the back of a windowless van.

But twenty seconds ticked by, thirty, and nothing changed. Nicole huffed impatiently. Cassidy took a sip from her glass. The lawn was a rich dark green, except in the corner centered in the camera. That part was patchy, more brown than green.

"This guy decided to videotape his lawn," Cassidy said. "He was sure that when his neighbor came home from work at 4:00 p.m. she let her dog out and let it—encouraged it, in fact—to poop on his lawn. So he set this up with an auto timer."

"And?" Allison prompted.

"And here's his proof. It's why he sent it to us."

A pretty young woman with a spaniel on a leash walked into the frame. She was bundled up in a long black down coat, but her legs were bare and she wore high-heeled pumps. No sound. But Allison could see her lips moving, see her bending down, and Allison knew she was urging the dog to hurry. Finally, it squatted and did its business. And then she pulled it out of the camera's view. As she did, she nearly collided with a man rushing down the sidewalk. He wasn't out for a jog, not in a suit and a heavy overcoat. His face was twisted, his eyes wild, his mouth open as if he were panting.

Senator Fairview. Running in a panic.

"Where is this?" Allison said sharply. "And what direction was he coming from?"

"Northwest Portland," Cassidy said. "And one block behind him is one of the entrances to Forest Park."

Allison thought of how Fairview had danced around, never telling them the truth. There was no way he could deny this videotape.

"Give it to me." She held out her hand. "I'm taking this to the grand jury so they can indict him."

Cassidy walked to the player, popped out the tape, and handed it over.

As Allison's hand closed on it, Nicole narrowed her eyes.

"That was easy. That's gotta be a big scoop. And you're just giving it up?"

Allison was about to defend Cassidy when she realized the other woman wasn't saying anything.

"Is this a duplicate?" Nic demanded.

Cassidy took a sip from her glass before replying. "It's not a dup." Another sip. "The dup's actually at work. That's the original."

Nicole wagged her finger threateningly. "You're *not* thinking of airing this!"

"Hey, it's my scoop." Cassidy's voice was mild. "I'm the one who found this tape, not you."

"I need to get ahead of Fairview on this, Cassidy," Allison said. "Every step of the way, he has misled us. All of us. Well, he can't with this. Not if we don't tip our hands. This is the evidence I need to get the grand jury to indict him. This guy's as slippery as a seal. With this tape, I can finally pin him down."

"I need the tape just as much as you do. If I don't keep coming up with scoops, the station is going to pull me off this story. They keep pressuring me to let Madeline McCormick take over the coverage."

Cassidy scrubbed her face with her free hand. She looked like an overtired child.

"Even though I'm the one who broke the story. I'm the one who made this story happen."

Allison knew she had the subpoena power to force Cassidy to turn over the tape to the grand jury. But the reality was that red tape would make it nearly impossible. The Department of Justice would have to green-light the idea, and by that time it would be too late. The station would air the tape now and claim freedom of the press later. The best she could do was to work out a deal.

"Cassidy—this is about a murder. Isn't that more important than ratings? I'm begging you—you have to hold on to this until after we arrest him. Once that happens, I'll give you a twenty-four-hour window before we give it to anybody else."

There was a long pause.

"Forty-eight," Cassidy said finally. "I need it to be forty-eight. With forty-eight I can tell the management and Maddy to take a flying leap."

Allison gritted her teeth. She didn't have many options. "Okay. Forty-eight. But you have to promise me it won't run until after he's arrested."

Cassidy finally seemed to come alive. "Thank you, thank you, I promise!"

She leaned in to give Allison a hug, and Allison could smell the wine on her breath and in her glass. Cassidy always had something to drink when the three of them were together, but even for Cassidy, a water glass full of wine seemed a bit much. But they were all under so much stress from the Katie Converse case that maybe it was understandable.

Cassidy pulled back, a smile on her face. "Are you going to have him arrested right away?"

"I'd like to, but it's probably not feasible." Allison ticked off the reasons on her fingers. "One, Fairview is a public figure. Two, he's shown no indication that he is likely to flee. Three, there aren't any allegations that he's a serial killer or in any way a danger to others. It's not like we need to get him off the street before he kills again. I'll take this to the grand jury first thing Wednesday and get him indicted."

"Wednesday? Why not tonight?" Cassidy's smile fell from her face like a plate from a shelf. "This man needs to be locked up. He killed a beautiful young girl."

"The only way I could do it tonight would be to take it to a judge. And a judge's standard is 'beyond a reasonable doubt.' Fairview knows all the judges in town—do you think any one of them is realistically going to say this tape is proof beyond a reasonable doubt? It doesn't show him with Katie. There are no marks on his hands, no pine needles on his clothes. Nothing to connect him to what happened. Michael Stone will say that all it shows is that his client was late for a meeting or something. Stone could even argue that the date in the corner is wrong. We all know that half the time the date on a video camera isn't right. But I can show the grand jury the tape, and it will establish his opportunity. Katie's blogs establish his motive. And the medical examiner has told us the means—that blow to the throat. Once we get the indictment from the grand jury, a judge will *have* to sign off on it. By this time Wednesday, Fairview will be locked up."

"And then they should throw away the key. That's what Rick says."

Allison said patiently, "Rick's been around the block enough to know that even once Fairview's arrested, he won't stay in jail long. He'll post bail."

"But he killed that girl. We all know he did it. I thought this would finally be enough to prove it." The glass slipped from Cassidy's hand and shattered into a dozen pieces. She started to cry. "I can't sleep. I can't eat. I can't think."

Cassidy wasn't a pretty crier. Her eyes immediately turned puffy, and snot leaked from her nose.

"Why?" Allison asked. "What's wrong?"

Was it Allison's imagination, or did Cassidy hesitate?

"Like I said, the station is pressuring me to step aside for Maddy. I'm making enemies, but if I don't hold on to my turf, I'll be nobody." She bent down and started to pick up the pieces of glass that lay around her bare feet.

"Here, Cass, let me," Allison said. "You'll cut your feet."

Together, Allison and Nicole picked up the biggest pieces of glass. In the kitchen, Allison opened the cabinet underneath the sink. Instead of table scraps, the garbage can was heaped with a half dozen silk bras and panties in shades of turquoise, silver, and pink.

Allison and Nicole exchanged a look. Allison set the pieces of glass on the counter and picked up a sky-blue bra. It had been sliced in several places.

Dear God, Allison prayed, *something feels very, very wrong about this. Help me to find the right words to help Cassidy.*

She took the bra out to the living room. Nicole followed after grabbing a broom and dustpan.

"Cassidy, what's this?" Allison held out the cut-up bra. "Your garbage can is filled with your underwear."

Cassidy bit her lip and looked away. "Oh, Rick says I dress too slutty. If I want to be taken seriously as a professional, he says I need to look more buttoned up. He says I'm insecure, and that's why I'm always flaunting myself."

There was more than a grain of truth to what Rick said. Still, wasn't it up to Cassidy to determine that?

"So he cut them up?" Nicole demanded.

"Of course not! I did it! He said if I was serious, I would cut them up. Then he would know that I meant it."

"But that's the kind of thing you should decide for yourself," Allison said.

"Rick loves me, and he doesn't want anyone to see me as a whore." Cassidy straightened up, although the bathrobe detracted from the effect. "I'm a professional broadcast reporter, not some little tart on an entertainment news program. I'm a serious journalist."

"And serious journalists can't wear pretty bras?" Nicole said with a deadpan expression.

"Not if they expect to be taken seriously." Cassidy sounded like she was parroting Rick.

What was happening to Cassidy was right out of the brochures they kept at the front desk of Safe Harbor: name-calling. Excessive possessiveness. Destruction of personal property.

And from experience, Allison didn't think it would stop with Rick making Cassidy get rid of her sexy underwear.

"Cassidy," Allison said carefully, "you have to promise me you'll think twice next time Rick wants you to change some part of your personality. It makes me nervous that he doesn't like you the way you are."

As she spoke, Nicole nodded.

Cassidy shook her head. "He likes me the way I *should* be." She managed a teary-eyed smile. "And isn't that better?"

"No," Allison said. "Frankly, it's not. You should only change for yourself. Not because someone tells you they won't love you unless you do. Let me ask you something, Cassidy, and you have to promise to tell me the truth."

"Okay," Cassidy said slowly.

"Has Rick ever hit you?"

"No." Cassidy laid her hand over her heart. "I promise you, Rick has never hit me. Ever."

Watching her, Allison felt sick. She had known Cassidy long enough to know when she was lying.

Allison had faxed a target letter to Stone. It told the lawyer that not only was his client the subject of a grand jury investigation, but Allison believed she had substantial evidence to link him to a crime. Fairview was now compelled to leave rehab and testify before the grand jury. He could still take the Fifth to any and all questions that might incriminate him, but he'd run a higher risk of being indicted because the grand jurors might think he was hiding the truth. And once you were indicted, the public decided you were guilty. As a politician, his life would be over.

And did Fairview even have a life outside of being a politician?

Allison figured that Fairview and Stone had to be weighing the odds. Did Fairview need to focus on saving his career—or on saving his skin?

What they didn't know was that she had a videotape that would be nearly impossible to explain away.

Although they would probably have rehearsed Fairview's testimony a dozen times, Stone would not be allowed to accompany his client into the grand jury room. Instead, he would be forced to sit in the hall, twiddle his thumbs, and hope that his client didn't open his mouth and hang himself. Inside the grand jury room, it was only the prosecutor, the jurors, and the witness. Grand juries were supposed to hold a prosecutor in check—but they also gave a prosecutor a lot of power.

Allison could have skipped the grand jury indictment and gone right to a probable cause hearing in front of a judge. But in that case, the

defendant and his lawyer were on hand to hear every word of her argument. And then the balance of power was tipped the other way. A
probable cause hearing gave the defense an early crack at the case, and an
opportunity to cross-examine the FBI agents who testified to the
evidence.

Allison began by bringing the grand jury up to speed on the events
of the last few days. She put Leif on the stand to set the scene by testifying
about what the ERT had found in Forest Park. But just as important, she
had him identify a photo of Katie's body. Behind her, she heard the jurors
gasp as the photo was passed from hand to hand.

In a way, it was overkill to show these photos to the jury. Given the
evidence of the videotape, Allison knew they would indict Fairview without them. But at the same time, she wanted to hear their reactions, gauge
how everything would go when it really came for trial.

Next, she called Nicole to the stand. Nicole testified about how the
Converses had taken the news that their daughter's body had been found.
While this was hearsay evidence that couldn't be used at trial, it was per-
missible at a grand jury hearing. At this point, with the facts of their
daughter's murder still fresh in their mind, it would be too volatile—as
well as too cruel—to call Wayne and Valerie to the stand. Nicole also identified autopsy photos of Katie's throat and the injuries it had received. By
the gasps Allison could hear coming from the jurors, these photos were
just as powerful as the previous ones. And Nicole explained that the
autopsy results meant that Katie had definitely been murdered.

Finally, Fairview was brought into the room and sworn in by the
court reporter. His face wore an expression that Allison was sure had
been practiced in front of a mirror. It mingled equal parts sorrow and
righteous indignation.

Allison got up to turn on the TV-VCR unit she had requested. "Senator,
I am going to show you a tape that was shot on December thirteenth. The
day Katie Converse went missing. The day, we now know, that she died."

Something in Fairview's eyes flickered, just for a second. The rest of his face remained impassive. As the tape began to play, he made his disinterest obvious, at one point even yawning as seconds ticked by and nothing happened.

But then the woman appeared with the dog. The jurors leaned forward in their seats. And finally, there he was, Senator Fairview, running in a panic. In a panic from the mess he had just left behind.

When the tape ended, Fairview was slumped in the witness chair. He looked, Allison thought, broken. In a voice so small she had to strain to hear it, he said, "I would like to consult with my attorney."

"All right, Senator." She turned to the grand jurors. "Okay, people, we'll take a ten-minute recess."

Allison remained at her table, although she could hear the excited babble of the grand jurors' voices as they took their chance to grab a snack and gossip about what they had just seen and heard.

When the break was over and Fairview had returned to the stand, she said, "Senator, would you care to explain what we just saw?"

He put his palm over his heart. "I swear to you, I am innocent. I did not kill Katie Converse. She was already dead when I found her."

Allison said, "Why do you expect us to believe that?" She would have loved to have leaned into his face when she asked the question, but in a grand jury trial the prosecutor always remained seated for the questioning.

Most people's inclination was to explain and convince and to try to make the prosecutor see it their way.

But Fairview said simply, "I expect you to believe me because I am telling the truth. I panicked when I found her body, and I ran away. You look at that videotape and you can tell that I was startled and afraid. But I did not kill Katie Converse. She took her own life."

They had not released the results of the autopsy publicly for this very reason—to help them flush out a killer. Katie's parents knew the truth, as did the investigators—and now the grand jurors—but no one else.

"Then tell us what happened," Allison said. "Tell us what really happened."

He sighed and pressed his hands against his face. "It's true that Katie and I had developed a relationship while she was a page. I didn't seek it out—it just happened. It was really more her idea than mine."

Behind her, Allison heard an angry hiss. Was Fairview testing his strategy for the future trial just as she was testing hers? Because if he was, it had just backfired.

"We met each other at that spot in Forest Park a couple of times over Thanksgiving break, when we were desperate to see each other. Katie knew the park well—she grew up only a few blocks away, and she and her dad went for walks there all the time. She had found this clearing that was off the main trails.

"But this time, instead of going there together, she called and demanded that I meet her there. She wouldn't take no for an answer. She was very angry. She threatened to tell my wife what had happened between us. So finally I agreed. The other times, we had walked there together. At first I thought I was lost. I couldn't see Katie anyplace. I was calling her name. And then the dog ran up to me. I wasn't even sure it was hers at first. It didn't have its leash. It was barking and running around in circles, all excited. And then it started racing up the path and stopping to look at me. Like it wanted me to follow. And so I did." Fairview's voice shook. "And—and there she was. Lying on the ground with a noose around her neck. Katie had killed herself. She had wanted me to find her like that. She was hell-bent on punishing me."

It would have been a clever twist—had the autopsy not put the lie to Fairview's claim.

"Punish you?" Allison echoed. "Why would she want to punish you?"

"Because earlier that day she had seen Nancy and me Christmas shopping. We were—we were holding hands. Katie called me, screaming that I was cheating on her." His voice rose indignantly. "Cheating on her? With my wife?"

And suddenly Allison knew that there had been something more. The blog entries, Katie's anger and sadness—it all added up.

"You got her pregnant, didn't you?"

A couple of the grand jurors gasped.

"And then you forced her to have an abortion."

"No! It wasn't like that at all." Fairview held his hands out, pleading with Allison and the jurors. "I tried to talk her out of having the abortion, but she wouldn't listen to me."

"So you paid for the abortion? Drove her to the clinic?"

"Katie was desperate. She said she would kill herself rather than have the baby."

"But, Senator Fairview, haven't you staked your professional reputation on being anti-abortion?"

He straightened up. "I've always favored an exemption when the life of the mother is at risk. And Katie was adamant that she would kill herself. She was so afraid of what her stepmother might do if she came home pregnant. She had two bottles of Tylenol, and she told me she was planning on taking both of them rather than go through with having the baby. I couldn't let that happen, so I took her to a clinic I knew about. At that point, my only thought was to keep her from killing herself. She was a bright, articulate young woman who was clearly going places." His voice wobbled. "I guess she was more emotionally unstable than I thought."

"Senator, the autopsy results show that Katie Converse was murdered. She didn't hang herself. Someone tried to make it look like a suicide." Allison took a deep breath. "And we believe that someone was you."

"No," he protested, his eyes widening. "I did not kill her! I did not kill Katie Converse!"

Looking directly into the camera, Cassidy said, "Late-breaking news tonight. Senator James Fairview has been indicted by a grand jury for the murder of Senate page Katie Converse."

As she was speaking, out of the corner of her eye Cassidy saw an intern with a tape come running into the room. By the time he realized he was running into a live shot, he was going too fast to stop. He tripped over a chair and landed just behind Cassidy. She hesitated for only a second, and in that second, if viewers had listened very carefully, they could have heard a whispered curse from the floor.

Cassidy smoothly resumed talking as if nothing had happened.

"The grand jury acted after seeing this exclusive footage, which you will see only on Channel Four. It was taken the same day that Katie Converse disappeared."

That night, Cassidy flipped from channel to channel. But Fairview's arrest didn't lead the news on a single station. Instead, each was extensively covering the same story, the story the intern had been rushing in. In Chicago, the roof of an ice-skating rink had collapsed under the weight of heavy snow. Three kids were missing and eight were confirmed dead. Many of them had been attending a birthday party for a five-year-old.

With a sinking feeling, Cassidy realized the media's great eye had just turned away from Katie to focus on another story.

The judge set Fairview's bail at a million dollars, so he was out within twenty-four hours. A million dollars might sound like a lot to the average person, but Allison knew that a defendant only had to come up with 10 percent. And for a man like Senator Fairview, she thought sourly, a hundred thousand was close to pocket change.

Under the conditions of his bail release, Fairview was not allowed to travel out of state. Release was determined by two considerations: risk of flight and danger to the community. But Fairview was so recognizable— he was currently on the cover of *Time*, *Newsweek*, and the *National Enquirer*—that he was not considered a flight risk, especially since the judge had confiscated his passport. And since it was allegedly a crime of passion, and not the act of a serial killer, Fairview was considered a minimal danger to the community.

As soon as Fairview made bail, he went back to the rehab center, which offered at least the illusion of privacy.

Chambers was out of jail, too, an idea Allison had a lot less trouble with. There was no way to tie the pot plants to him, and Starshine's story backed him up. After Cassidy's piece had run, offers to help had poured in from Channel Four viewers. One had offered Chambers a job and a place for him and his daughter to live on a horse farm in rural Washington County. Now they were staying in a mobile home and getting used to having heat, electricity, and running water—all things they had survived without for the past three years.

Allison had just sat down in front of her overflowing inbox when the phone rang.

"Allison Pierce."

"Ally—it's Lindsay."

The first emotion Allison felt was annoyance. The second was guilt.

Lindsay was her sister. She had to be there for her. Even when everyone else had given up on her.

"What's up, Lindsay?" What she meant was *What's wrong, Lindsay?* Because something had to be. For one thing, her sister had never come home for Christmas.

"I've been arrested."

"Are you still in Tennessee?" Or had it been Alabama?

"No, I'm here in Portland. Chris took me back."

Allison couldn't believe it. Was there a note of joy in her sister's voice?

"So what were you arrested for?"

"Selling meth. But I—"

"Don't say any more, Linds." Phone calls from jail were routinely recorded. Allison would rather not have to argue about whether a conversation with her sister fell under attorney-client privilege. "I'll come down and talk to you. I can be there in less than an hour."

She was resting her head in her hands when the phone rang again. She said hello and braced for some new revelation from Lindsay. Instead, she heard a man's rough voice.

"I'm going to kill you."

"What?" Electricity shot down her spine.

His voice rode inexorably over hers. "Don't think you can ever be safe. No matter where you try to hide, I will find you. I don't care how long it takes. No matter where you run, I will hunt you down. And then I will cut your head off. Or do you want me to tear your heart out? I'll do it while your heart is still beating." He laughed. "How's your husband going to feel when he finds you dead, with no heart?"

He was still laughing when Allison hung up. Her hand was trembling so hard she had trouble replacing the phone in its cradle.

Kira Dowd was walking up the Wildwood Trail, enjoying the pull in the back of her legs and the sounds of Wilco in her headphones. The sky had cleared overnight and was now a bright blue. The curling ferns were a beautiful emerald green, the air crisp. The ground had frozen enough that the mud was nearly solid underneath her Timberland boots.

Suddenly someone grabbed her from behind. Powerful hands squeezed her neck.

Two years ago, when she was a freshman at Portland State, Kira had taken a women's self-defense class. But then the attacker had been some guy lumbering around in a face mask and six inches of white padding, and she had had a cheering section.

Now she knew she was probably going to die all alone, with no one to hear, no one to help.

She kicked back and connected with the guy's shin, but it had hardly any force. The hands tightened. One of her headphones popped loose. What was she supposed to do? Kira couldn't remember. All she could think of was air and how badly she needed some.

She grabbed her attacker's wrists and pulled, but they were strong and wiry. Kira clawed at her own neck, ignoring the pain, until she was finally able to grab a gloved index finger. Her lungs were on fire, and the edges of her vision went black. Still she yanked and twisted until finally the hands fell away.

Her first breath was so sweet, even squeezing through her bruised throat.

And with her second breath, Kira began to scream and scream, not even stopping when she saw her attacker, dressed in dark clothes and a black ski mask, crashing away from her through the brush.

TOMMY'S BAR-B-Q
January 17

Allison parked a block away from Tommy's Bar-B-Q. As she got ready to leave her car, she glanced in her rearview mirror. Her blood chilled. A block behind her, a man in a blue parka was getting out of a nondescript older model car. She looked closer. It wasn't just any man in a blue parka. He had a square, blocky build, and his jacket hood was cinched tight so that she couldn't see his face.

Frantic, Allison looked up and down the empty street. No pedestrians and no other open businesses. Tommy's Bar-B-Q was in a part of North Portland that gentrification hadn't reached yet, between a burnt-out lot and a storefront that advertised appliance repair in one window and a no-kill cat shelter in the other.

Slow nausea rose in her throat. What was he planning to do to her? Would he really rape her and kill her? Or would he just beat her up? Even if he only left another note on her car while she was inside eating, she couldn't take it anymore. Couldn't take not feeling safe. Couldn't take not knowing what was going to happen next.

And this wasn't just about her. This was about the baby. She had to do what she needed to do to keep the baby safe.

Pretending to look for something in her purse, Allison pulled out her cell phone and called Nicole. She pressed the button for speakerphone and left the phone on her lap where her pursuer wouldn't see it.

Nicole's voice floated up to her. "You running late?"

"No," Allison said. "I'm right outside. But you know that guy who's been threatening me? Well, he's out here right now. He just parked on the corner about a block behind me. I don't think he knows I've spotted him."

Nicole's voice was sharp with urgency. "Where are you?"

"In my car on the corner of Vancouver."

"Turn on your dome light and pretend like you're putting on lipstick. Keep an eye on him, though, and if it looks like he's coming for you, start the car and drive off. I don't want you getting hurt. I'll call for backup and then go around the corner and come up behind him."

A minute later, Allison watched the whole thing unfold in her rearview mirror. The guy shifting from foot to foot, his eyes on her car. Nicole popping around the corner, running up behind him with her gun drawn, and then her yell worthy of a warrior.

"FBI. Put your hands up!"

The man's body jerked in surprise. But his hands didn't move. Allison had her fingers on the ignition key, ready to turn it if he made a single step toward her. In the distance she heard sirens.

Nicole screamed, "Get your hands up right now or I will light you up!"

Instead of obeying her, he started running—right toward Allison's car.

With a shaking hand, Allison quickly turned the key. But she turned it too far. The engine made a grinding shriek, shuddered, and fell silent. Her eyes flashed up to the rearview mirror. He was only ten feet from her car.

She turned the key again. Now there wasn't even a noise.

Nicole made a flying tackle and slammed the guy against Allison's trunk. Even inside the car, Allison could hear his grunt of pain.

With a cough and a whine, the car finally started. Her foot hovered over the accelerator. Should she still drive off? In her rearview mirror, she saw Nicole handcuff her would-be assailant, none too gently, and begin patting him down. In a second, one, two, three cop cars screamed around the corner.

Allison turned off the car. She had to see his face. She had to know who had been doing this to her. She opened the door.

Three curious diners had come out of Tommy's and were gathered on the sidewalk. Cassidy was snapping photos with her cell phone.

As Nicole leaned Allison's pursuer over the trunk of her car, his hood fell back, allowing Allison to finally see the man she had been running from.

Only it wasn't a man.

It was a woman.

"That's a surprise," Cassidy said, touching Allison's arm. "Do you know her?"

She had difficulty finding her voice. "It's . . . it's Vanessa Logue. I prosecuted her date rapist. But the jury found him not guilty."

Allison walked around the car until she could look into the woman's eyes, snapping with anger.

"Vanessa—*you're* the one who's been following me? Leaving me threats? But why?"

The woman's face was creased into a snarl. "If you had done your job the way you should have, the guy who raped me would be in jail. Instead, he's walking around free, and I'm the one living in fear. Because of your incompetence." Vanessa took a ragged breath. "I just wanted you to see what it was like to have to watch your back all the time. To never feel safe."

"But who placed all those phone calls?"

It had been a man's voice on the phone. Allison was sure of it.

"My brother," Vanessa said as sirens began to fill the air. "He hates you as much as I do."

Allison hoped the brother could be found soon enough.

T hat was an exciting way to begin the evening," Cassidy said dryly, when the three women were finally settled in at Tommy's an hour later.

She seemed different somehow, but in ways Allison was having trouble putting a finger on. It was more than just her high-necked blouse or her uncharacteristically subdued manner. Normally she would have been unable to sit still after all the excitement, would have flirted with the cops before they left. Instead, she somehow just seemed . . . flat.

Tommy's Bar-B-Q wasn't long on looks. Once it had been a dry cleaners, but Tommy had remodeled it by adding a tiny open kitchen on the other side of the front counter. Three wooden picnic tables had been squeezed into the former waiting area—and that was the extent of the seating.

But the smell of barbecue had made Allison's mouth start watering when she was still out on the sidewalk. She had decided that tonight, of all nights, she could afford to deviate from her diet.

"So what's Channel Four's take on that woman who was attacked in Forest Park? Do you think it's related to Katie's murder?"

The Oregonian's top headline that morning had read DOES SERIAL KILLER STALK FOREST PARK? in forty-eight-point type, accompanied by a boxed sidebar titled RUSH TO JUDGMENT?

"Senator Fairview has been my bread and butter," Cassidy said, "but there's no way he could have attacked this girl. He's still in rehab, and he's watched 'round the clock."

"Maybe he found a way to bribe one of the staff," Nicole said.

"And what—just sneaked out to go grab a girl?" Cassidy shook her head. "That doesn't make any sense. Maybe everything did happen the way Fairview said it did. He went up to Forest Park to talk to Katie, but when he arrived, she was already dead. And he panicked and ran."

Putting down the rib she had been nibbling, Allison said, "I still think Fairview killed Katie. He got scared that she was going to tell people about their relationship. People were willing to look the other way about his womanizing, but if they found out his latest was underage, that could have blown his career out of the water."

"Yeah—but murder?" Cassidy asked skeptically. "That's a bigger career-breaker than a little indiscretion. Even if people did find out about the abortion. And there are other suspects. Take Nancy Fairview—if she found out this girl was sleeping with her husband, she could have snapped. And what about Chambers? He was living out in the woods with his kid, afraid people were going to take her away. Maybe it's not a coincidence that her body wasn't far from where they lived."

Nicole dropped one more bone onto the pile on her plate. "Hey, aren't you the one who did the whole story about how noble Chambers was, looking after his kid, keeping her away from the influences of the street? Didn't you help him get a whole brand-new shiny life?"

Cassidy shrugged. "I was just covering all the angles. Just because he was looking after his kid doesn't mean he didn't do it. In some ways, it makes it more likely." She looked down at her plate. "People aren't always what they seem."

Allison said, "The problem is that Fairview's lawyer will say that who-ever was growing the pot—whether it was Chambers or not—could have been the one who killed Katie. Or he'll say it could even be someone we haven't looked at yet—some kid who knows Katie here in Portland. Stone will say it's possible they ran into each other while she was walking down Twenty-third, they went for a walk up the trail, and something went wrong, there was a fight, and he accidentally killed her." She sighed. "The trouble with all the evidence is that it's circumstantial. We have no eye-witnesses. No physical evidence. 'Beyond a reasonable doubt' is a high standard of proof. We don't have a smoking gun."

Tommy came over to take Nicole's plate, empty of everything but bones.

"You're all talking about that dead girl, right? That Katie Converse?" They nodded.

"Well, have you looked at what happened to Janie Peterson?"

"Janie Peterson?" The name teased the edge of Allison's memory.

"She grew up in my neighborhood," Tommy said, "but I never knew her. After college, she came back to Portland and lived over by Good Sam. She went out to a movie with some friends about eight or nine years ago. One of them gave her a ride home. She asked if they could drop her off at Quality Pie, you know, that place that used to be on Lovejoy across from the hospital? She said she could walk to her apartment from there."

"I remember that case, " Allison said slowly.

Neither Cassidy nor Nicole had been living in Portland then.

"She was around my age," Allison said. "They found her body months later, like in a creek or something, right?"

"Yup. A couple of folks who were canoeing found part of a leg. Eventually, they found the rest of her body scattered for miles along the creek. They had to use that DNA testing on it to see who she was. They never figured out how she died. Murder, suicide, some kind of accident—nobody knows."

Cassidy said. "Three girls. All in Forest Park." Her eyes widened. "Do you think it's a serial killer?"

Tommy shrugged one shoulder and turned to go back to the kitchen.

"I'll look up more about it tomorrow," Nicole said. "But this doesn't feel like a serial killer to me. These aren't prostitutes or runaways. No signs of rape. And there's way too long a gap in between. Serial killers kill and keep killing. They don't take years off."

"Maybe the guy was in prison for a while," Cassidy said. "That would explain the gap."

"It's possible," Allison said, but like Nicole, she didn't feel it in her gut. She wouldn't be surprised if Cassidy didn't feel it either—she was probably just happy to be handed a way to refresh the story.

Allison's phone began to vibrate across the table. The name on the display was familiar, but she still couldn't place it.

"Allison Pierce."

"It's Mrs. Rangel."

She had to think. Lily Rangel. Katie's oldest friend.

"Hello, Mrs. Rangel, what can I do for you?"

"It's Lily. She's gone."

Allison straightened up. "What do you mean, Lily's gone?" She watched the other two women exchange glances.

"She never came home last night."

"When did you last see her?"

"I dropped her off at a movie at Cinema Twenty-one. She was supposed to call me when it was over. But she never did. And whenever I call her, her cell phone goes straight to voice mail. Like it's been turned off."

Cinema Twenty-one was less than two dozen blocks from Forest Park. But who said a killer had to stop at its borders?

As soon as she let herself in her front door, Cassidy kicked off her high heels. It had been a long day, especially with the excitement of watching Nicole catch Allison's stalker. Her feet were killing her. You couldn't spend sixteen hours in four-inch heels and not pay the price. But they did make her legs looks good—long and muscular.

Without turning on the lights, Cassidy dropped her purse and keys on the front table, next to the white vase filled with fresh-cut flowers that were supposed to bring abundance. The flowers had been fresh a week ago, so now they smelled more rotten than sweet.

But it seemed like they were working. Other stations were calling her nearly every day now, feeling her out about whether she might want to work in Las Vegas or San Francisco or Boston. Cassidy was spunky, they said. They liked that she wouldn't take no for an answer. They flattered her, complimenting her voice, her writing, and her feel for a story. They told her she was sure to win an Emmy for her coverage of the Katie Converse case.

It had taken eleven years, but now Cassidy was finally at the place she had been daydreaming about since she graduated from college. She had started her career in Medford, a small town just above the California border, beginning as little more than a glorified gofer. But the good thing about being at an undersized station was that you got a chance to do a lot—even if it was for a salary that worked out to far less than minimum wage when you factored in all the hours. Then she had moved on to Eugene, a slightly larger town midway between Medford and Portland. She was again lowest on the totem pole, getting the worst segments, the middle-of-the-night stories, the drudge assignments, the silly lifestyle pieces. Once she had done a stand-up at the state fair holding a fourteen-foot python. They had had to stop taping four times because the snake kept wrapping itself around her neck. The whole time, she had been expected to keep smiling.

Eventually Cassidy had been able to take the next step and move on to Portland. If you wanted to get ahead in broadcast, you had to move again and again. With every move, you landed in a bigger media market and worked your way up once more. And if you were very, very lucky, as well as exceptionally good, you might make it to the networks.

Cassidy had paid her dues at Channel Four. To take the next step, she had needed a big story. And the universe had handed it to her in the form of Katie Converse. If she were going to make her move, she had to make it soon, while people still remembered who Katie Converse was. Because right now there was surely a reporter in Chicago who was riding the tiger of the stories of the kids in the collapsed skating rink.

In the kitchen, she poured herself a glass of wine without bothering to turn on the lights. She picked up the glass and carried it into the bathroom, then stripped and climbed into the shower.

Cassidy was rinsing the shampoo from her hair when she heard a sound. She didn't know what the sound was, just that there was a noise that didn't belong. It seemed to be coming from the living room. Maybe she was imagining things. Sound carried weirdly in these condos. Half the units were unoccupied, bought by real estate speculators who had been unable to sell when the bottom fell out of Portland's condo market.

There. She heard it again. Even though she hadn't finished rinsing her hair, she turned off the shower and held her breath. Now the sound was clear.

Footsteps. In her living room.

If she screamed, what would happen? How long would it take one of her few neighbors to respond? Would they even hear her? Many of them were probably asleep. A scream might not even register.

In her head she replayed the latest threat from her voice mail. *Stop asking so many questions about that Katie Converse. It's none of your business anyway. Back off that story or you'll be sorry.* She had become blasé about angry viewers. Could it be that someone had really gone so far as to break into her apartment?

Another thought occurred to her. Living alone, she never locked the bathroom door. In fact—Cassidy peeked out of the shower curtain to double-check—tonight she hadn't even closed the door all the way. Long before anyone could help her, whoever was in the living room would get to her first.

How had they even gotten in? Hadn't she locked the front door behind her? She thought she had, but she couldn't be sure. After weeks of long days and this evening's excitement, she was so tired that she was moving on autopilot.

The footsteps sounded closer. Could she get to the bathroom door before the intruder did? And if she did manage to lock it, how long would it hold?

Cassidy took stock. She had no phone, no gun, no weapon of any kind. She had a half dozen bottles of shampoo and conditioner, a loofah, and a bar of soap. She had a razor that she kept meaning to replace because it was barely up to the job of scraping the stubble off her legs.

She was a naked, wet woman trapped with an intruder and no one to hear her.

Cassidy took a deep breath and stepped out of the shower.

I'm home now. It's so weird to be back. When I left, I was a little girl. Now I'm a woman.

I feel like a stranger. I don't belong here. Maybe I can talk Daddy into sending me to boarding school. I wish I were already in college.

I need to go shopping. I think I'll go to Nordstrom today. I have lots of presents for my sister & my dad doesn't honestly care, but I still need something for V. Although part of me doesn't feel like doing it. She's such a fraud. She always acts all high & mighty, but now I know the truth.

Standing outside the tub, Cassidy reached in and turned the shower back on. Let whoever had broken into her apartment think she was preoccupied and vulnerable. Two could play this game. The sounds of falling water would also provide her with some camouflage.

Gently easing open the cupboard door under the sink, she grabbed the bottle of tile cleaner. Experimentally, she pressed the trigger. With a hiss, the spray shot out three feet. It was something. But was it enough?

Cassidy looked around the room again. What could she turn into a weapon? Her hair straightener would take too long to heat up. If she broke her wine glass, she would probably just cut herself and still not end up with a piece big enough to hurt anyone else. Then her gaze settled on the top of the toilet tank. Heavy porcelain. She hefted it experimentally, then tucked it under her arm, grabbed the spray bottle again, and stationed herself on the far side of the door.

A man's hand appeared, slowly pushing open the door. Should she try to slam it closed, break his fingers? But before she could decide, the hand was followed by an arm and shoulder.

Screaming like a banshee, Cassidy jumped out from behind the door, pressing the trigger on the tile cleaner over and over. The man reeled backward, cursing. She dropped the bottle and lifted the toilet tank over her left shoulder, ready to swing it like a bat.

But instead she let it slip from her fingers to the floor, where it thumped on the bath mat.

Because the man scrabbling at his eyes, pulling off his glasses and running to the sink, was Rick.

A relieved laugh spurted from her.

Rick. It was Rick.

Cassidy didn't know how he had gotten in, but it didn't matter. Because she was safe.

Then Rick, his face red and wet, whirled and grabbed her wrists. He slammed her back against the wall.

"What in the hell do you think you're doing?" he roared.

And the next thing Cassidy knew, she was staring down the barrel of his gun.

What are you guys doing here?" Cassidy's smile didn't reach her eyes. She was dressed in a well-worn gray sweatshirt and sweatpants.

Behind her, Allison could see a nearly empty glass of wine on the table in the entryway. She would bet anything that the glass wasn't left over from the night before, but had only just left Cassidy's hand.

"Are you alone?" Allison asked.

Cassidy nodded. Her eyes looked wary.

"We're here to do an intervention," Nicole said.

"That's ridiculous," Cassidy said. Her eyes went to her glass.

"Not for drinking," Allison said. "To make you see the truth about Rick."

"What are you talking about? You guys are crazy."

Nicole reached out for Cassidy's wrist, catching it even when she tried to hide it behind her back, like a little kid.

"Crazy? Then why do you have these bruises?" She pushed up the sleeve so they could all see the clear ovals where a thumb and finger had left their mark. "Something about the way you've looked lately has been bugging me. And after we saw you at Tommy's, I realized what it was—you've been putting makeup on your wrists."

"We were just playing around, the way two consenting adults can." Cassidy lifted her chin. "Maybe I like it a little rough."

"Oh, Cassidy," Allison breathed. She had to blink back tears.

At the sight of Allison's emotion, something inside Cassidy broke. Her own eyes grew red. "But Rick loves me. He only acts the way he does sometimes because he loves me so much."

"Ha! He can call it whatever he wants to, but it's abuse," Nicole said. "He's trying to control you."

"He just wants me to be happy."

"No, he doesn't. He just wants you to obey him," Allison said. "That's why we want you to go with us to Safe Harbor. Some of the women there have agreed to tell you their stories. Not as a reporter, but as a human being. They've been down the same road, Cass. They know exactly what could happen if you don't get free of Rick."

"This is ridiculous," Cassidy said, but there was no force behind her words.

"Just come with us and listen. If you don't believe them, you can walk away. But just promise you'll listen for a little while."

Cassidy sighed. "Okay. But I tell you, Rick's not like those other guys. And I'm not like those women."

The director met them in the lobby. "You're Cassidy, yes?" she asked, shaking her hand. "We only use first names here." She ushered Cassidy down the hall.

Allison figured the women at the shelter didn't need anyone else there, eavesdropping on their own personal horrors, so she went out into the dayroom, with Nicole following. The TV was on, the sound turned down to a low murmur. Katie's parents were being interviewed by Madeline McCormick. Was this the bigfooting thing Cassidy was always going on about?

Eliana, who worked the front desk, came in with an armful of dog-eared donated magazines. She began to sort through them, putting most of them on a low table in the middle of the room, pausing every now and then to reject copies of *The Watchtower*, *Opera Today*, and *Golf Digest*.

Then she glanced up at the screen.

"Huh!" she said in a tone of surprise.

"What?" Allison asked. "Do you know them?"

Eliana glanced sideways at Nicole and then looked back at Allison. "It's confidential. You know I can't talk about clients."

Clients? Allison and Nicole exchanged surprised looks. This changed everything. Wayne had abused his wife, maybe his children?

If so, Wayne Converse had just changed from a grieving father to the number one suspect.

"Eliana," Allison said carefully, "this is Nicole Hedges. She's an FBI agent. And you know that I'm a federal prosecutor. We are both working an active murder case that involves their daughter, Katie Converse. So if they were clients, we need to know."

"It wasn't under that name, but yeah, I recognize them."

"So Valerie Converse came here for services?" Nicole asked.

"No," Eliana said. "Not the mom. The *dad*. We see that every now and then. He came here a few times a couple of years ago because his wife was beating him. It was the wife who was the bad guy."

Allison gave Eliana a twenty-dollar bill to give to Cassidy for cab fare and asked her to apologize and say that something had come up. Then Allison and Nicole drove to the Converses' house.

"Are you thinking what I'm thinking?" Allison asked. She threw a quick glance at her friend.

"We never looked at the mom," Nicole answered. "Not for a second. But now I'm thinking we made a big mistake."

"But why would she kill her own daughter?"

Nicole shook her head. "The autopsy showed it was a blow to the throat. Maybe it was an accident."

"What about the necklace? Why leave it at the vigil?"

"Maybe she realized later that she had taken it with her," Nicole said, "and then couldn't think of how to get rid of it."

They pulled up beside the house. The media crowds were gone now. So was Valerie's car. Wayne answered the door.

"Hello, Wayne," Nicole said.

Jalapeño pushed himself forward and began nosing the two women's hands.

"Is your wife home?"

He straightened up. His cheeks were hollow, his eyes haunted. "Why? Do you have news? Has Fairview confessed?"

"Is Valerie here?" Allison repeated.

"No—she took Whitney to school, but she should be back pretty soon."

Nicole said, "Maybe we can talk to you for a second, then."

"Of course." He stepped back. "Come in."

Once they were in the living room, Allison said, "Wayne, we were just over at Safe Harbor shelter."

"Oh?" His face was carefully bland.

"Have you ever been there?"

"No, I don't believe so."

No longer anxious to talk to them, Wayne busied himself lining up the fan of magazines on the coffee table.

"Is that the name of the animal shelter that had Jalapeño?" At the sound of his name, the dog pushed against Wayne's thigh, and Wayne stroked the dog's ears.

With a sigh, Nicole said, "Wayne, just—just stop. You know what kind of shelter it is. One of the women who works there recognized you on TV. She said you had come in for help a couple of times, but you used a fake name. So we need to ask you, Wayne—has Valerie ever hurt you?" A beat. "Or hurt your girls?"

He tried to look bewildered. "What are you talking about?"

Nicole said, "Wayne, please. Why didn't you tell us about your wife? About Valerie?"

He looked down at his hands, which were still now. "Look, let me tell you something. When I was growing up, there were a couple of rules: you never hit anyone smaller than you, and you never, ever hit a woman."

Allison felt more confused. Was Wayne saying *he* had been the one who had been abusive?

"So say your wife throws a telephone at you and it hits you in the head, then what do you do? Call the police?"

He looked back up at them with reddened eyes. "Valerie told me if I did that, she would tell them that I was the one who hit *her*. Was I supposed to throw a phone back at her? I couldn't do that. Try to talk it out with her? Have you ever tried to talk anything out with Valerie? File for divorce? She would have killed me."

"Wayne," Nicole said. "Wayne, do you think Valerie is capable of murder?"

His face morphed with shock as he realized what Nicole was implying.

"What are you saying? Are you thinking she had something to do with what happened to Katie? That's impossible. She would never hurt the girls. She loves them so much. She raised Katie like she was her own mother, and of course Whitney is the most important person on the planet to her."

"Okay," Allison said carefully. "So she wouldn't hurt the girls. But she would hurt you? Why do you think she did that?"

"Because she's always held it over me that it was my fault that we had to get married. I got her drunk after my first wife's funeral, I couldn't control myself, I got her pregnant, and I left her no choice. She's still so angry about it. She moved out of her parents' house and straight into mine. She never got to go to college. She never even dated. And sometimes that comes out as rage."

He wiped his nose with the back of his hand. Jalapeño regarded him anxiously, tail thumping lightly on the floor.

"And she's right," Wayne continued. "It *is* my fault. I stole Valerie's childhood from her. And as she got older, she realized how much she had missed, and she got angrier and angrier. It started with little things. If she thought I didn't like the dinner, she would tip the plates on the floor. Then she started throwing the plates at me. And then just whatever was handy."

"If you went to the shelter, why didn't you let them help you?" Nicole asked quietly.

"If we both got up in court and each said the other one was beating us—who do you think most judges would believe? And then I wouldn't see my girls again. And Valerie's not always like that. Sometimes she can go for months and everything's great, and I think she's finally healed. But then something will happen to set her off again."

They heard the sound of the front door opening. Nicole got to her feet, with Allison following a beat later. But it wasn't just Valerie who walked around the corner. She had one arm around Cassidy's stiff shoulders. And Valerie's other hand pressed a gun against Cassidy's ribs.

"Valerie—what are you doing with my gun?" Wayne asked.

Valerie didn't answer. Instead, she said in a bright voice, "Wayne—look who I found trying to listen at the window outside! Isn't this a nice surprise? Cassidy, the reporter who helped us." Her voice tightened. "Cassidy, the reporter who is building her career on our tragedy."

Sensing the rising tension, Jalapeño began to whine.

Wayne said, "Look, Valerie, they know."

"They know?"

Allison had expected her to grow even angrier, but instead her shoulders slumped as if in relief. But the gun didn't budge.

"Then they have to understand it was an accident. I just snapped. She knew how to push my buttons, and she just kept pushing and pushing them."

"Wait—are you talking about Katie?" Wayne's voice rose and broke. "I meant they knew that you beat me. What are you saying? Are you saying you killed Katie?"

Valerie lifted her head. "You don't understand. All I wanted was for her to be quiet. If she had only been quiet, nothing would have happened."

"Tell us what happened, Valerie," Nicole said soothingly. "We want to know. We want to hear your side of the story."

Her words tumbled out. "I followed Katie that day. I thought she was meeting a boy. When she heard me coming down the path, she said"— Valerie made her voice high and mincing—"'What took you so long, James?' There's only one James we know. Our senator. A man old enough to be *my* father, let alone her father. So I slapped her. I slapped her and called her a fool."

Jalapeño growled as if he could understand her, but Valerie paid him no mind, lost in the details of what had happened the month before. She had taken her arm from around Cassidy's shoulder. But now, Allison noted with horror, the gun was pointed squarely at her. At her belly.

"But Katie told me they were in *lo-ove*." The word was loaded with sarcasm. "Love! Like she would know what that word meant! She's seventeen! She knows nothing! I told her she was going to ruin her life. That she would turn up pregnant and have to walk around with her belly showing and her shame for everyone to see."

Valerie's eyes narrowed. "And then she told me that she was smarter than me. Smart enough to have taken care of it. Unlike me. And then I thought I heard someone. She was still shouting about things no one else had any business knowing about, so I told her to be quiet. But she wouldn't. So I tried to put my hand over her mouth. Just to shush her. But she pushed me away. And the side of my hand hit her throat. And then suddenly she was on the ground making this terrible whistling noise. And her eyes—her eyes were so big. And then the whistling stopped."

The room was absolutely silent, all of them staring at Valerie.

"And I knew"—her voice was close to a whisper—"I knew that if I didn't act fast, Whitney would not only lose her sister, but also her mother. So I put the leash around her neck. I tied it to a branch, but it broke. And then I heard someone coming, so I left."

While she was listening, Allison had been slowly edging away from Valerie, so that the gun was now pointing somewhere between her and Nicole. At least she hoped it was.

Cassidy had watched her captor's confession with darting eyes. Allison could tell her attention was torn between thinking what a great scoop this would make and wondering whether she would die before she ever got to serve it up to viewers.

In that moment, when they were all digesting the news, Nicole made her move. Her gun was in her hand so fast it seemed like a magic trick. And after that, everything happened so fast. Jalapeño jumping, Nicole's gun firing, Valerie's going off at the same time, Cassidy screaming, Wayne shouting, "No!"

And then Nicole was on the floor with bright red blood quickly drenching her white blouse. With the dog lying next to her, whining and biting its flank.

And Valerie still standing, unscathed. If she hesitated, it was only because she couldn't decide which of them to shoot next.

The only time Allison had fired a gun was when Nicole had invited her to spend a few hours at the FBI range in rural Washington State. The weight of Nicole's Glock had surprised her, as had the way it kicked up with every shot. She had flinched and blinked each time she pulled the trigger. And she hadn't been very good.

But now without hesitation she grabbed Nicole's gun from her slack hand. She remembered her friend's advice. *You aim at the largest part of the body and pull the trigger until the subject goes down.*

The shot threw Valerie back against the wall. Red bloomed on her chest. Her eyes widened in surprise. The gun fell from her hand to the floor. She raised her hands to the wound, her fingers dabbling the blood. Her body turned boneless and she slid down the wall, leaving a long smear of blood. Raising her shocked eyes to their faces, she said, "I had to think of Whitney." She wheezed, gasped, tried to breathe, but blood bubbled from her lips. And then she slumped over sideways.

Cassidy grabbed a dishcloth from the kitchen and pressed it to Nic's shoulder as she yanked her cell phone from her belt and dialed 911.

Allison fell to her knees. She moved her fingers around Valerie's wrist, but even as she found it, the pulse eased and then vanished altogether. She had no clue how to get it back.

Allison was the first person to arrive at Fong Chong in Portland's Chinatown. While she waited for her friends, she thought about all the changes the last six weeks had brought. A new life had begun within her and she had killed a woman. And in different ways, she had saved both of her closest friends.

Wayne and Whitney were in seclusion, getting used to Valerie's absence and the reality of what she had done.

Lily Rangel was safely back at home, after having gotten drunk at a party and then deciding to lie low rather than face her parents.

Senator Fairview was facing the Senate Ethics Committee, but there was talk that he might escape with a censure.

His wife, however, had been charged with hiring a transient to attack the first young woman he could find hiking alone in Forest Park. Nancy hadn't really known whether her husband was guilty, and had been trying to cloud the case as much as possible.

Allison's stalker was in a mental hospital.

Nicole came in the door. Uncharacteristically for her, she immediately gave Allison a hug that was only a little awkward because her right arm was in a sling. The bullet had gone through her arm, somehow managing to miss anything important.

"Thank you again for saving my life," Nicole whispered in her ear.

"Just returning the favor after you saved mine," Allison said, giving her good shoulder a squeeze.

As they released each other, Cassidy walked in the door of the restaurant, blinking rapidly. She said, "There's something really strange in the sky."

"What?" Allison asked, looking past her.

"It's a big bright disk of light."

"Very funny," Nicole said, but she smiled nonetheless.

"For three?" the waiter asked.

They nodded, and he led them to one of the brown and orange vinyl booths. He poured them each a cup of tea.

"The floor looks kind of dirty," Nicole whispered as soon as he was out of earshot.

"You don't come here for the *floor*," Cassidy said. "You come here for the food. I still can't believe you haven't eaten here before."

Nicole looked offended. "I've had Chinese food."

"Yeah, but if you've never had dim sum, it's not the same."

"You have to admit this place doesn't look like much from the outside." Nicole looked around pointedly at the bucket swivel chairs, the Formica tables, and the two surly waiters yelling at each other across the room in what might have been Cantonese.

"I think it's the perfect place for the Triple Threat Club to meet," Allison said. "It symbolizes that we need to be open to trying new things. And," she added, "that life is full of delicious, mysterious morsels."

As she spoke, women piloting silver carts piled high with tiny plates circled the tables, calling out the names of their wares.

"Hum bao!"

"Pork shu mai!"

"Ha gow!"

Allison and Cassidy immediately pointed at four or five plates. At first, Nicole tried to ask questions about each dish, but since none of the servers seemed to speak English as a first language—or even a second or third— she soon followed their lead.

Since she couldn't use her right hand, the waiter brought her a fork.

It only took about three or four bites before she said, "Okay, okay, I take it back. You come here for the food." Speaking around a mouthful of shrimp dumpling, she asked Allison, "So how are you doing?"

Allison could feel both her friends regarding her closely. "It's a bit of a roller coaster. Killing someone sure isn't like shooting holes in a target. But I've been going to my pastor, and he's been talking through it with me. It turns out he's a Vietnam vet. He's helping me understand there's no burden too heavy for me to carry. Not with God's help."

She felt a little self-conscious being so open about her beliefs, but instead of being sarcastic or snarky, the other two women regarded her thoughtfully.

Allison pointed her chopsticks at Cassidy. "How about you? Have you decided which offer to take? Boston? LA?"

Cassidy sat back, a private smile playing about her face. "Actually, I've decided to stay in Portland. The ratings have been so high that Channel Four made me an offer I couldn't refuse. The only other news I have is that I went back to the shelter, and they helped me decide to press charges against Rick. It might not work, given that he is employed by the very organization that's in charge of investigating him. But I hear he's running scared. And if nothing else, it will give them a heads-up in case he ever tries it with another woman. As a result, I've officially sworn off men." She leaned toward Nicole and mimed a leer. "But women, however . . ."

With a laugh, Nicole pushed her back. "You're too late."

It was hard to startle Cassidy, but this news did it. "What do you mean?"

"I actually went out with someone last weekend." Nicole smiled a Cheshire grin. "I'm not sure I would even call it a date. Let's just say he's a friend. But I'm not answering any questions about who, why, what, or how."

Allison lifted her cup of tea. "This calls for a toast. To Nicole, for taking the plunge."

Nicole clinked her cup against Allison's and then Cassidy's. "And to

Cassidy for being smart enough to get out of the pool." She looked at Allison. "And to Allison for saving my life—and creating a new life. And to the Triple Threat Club, for living up to its name."

"And to the memory of Katie Converse," Allison said.

"To Katie," they all echoed solemnly and raised their cups to their lips.

1. At its heart, *Face of Betrayal* is about three friends who love each other—and their work. Do you have any friendships like that?

2. When the book opens, the man Allison prosecuted for hiring someone to kill his wife is sentenced. He had hired a hit man to kill his wife. Should hiring a hit man carry the same penalty as committing murder yourself?

3. When Katie disappears, her parents work to get attention from the media and law enforcement. Do you think that if a girl disappeared who wasn't white or upper class, or whose parents weren't as savvy, the case would get as much media attention? If not, is there anything that can be done about it?

4. Allison has been trying for two years to get pregnant. Do you know people who have struggled with infertility?

5. Nicole works with the FBI's Innocent Images to catch online pedophiles. Do you think the Internet has led to an increase in the number of pedophiles, or that it has simply given them new tools?

6. Cassidy is a spiritual seeker. Do you know women like her?

7. Katie's parents were unaware of her MySpace page. If you have kids, do you let them have a MySpace or Facebook page? Do you monitor

it? Why or why not? Is it snooping for parents to look through their kids' e-mails? Is it any different than reading letters that they get in the mail?

8. Nicole has to send her daughter to live with Nic's parents while the case is at a fever pitch. Is it possible to hold a demanding job and still be a good mother? Do we ask the same question of fathers? Should we?

9. As a black woman working in a white man's world, Nicole feels she has to be twice as good to be treated as an equal. Do you think there still is a double standard for race? For sex?

10. Cassidy's station devotes a lot of resources to the story of the missing Senate intern. Do you think TV news is catering more and more to sensationalism and celebrities and doing fewer in-depth, well-researched stories? Has the way you get your news changed in the past few years?

11. In desperation, Katie's parents contact a woman who says she can get in touch with Katie's spirit. Do you think there are people who really have such powers?

12. Allison knows that domestic violence accounts for more injuries to women in America than heart attacks, cancer, strokes, car wrecks, muggings, and rapes combined. Do you know anyone who has been affected by domestic violence? Have you ever tried to help someone you suspected was being abused?

13. Senator Fairview is revealed to be a man who lies, cheats, and ratio-nalizes. Do you think it's possible to be a politician while still retain-ing your principles? Or does "power corrupt, and absolute power corrupts absolutely," as Lord Acton said?

INTERVIEW WITH LIS WIEHL, CONDUCTED BY BILL O'REILLY

Q: You've written non-fiction, and now this novel. Why'd you decide to do that . . . inspired by my novel *Those Who Trespass*, right?

A: With all due respect, no not really. In my time away from you, I like to hunker down with a good mystery. But I had an increasingly hard time finding stories I could relate to. And I wanted to read about strong women solving crimes. So, I thought, why not create my own mysteries . . . fiction stories with a slice of reality about how law and journalism really work.

Q: Describe a day in "Lis Land."

A: Let's pick a typical Tuesday. After I make fruit smoothies and oatmeal or whatever else (fast) for the kids, get a load of wash in the laundry, and pack the kids off to school . . . I get to work to start my day. On the way in to work, I'm reading up for the 10:30 a.m. TV show, figuring out which side I want to take on the daily debate. I go directly from that to a FOX streaming Internet show, where we talk about the news of the day. I leave that show early explaining that I'm doing radio with you, Bill, grab a quick bite to eat (so my stomach doesn't rumble during radio), and then get to spend the next two hours doing radio with you. While I'm doing the radio show, your TV producers are sending me the topics for your TV show that night. They want me to study up and then send them my point of view for the program. So I try to answer their questions while paying attention to the radio show—women know how to multitask! From radio I have a little downtime to work on my column for Foxnews.com, do more research for TV that night, and call the kids to bug them about their homework and make a dinner plan. TV with you is the next highlight (smile), and then it's home to make dinner, check homework, make kid lunches for the next day, and start the whole process all over again.

Q: Everyone knows I'm the most boring guy around, but tell us something about you that we'd never guess.

A: I hate to shop for clothes. I won't even look at something unless it's at least 50 percent off, so that means sorting through a lot of piles, which I really don't like. I'd rather wear sweats. Fortunately, FOX has a wardrobe department, so I can at least look presentable at work. But if you see me in the supermarket, you'll see me in sweats.

Q: You were a federal prosecutor, now you work in TV, and your dad was an FBI agent. So you're taking your material from your own background?

A: I figured with this personal background I could create fictional characters who work together, and I could give readers a true sense of what goes on in a TV station and in a courtroom. Although the overall book is fiction, many of the scenes are based on cases I've actually had—though I am careful to change the names to protect the guilty. And the crime-solving techniques, including forensics and grand jury methods, are based on my own experience along with consulting experts in forensics, pathology, defense lawyering, etc.

Q: You've been all over the place—Prosecutor, Pundit, and Professor. Which job best prepared you to write fiction?

A: All of my experiences in the law and on television prepared me for *Face of Betrayal*. As a prosecutor and pundit, you have to be quick on your feet, and a good judge of character. As a professor, you have to be measured and systematic. This all helps with storytelling. And it's so fun to bring these worlds together in fiction format.

Q: *Face of Betrayal*. Tough sounding title. Why?

A: I think betraying someone who trusts you is one of the worst sins a person can commit. And Katie Converse comes face-to-face with that sin, so the title just makes sense.

Q: We're living in a society where secularism is combating traditional religion. Most Americans are facing that struggle on a regular basis. This important to you, your characters?

A: Absolutely critical. All three women in the book struggle with issues of what to believe and why. For Allison especially, it's difficult to reconcile a loving God with what she sees everyday at work. For me, my faith is an integral part of who I am, and my own moral compass. As a Christian writing fiction I deal with issues of faith. And I think most Americans can relate to that.

Q: So what do you want readers to get out of the book?

A: First off, I hope readers will have a fun read. This can be "me" time to just enjoy a good mystery—see if you can figure it out kind of thing. And then, because the characters are based on my own background, I hope that readers will learn something about the behind-the-scenes world of a TV station and a criminal courthouse.

Q: I'm almost afraid to ask—what's next, Wiehl?

A: You should be very afraid, Bill! The next book, *Hand of Fate*, opens
         with the murder of Jim Fate, a radio and TV show host, with strong
         opinions and lots of enemies. Sound like someone you know? And
         the way he is murdered sets the whole town into chaos. One of the
         immediate suspects is his smart and witty female radio co-host.
         Again, sound like someone you know? Turns out Cassidy had been
         dating Fate, and she may have the critical clue. But I can't give away
         any more. You'll just have to tune in to see how it turns out!

ACKNOWLEDGMENTS

This book would not have been possible without the unwavering support and encouragement from Bill O'Reilly (really!). Roger Ailes and Dianne Brandi at the Fox News Channel paved the way. And my office buddy, Gregg Jarrett, listened and offered wise guidance along the way.

Although this is a book of fiction, we relied on expert research help to get the facts right. Thank you Dr. Michael Baden, forensic pathologist; Robin Burcell, police investigator/author; Dr. David Farris; George Q. Fong, FBI Unit Chief for Safe Streets and Gang Unit; James Kotecki, former congressional page; and many unnamed law enforcement who asked not to be identified but were incredibly helpful in making sure we got this right. All errors are our own.

Our book agents were absolutely instrumental from inception to execution of this book . . . Wendy Schmalz of the Wendy Schmalz Agency and Todd Shuster and Lane Zachary of Zachary, Shuster, Harmsworth Literary & Entertainment Agency found the perfect home at Thomas Nelson for Allison, Nicole, and Cassidy. Allen Arnold, senior vice president and publisher, got the idea right away . . . as did Ami McConnell, senior acquisitions editor, who provided expert guidance. L.B. Norton helped us fine-tune the plot and the prose. And the enthusiasm of Jennifer Deshler, Natalie Hanemann, Becky Monds, Mark Ross, Katie Schroder, and the other good folks at Thomas Nelson is both infectious and inspiring. Thank you.

When the host of a popular radio show is murdered,
the Triple Threat Club must narrow down
the lengthy list of suspects who want him dead.

Excerpt from *Hand of Fate*
Chapter 1

KNWS RADIO STUDIO
February 7

J im Fate bounced on the toes of his black Salvatore Ferragamo loafers. He liked to work on his feet. Listeners could hear in your voice if you were sitting down, could detect the lack of energy. He leaned forward, his lips nearly touching the silver mesh of the mike.

"Global warming may well be real. But there's no evidence that the main cause is carbon emissions. This is a natural cycle that's been occurring long before mankind built the first combustion engine. Carbon dioxide emissions play, at most, a minor role. And we *need* energy, people. It's what makes America great. Economies need energy to grow. How are people going to get to work if they can't afford gasoline? We can't all get to work by bicycle. For the past umpteen years, environmental extremists have driving energy policy in this country, saying no to everything. Well now the chickens have come to roost."

"So what are you suggesting, Jim?" Victoria Hanawa asked. She sat on a high stool on the other side of the U-shaped table, her back to the glass wall that separated the radio studio from the screener's booth. To Jim's right was the control room, sometimes called the news tank, where the board operator worked his bank of equipment and then was joined at the top and the bottom of the hour by one or more local reporters. "Are you saying we can just drill our way out?"

"What I'm saying, Victoria, is that we're in a situation now where we're buying too much energy from foreign dictatorships. We ought to be producing a lot more energy here at home."

While he spoke, Jim eyed one of the two screens in front of him. One displayed the show schedule. It was also hooked up to the Internet so he could look up points on the fly. The other screen showed listeners holding for their chance to talk. On it, Chris, the call screener, had listed the name, town, and point of view of each caller. Three people were still on the list, meaning they would hold over the upcoming break. As Jim spoke, he saw a fourth caller and then a fifth join the queue.

"What we need is to open up the coast to drilling, and open up the Rocky Mountains for shale oil. The Rocky Mountains have three times the amount of oil that the Saudis have in their entire reserve. And yet it's currently illegal for Americans to get oil from American territory in the Atlantic, the Eastern Gulf of Mexico, the Pacific, northern Alaska. We should have been drilling in ANWR fifteen, twenty years ago. I mean, it's insane."

"What about the wilderness?" Victoria said. "What about the caribou?"

"If the caribou don't like it, we'll relocate them."

Victoria's mouth started to form an answer, but it was time for the top of the hour break, and he pointed at the clock and then made a motion with his hands like he was snapping a stick.

Jim said, "And you've been listening to *The Hand of Fate*. We're going to take a quick break for a news, traffic, and weather update. But before we go, I want to read you the email from The Nut of the Day: 'Jim—you are a fat, ugly, liar who resembles the hind-end of a poodle. Signed, Mickey Mouse.'"

He laughed. "Fat? Maybe. Ugly? Well, I can't help that. I can't even help the hind-end of a poodle business, although I think that's going a bit far. But a liar? No, my friend, that's one thing I am not. Come on, all you listeners who just tune in because you can't stand me, you are going to have to get a little more creative than that if you want to win the NOD award. And for the rest of you, when we come back, we'll be opening up the lines for more of your calls." He pushed back the mike on its black telescoping arm.

As the first notes of the newscast jingle sounded in his padded black headphones, he pulled them down around his neck. He and Victoria now had six minutes to themselves, before the second and final hour of *The Hand of Fate* was broadcast.

"I'm going to get some tea," Victoria said without meeting his eyes. Jim nodded. In the last week, there had been a strained civility between them when they were off mike. On air, though, they still had chemistry. Even if lately it had been the kind of chemistry you got when you mixed together the wrong chemicals in your junior scientist kit.

Everything was different on air. Jim was more indignant and mocking than he ever was in real life. Victoria made vaguely dirty jokes that she wouldn't tolerate hearing off mike. And on air, they usually got along great, bantering and feeding each other lines.

Victoria grabbed her mug and stood up. Even though she was half-Japanese, Victoria was five foot ten, with legs that went on forever. "Oh, this was in my box this morning, but it's really yours," she said, handing him a padded envelope from a publisher.

When she pushed open the heavy door to the screening room, the weather strip on the bottom made a sucking sound. For a minute, Jim could hear Chris talking to Willow and Aaron in the screener's booth. Then the door closed with a snick—there were magnets on the door and frame—and Jim was left in the silent bubble of the radio studio. The walls and ceiling were covered with blue textured soundproofing material that resembled the loop side of Velcro.

Jim grabbed the first piece of mail from his inbox and slit it with a letter opener. He scanned the note inside. *Dad's seventy-fifth birthday, would love to have a signed photo, yada yada.*

Happy Birthday, Larry! he scrawled on a black and white head shot he pulled from dozens kept in a file folder. *Your friend, Jim Fate.* Paper clipping the envelope and letter to the photo, he put them off to the side for Willow to deal with. Three more photo requests, each of which took about twenty seconds to deal with. Jim had signed his name so many times in the last couple of years that it should have been routine, but he still got a secret thrill each time he did it.

There were less than three minutes left, so he decided to open the package from the publisher. He liked books about true crime, politics, or culture—with authors he might be able to book on the show.

Fans also liked to send him things. All kinds of things. Party invitations. A bikini, once. Death threats. Naked Polaroids of themselves. Marriage proposals. T-shirts. In honor of the show's name, he had gotten more than a dozen hands made of wood, plastic, and metal. Poems. Pressed flowers. Brownies. He had made enough enemies that he never ate any food from a fan, even if was still sealed in a package. He figured that a determined person might still be able to inject something toxic through layers of plastic and cardboard. But Jim also liked to handle his own mail, just in case it contained items of a more, say, *personal* nature.

Jim pulled the red string tab on the envelope. It got stuck half way through and he had to give it an extra hard tug. There was an odd hissing sound as a paperback—*Talk Radio*—fell onto his lap. A book of a play turned into a movie—both based on the true-life killing of talk show host Alan Berg, gunned down in his own driveway.

What the?

Jim never got to finish the thought. Because the red string had been connected to a small canister of gas hidden in the envelope—and it sprayed directly into his face.

He gasped in surprise. With just that first breath, Jim knew something was terribly wrong. He couldn't see the gas, couldn't smell it, but he could feel the damp fog coat the inside of his nose and throat. His eyelids sank to half-mast. With an effort, he opened them wider.

He swept the package away. It landed behind him, in the far corner of the studio.

Whatever it was, it was in the air. So he shouldn't breathe. He clamped his lips together and scrambled to his feet, yanking off the headphones. The whole time, Jim was thinking about what had happened in Seattle. Three weeks earlier, someone had spilled liquid sarin on the third floor of a 15-story downtown office building. Fifty-eight people had died, including an unidentified, Middle Eastern-looking male dressed in a janitor's uniform. Was he a terrorist? Had he been in the process of putting the sarin into the ventilation system and then literally taken a wrong step? No one knew. Authorities had still not identified the culprit, and no one had claimed responsibility. But up and down the west coast and across the nation, people were on a heightened state of alert.

And now it was happening again.

His chest already started to ache. Jim looked out through the thick glass wall into the control room on his right. Greg, the board operator, was turned away from the glass, gobbling a Payday bar, watching his banks of equipment, ready to press the buttons for commercials and national feeds. Bob, the reporter, had his back to Jim, his head down as he reviewed his copy for the local segment of the news. In the call screener's room directly in front of Jim, Aaron, the program director, talked rapidly to Chris and Willow, waving his hands for emphasis. None of them had seen what was happening. Jim was unnoticed, sealed away in his bubble.

He forced himself to concentrate. He had to get some air, some fresh air. But if he staggered out to the screener's room, would the air there be enough to dilute what he had already breathed in? Would it be enough to clear the sarin from his lungs, from his body?

Would it be enough to save him?

But once the door was open, what would happen to the people out there? Chris, Willow, Aaron and the rest? He thought of the firefighters who had died when they responded to the Seattle attack. Would invisible tendrils of poison snake out to the dozens of people who worked at the station, the hundreds who worked in the building? The people in the control room, with its own soundproofing, might be safe if they kept their door closed. For a while, anyway. Until it got into the air ducts. Some of the people who died in Seattle had been nowhere near the original release of the gas. If Jim tried to escape, then everyone out there might die, too.

Die too. The words echoed in his head. Jim realized that he *was* dying, that he had been dying from the moment he first sucked in his breath in surprise. He had the innate sense of timing that you developed working in radio. It had been, he thought, somewhere between fifteen and twenty seconds since the gas sprayed into his face. No more.

Every morning, Jim swam two miles at the MAC club. He could hold his breath for more than two minutes. The magician on Oprah had done it for, what? Seventeen minutes, wasn't that it? Jim couldn't hold his breath for that long, but now that he had to, he was sure he could hold it longer than two minutes. Maybe a lot longer. The first responders could surely get him some oxygen. The line might be thin enough to snake under the closed door.

Jim pressed the talk button and spoke in a slurred, breathy voice. "Sarin gas! Call 911 and get out! Don't open the door!"

They all swung around to look at him in surprise. Without getting any closer, he pointed to the book and wrapper that now lay in a corner of the room.

Chris sprang into action. He had the catlike reflexes of someone who worked in live radio, dealing with the crazies and the obscenity spouters before their words got out on the airwaves and brought down a big fine from the FCC. He punched numbers into the phone and began shouting their address to the 9-1-1 operator. At the same time, he pressed the talk button, so Jim heard every word. "It's sarin gas. Yes, sarin! In the KNWS studio! Hurry! It's killing him! It's killing Jim Fate!" Behind Chris, Willow took one look at Jim, her face a mask of fear, and turned and ran.

In the news tank, Greg and Bob backed away from the window. But in the screener's booth, Aaron moved toward the door with an outstretched hand. Jim staggered forward and held the door closed with his foot. His eyes met Aaron's through the small rectangle of glass set in the door.

"Are you sure? Jim, come out of there!"

Jim knew Aaron was yelling, but the door filtered it into a low murmur, stripped of all urgency.

He couldn't afford the breath it would take to speak, couldn't afford to open his mouth in case he accidentally sucked in air again. His body was already demanding that he stop this nonsense and breathe. All he could do was shake his head, his lips clamped together.

Chris pressed the talk button again. "9-1-1 says they're sending a special hazmat team. They should be here any second. They said they're bringing oxygen."

Jim made a sweeping motion with his hands, wordlessly ordering his coworkers to leave. His chest ached. Greg grabbed a board and a couple of microphones and left the news tank at a run, Bob on his heels. Aaron took one last look at Jim, his face contorted by fear and regret, and then left. A second later, the fire alarm began to sound, a low pulse muffled to near nothingness by the soundproof door.

Chris was the only one left, staring at Jim through the glass. The two of them had been together for years. Every morning Chris and Jim—and more recently Victoria—got in early and put the show together, scouring the newspaper, the Internet and TV clips for stories that would light up every single one of the lines. "I'm praying for you, man," Chris said, then released the talk button. He gave Jim one more anguished look, and then turned and ran. Jim wished he could run away. But he couldn't run away from what the poison had already done to him. Now the muscles in both arms and in the tops of his thighs were twitching. He was so tired. Why did he have to hold his breath again? Oh yes, poison.

When he looked back up, Victoria was in the screener's room. She moved close to the glass, her wide dark eyes seeking out Jim's. Angrily, he shook his head and motioned for her to go.

Victoria pressed the talk button. "They say there's gas, but I don't smell anything out here. The booth is practically airtight, anyway."

Jim wanted to tell her that "practically" wasn't the same as really and truly. It was the kind of argument they might have on air during a slow time, bantering to keep things moving along. But he didn't have the breath for it.

A part of Jim's brain remained coldly rational even as his body sent more and more messages that something was badly wrong, and that things were only getting worse. He had not breathed since that first fateful gulp of air when he opened the package. A vacuum was building up in his head and chest, a sucking hollowness, his body screaming at him, demanding that he give in and breathe.

But Jim hadn't made it this far by giving in when things were tough. It had been a minute, a minute ten maybe, since he opened the package. But then he did give in to another hunger—the hunger for connection. He was all alone and he might be dying and he couldn't stand that thought. Jim moved to the glass and put his hand up against the glass, fingers spread, a lonely starfish. And then Victoria mirrored it with her own hand, everything between them forgotten, their hands pressed against the glass.

There was a band around Jim's chest, and it was tightening. An iron band. It was crushing him, crushing his lungs. His vision was dimming, but he kept his eyes open, his gaze never leaving Victoria. Their matching hands pressed on either side of the glass. They were just two human beings, reaching out for each other, but destined to never touch.

With her free hand, Victoria groped blindly for the talk button, found it. "Jim, you've got to hold on. I hear sirens. They're almost here!"

But his body was ready to break with his will. It hadn't even been two minutes yet, but he had to breathe. Had to. But maybe he could filter it, minimize it.

Without taking his eyes from Victoria, Jim pulled up the edge of his shirt with his free hand, and pressed his nose and mouth against the fine

Egyptian cotton cloth. He meant to take a shallow breath, but when he started, the hunger for air was too great. He sucked it in greedily, the cloth touching his tongue as he inhaled.

He sensed the shoots of poison wind themselves deeper within him, reaching out to wrap around all his organs. His head felt like it was going to explode.

No longer thinking clearly, Jim let his shirttail fall away. It didn't matter, did it? It was too late. Too late.

He staggered backward. Tried to grab his chair and missed. Fell over.

Horrified, Victoria started screaming. She watched Jim convulse, his arms and legs twitching and jerking, foam bubbling from his lips.

And then Jim Fate was still. His eyes, still open, stared up at the soft fuzzy blue ceiling.

Two minutes later, the first hazmat responders, suited up in white, burst through the studio door.

Chapter 2

F ederal prosecuting attorney Allison Pierce eyed the 150 prospective jurors crowded into 16th floor courtroom in the Mark O. Hatfield Federal Courthouse. No one had yet been called into the jury box or two of cherry-wood benches marked "Reserved" via scrawled notes on taped up pieces of paper. There were so many jurors that a few dozen were forced to stand, so many jurors that Allison could smell unwashed bodies and unbrushed teeth. She swallowed hard, forcing down the nausea that now plagued her at unexpected moments.

The would-be jurors carried backpacks, purses, coats, umbrellas, bottled water, books, magazines, and—this being Portland, Oregon—the occasional bike helmet. They ranged from a hunched over old man with hearing aids on the stems of his glasses to a young man who immediately opened a sketch book and startled doodling an eight-armed monster. Some wore suits while others looked like they were ready to hit the gym, but in general they appeared alert and reasonably happy.

There would have been more room for the potential jurors to sit, but the benches were already packed with reporters who had arrived before the jury was ushered in. Among them was a fortyish woman who sat in pride of place directly behind her daughter at the defense table. She wore far too much makeup and a sweater with a plunging neckline.

Everyone rose and the courtroom deputy swore the prospective jurors in en masse. After those lucky enough to have seats were settled in again, Judge Fitzpatrick introduced himself and told the jury that the defendant had to be considered innocent until proven guilty beyond a reasonable doubt, and that she did not need to do or say anything to prove her innocence. It was solely up to the prosecution, he intoned solemnly, to prove their case. Even though she had heard the same words many times, and the judge must have said them hundreds of times over his nearly twenty years on the bench, Allison found herself listening. Judge Fitzpatrick never lost sight of the meaning behind the words.

When he was finished, he asked Allison to introduce herself. She stood and faced the crowded room, trying to make eye contact with everyone. It was her job to build a relationship from this moment forward, so that when the time came for the jury to deliberate, they would trust what she had told them. "I am federal prosecuting attorney Allison Pierce." She gestured toward Nic. "I'm assisted by FBI Special Agent Nicole Hedges as the case agent."

On some of the potential jurors' faces, Allison saw surprise when they realized that the young woman with the pinned back dark hair was actually the federal prosecutor. She was thirty-three, but people always seemed to expect a federal prosecutor to be a silver-haired man.

Nicole was only four months older than Allison, but with her unlined dark skin and expression that gave away nothing, she could have been any age from twenty-five to forty. Today, Nic wore her customary dark pantsuit and flats.

Allison was dressed in what she thought of as her court uniform: a blue suit from JCPenneys, low pumps, and little makeup. Underneath her ivory silk blouse was a silver cross on a fine chain. Her father had given it to Allison for her sixteenth birthday, six weeks before he died.

The judge then pointed out the defendant, Bethany Maddox, dressed today in a demure pink and white dress that Allison was sure someone else had picked out for her—and that Bethany was wearing only under protest. The courtroom stirred as people craned their necks or stood up to get a glimpse of her. Bethany smiled, looking as if she had forgotten that she was on trial. Her defense attorney, Nate Condorelli, stood and introduced himself, but it was clear that the would-be jurors weren't nearly as interested in Nate as they were in his client.

Today was the first step in bringing to justice the pair the media had dubbed the Bratz Bandits, courtesy of their full lips, small noses, and trashy attire. For some reason, the media loved to give bank robbers nicknames. The Waddling Bandit, the Grandmother Robber, the Toboggan Bandit, the Runny Nose Robber, the Grocery Cart Bandit—the list went on and on.

For a few weeks after their crime, grainy surveillance video of the pair had been in heavy rotation not just in Portland, but nationwide. The contrast between two nineteen-year-old girls—one blonde and one brunette, and both wearing sunglasses, short skirts, and high heels—and the big black guns they waved around had seemed more comic than anything else. On the surveillance tape, they had giggled their way through the robbery.

Even after they had been arrested—and of course they had been, the robbery had had about five seconds of planning behind it—the two of them had remained in the public eye, as family and friends stepped forward to plead their innocence or peddle tales of their unsavory past.

The week before, Allison had heard Bethany's parents on *The Hand of Fate*, the radio talk show. The mother had told listeners that the two young women were not bandits, but rather, "little girls that made a bad choice."

Bethany's mother had seemed surprised when Jim Fate laughed.

The father, who was divorced from the mother, had seemed a little more in touch with reality, and Allison had made a mental note to consider putting him on the stand. "God gives us free will and it's up to us what we do with it," he had told Jim Fate. "Any adult has to make decisions and live with them—good, bad or indifferent."

The girls weren't the innocents they were now painting themselves. They had dropped out of college and started stripping and using drugs. With a male friend who worked as a bank teller, they began to plan a robbery. Incredibly, on the day of the crime they made a wrong turn and robbed the wrong bank. Things got more confusing when the teller panicked and threw the money at the girls. They giggled and scooped it up in pillowcases and even stuffed some down their surgically enhanced cleavage. But they had never stopped waving their guns (which they had borrowed from another girl at the strip club), at the terrified patrons lying trembling on the floor.

They had done it for the money, of course, but now it seemed they welcomed the fame that came with it even more. On their Facebook pages, the girls now listed more than a thousand "friends" each. Allison had even heard a rumor that Bethany—the blonde half of the pair and the girl who was on trial today—would soon release a hip-hop CD.

The challenge for Allison was getting a jury to see that what might seem like a victimless crime—and which had only netted eleven thousand dollars—deserved lengthy jail time.

The courtroom deputy read out fifty names, and the congestion eased a little bit as the first potential jurors took seats in the black swivel chairs in the jury box and in the much-less comfortable rows of benches that had been reserved for them.

Now the judge turned to the screening questions. A high-profile case like this necessitated a huge jury pool. One reason was that many of them might already have formed opinions on the case and therefore could not be unbiased. "Has anyone heard anything about this case?" Judge Fitzpatrick asked. "If you have responses please hold up your hand and we'll pass a microphone to you so you can state your name and answer the question."

Half the hands in the jury box went up. The law clerk handed the microphone to the first person in the first row. "My name is Melissa Delphine and I remember reading about it in the paper."

"Did you form any opinions, Miss Delphine?" In Judge Fitzpatrick's courtroom, the women, no matter how old or how married, were always "Miss."

"Mild ones."

"Could you put them aside?"

"I think so."

"Then forget what you read in the paper. It might have been incomplete. It might have been wrong. It might even have been about completely different people." No one expected jurors to have lived in a vacuum, but Judge Fitzpatrick would dismiss those who said their minds were made up. It would be an easy out, if anyone was looking for an out.

But many weren't. Twenty-four hour news cycles and the proliferation of cable channels and Internet sites meant that more and more people might be interested in grabbing at the chance for their fifteen minutes of fame. Even the most tangential relationship to a famous or infamous case could be parlayed into celebrity. Or at least a stint on a third-rate reality show. Britney's nanny or Lindsay's bodyguard might be joined by a Bratz Bandits juror—all of them spilling "behind the scenes" stories. Allison wanted to make sure that none of the jurors wanted to sit in the box just for the media attention they might later receive.

The jurors listened to each other's answers, looking attentive or bored or spacey. Allison took note of the ones who seemed most disconnected— she didn't want any juror who wasn't invested. Like a poker player, she was looking for signs or tells in the behavior of a prospective juror. Did he never look up? Did she seem evasive or over-eager? Allison also made note of the things they carried or wore: Dr. Pepper, *Cooking Light* magazine, tote bag from a health food store, *Wired* magazine, brown shoes worn to white at the toes, a black jacket flecked with dandruff. Together with the written questionnaire the prospective jurors had filled out earlier, and how they answered questions now, the information would help Allison decide who she wanted—and who she didn't want—on the jury.

It didn't take a mind reader to guess that Nate would plead that his client was too young—and quite possibly too stupid—to fully grasp what she had done. That it had all been a joke. That she had fallen in with a bad crowd. In their separate trials, the two girls would each claim that it was the other's idea.

There was an art to picking a jury. Some lawyers had rigid rules: no postal workers, no social workers, no engineers, and/or no young black men (although the last rule had to be unspoken, and denied if ever suspected). Allison believed in looking at every person as a whole, weighing each prospective juror's age, sex, race, occupation, body language.

For this jury, she thought she might want middle-aged women who worked hard for a living and who would have little sympathy for young girls who had literally laughed all the way to the bank. Nearly as good would be younger people who were making something of their lives, focusing on good grades or climbing the career ladder. What Allison wanted to avoid were older men who might think of the girls as "daughter" figures.

"Barp . . . barp . . . barp." Everyone jumped and then looked up at the ceiling, where red lights were flashing. It was a fire alarm. Allison and Nicole exchanged a puzzled look. Judge Fitzpatrick announced calmly, "It looks like we're having a fire drill, ladies and gentleman. We'll all need to take the stairs which are directly to your left as you exit the courtroom." His voice was already beginning to be lost as people got to their feet, complaining and gathering their things. "Once the drill is over we'll all reconvene here and began where we left off."

"Kind of odd," Nicole said as she collected her files. "I hadn't heard we were going to have a drill today."

Allison's stomach lurched as she thought of Seattle. She clutched the sleeve of Nicole's jacket. "Maybe it's not a drill?" For an answer, Nic patted her arm.

As Allison and Nicole turned toward the exit, they saw that one of the prospective jurors sitting in the row directly behind them, a hunched old lady with a cane, was having trouble getting to her feet. Allison and

Nicole helped her up and then Allison took her arm. "Let me help you down the stairs," she said.

"No, I'll take care of her, Allison," Nicole said. "You go on ahead. Remember, you're evacuating for two now."

Allison had been so busy concentrating on the jury selection that had actually managed to forget for a few hours that she was pregnant. Eleven weeks along now. She didn't quite show when she was dressed, but her skirt was only fastened with the help of a rubber band looped over the button, threaded through the button hole and back over the button.

"Thanks." She decided not to argue. Nicole was a single mom to nine-year-old Makaylah, but at least she knew her child was safe. What if this wasn't just a drill?

Allison went through the double black padded doors, past the elderly bailiff with his plastic name badge clipped to his chest, and hurried toward the stairs.

THE STORY CONTINUES IN *HAND OF FATE*.

AVAILABLE EVERYWHERE APRIL 2010

HUNGRY FOR MORE

ABOUT THE AUTHORS

Lis Wiehl is a *New York Times* bestselling author, Harvard Law School graduate, and former federal prosecutor. A popular legal analyst and commentator for the Fox News, Wiehl appears on The O'Reilly Factor and was co-host with Bill O'Reilly on the radio for seven years. Visit liswiehlbooks.com.

April Henry is the *New York Times* bestselling author of mysteries and thrillers. Her books have been short-listed for the Agatha Award, the Anthony Award, and the Oregon Book Award. April lives in Portland, Oregon, with her husband and daughter.

HUNGRY FOR MORE?

For the latest insights from Lis Wiehl
and exciting news about
the Triple Threat series . . .

Visit LisWiehlbooks.com